Cecil the Lion Had to Die

Ukrainian Research Institute
Harvard University

Harvard Library of Ukrainian Literature 11

HURI Editorial Board

Michael S. Flier
Oleh Kotsyuba, *Director of Publications*
Serhii Plokhy, *Chairman*

Cambridge, Massachusetts

OLENA STIAZHKINA

CECIL
THE LION
HAD TO DIE

A Novel

Translated from Ukrainian and Russian by
Dominique Hoffman

50 years ■ 1973–2023

Distributed by Harvard University Press
for the Ukrainian Research Institute
Harvard University

The Harvard Ukrainian Research Institute was established in 1973 as an integral part of Harvard University. It supports research associates and visiting scholars who are engaged in projects concerned with all aspects of Ukrainian studies. The Institute also works in close cooperation with the Committee on Ukrainian Studies, which supervises and coordinates the teaching of Ukrainian history, language, and literature at Harvard University.

Translation of the excerpt from the song "U mene nemaie domu" (2019) by Odyn v kanoe is by Michelle R. Viise. Translation of the excerpt from Lesia Ukrainka's (Larysa Kosach's) poem "Khotila b ia tebe" (1900) is by Oleh Kotsyuba.

Book chapters, passages, and phrases of the text written in Russian in the original publication are rendered here in white font on black background.

ISBN 9780674291645 (hardcover), 9780674291669 (paperback), 9780674291676 (epub), 9780674291683 (PDF)

Library of Congress Control Number has been applied for and can be found at https://lccn.loc.gov

Cover image by Anya Styopina, https://zemla.studio
Book design by Andrii Kravchuk

Publication of this book has been made possible by the generous support of publications in Ukrainian studies at Harvard University by the following benefactors or funds endowed in their name:

Ostap and Ursula Balaban
Jaroslaw and Olha Duzey
Vladimir Jurkowsky
Myroslav and Irene Koltunik
Damian Korduba Family
Peter and Emily Kulyk
Irena Lubchak
Dr. Evhen Omelsky
Eugene and Nila Steckiw
Dr. Omeljan and Iryna Wolynec
Wasyl and Natalia Yerega

The publication of this book was made possible, in part, by a generous contribution from Razom for Ukraine. Since 2014, Razom has been working to provide support for Ukraine on the ground and to amplify Ukrainian voices in the West.

You can support our work of publishing academic books and translations of Ukrainian literature and documents by making a tax-deductible donation in any amount, or by including HURI in your estate planning.

To find out more, please visit
https://huri.harvard.edu/give.

CONTENTS

Main Characters • IX

Timeline of Events • X

Maternity Ward. 1986 • 1

Papa Korniyenko. The First Seven Years • 11

Fink. Munich. 2019 • 19

Tanya Nefyodova. The End of the Millennium • 27

Thelma. Around the Millennium • 35

Lischke. Donetsk. Trolley • 41

Angelina. Before Thelma and a Bit After • 49

Call Sign "Marshal" from 2014 on • 57

Maria. Life as War • 65

Nefyodov. Borders of Time • 73

Ernest. Donetsk. Cartoons • 81

Bohdan Korniyenko. January 2000 • 89

Tanya Nefyodova Is Fifty • 97

Fink. Kyiv. 2019 • 105

Thelma. 2004–2006. Escapes • 113

Nefyodov. 2004–2011. Watercolor • 121

Petro. Off the Trolley at the Start of the Millenium • 129

Angelina. Pregnancy • 135

Maria. Shot at the Divan • 143

Lyosha. War. On Leave • 151

Bohdan. A Letter. December 2015 • 159

Petro Lischke. The Number 17 Trolley. 2014–2015 • 167

Tanya Nefyodova. Alien. 2014 • 175

Thelma. 2015–2020 • 183

Oleksii. Munich. 2019 • 191

Angelina. Daughters. 2011–2020 • 199

Maria. On Leave and a Little Before. 2015–2016 • 207

Nefyodov. 2015–2020 • 215

Ernest. Swings. Occupation • 223

Dina. Tree. 2020 • 231

MAIN CHARACTERS

Fink (also Heinrich, Henya)

Andrey Nefyodov

Tanya Nefyodova (also Tata, Tanya Shvets)

Aleksei Nefyodov (also Lyosha [Russian]; Oleksii, Les [Ukrainian])

Angelina Pahutiak

Thelma Pahutiak

Petro Lischke

Maria Lischke

Halya Lischke (also Halyuska, Haska)

Bohdan Korniyenko

Alla Korniyenko

Ernest Korniyenko (also Ernie)

Khrystyna (also *pani* Khrystyna)

Dina Pahutiak

TIMELINE OF EVENTS

1986:   100th anniversary of Ernst Thälmann's birth

1991:   Collapse of the Soviet Union and re-establishment of Ukraine's independence

2000:   Dawn of the new millennium

2013:   Start of the Euromaidan Revolution (Revolution of Dignity)

2014:   Russia's war against Ukraine begins with the invasion of Crimea and the Donbas

2015:   Cecil the Lion's death

MATERNITY WARD
1986

"In honor of the 100th anniversary of the birth of Ernst Thälmann, new mothers in the Lenin District have chosen to name their children after that heroic German Communist viciously murdered by the Fascists in Buchenwald." This caption to the photograph in the local paper contained little specificity, some untruths, and a bright spot in the corner.

The photographer from the local paper arrived on time but was in a rush. The new moms and dads couldn't reach a decision on which of the newborns would bear the name of the German Communist. Fink was tired of trying to convince them and almost gave up entirely. But it would be a shame to give up on such a good idea. And that's why Fink just had him photograph the whole group. The Pahutiak girl and one half of the Lischke twins, the unfortunate little Korniyenko boy, well, really, the two unfortunate Korniyenko boys, and the fortunate Nefyodov boy, at least as far as parents go—though, really, who can say for sure. At that time, it didn't occur to anyone that the children could be photographed individually. Now? Sure, now it's possible. But Fink's not sure it's actually better. A modern-day diapers commercial is just as much a violation of children's rights as names assigned based on directives from the local Communist Party administration, or in honor of a favorite relative or a character in a book. The children can't refuse. Sometimes a name fits quite well, but it can also pinch, lack a good nickname, prove dangerous, be hard to pronounce in another language, or fail to resonate with one's sense of self. Of course, adults have the right to change their names, but there's no guarantee that a new, consciously chosen name won't pinch, tear, or bother them. Moreover, society is of the opinion that only weirdos, spies, cowards, and immigrants change their names. Other people—"normal" people—don't even think about their name. It is what it is. In the worst case, they just get used to being called "honey."

Now when Fink looks at the newspaper clipping or shows it to someone, he can't find the language to describe it. There are plenty of words, but they clump together into a crowd without any rules because the rules have been forgotten, and the explanations are just plain ridiculous. Too ridiculous or inadequately obscured (what does it matter now), carelessly interred, and relevant to no one. Whenever Fink tries to describe it, whether to himself or the rare interlocutor, he can taste coal dust and newspaper ink on his tongue. The crowd of words scatters, and he doesn't know which to pursue, which words to consider his own. He goes wrong every time. The words mock him with their disobedience and the discarded meanings, meanings they may never have actually possessed. So he talks as best he can, bouncing along bureaucratic bumps, tangling the time loops, baffled by the blank spots that just yesterday were so significant, and now proffer only shame—or indifference at best. He allows himself, really forces himself, to speak and frequently uses random words that he seizes just as they slip by or pop out from a corner. It's embarrassing, but he promises to explain anything that's confusing.

At the beginning, Fink wanted them to be Germans. He was born in Ukraine in 1940, so, before he could be a German for even a little while, he was instantly a Fascist. He wanted a different childhood for other little German Soviet children. Completely different. He wanted annual gifts from the Soviet-German Friendship Club to lift the children up to fantastic heights, for letters from Germany to silence the bullies, for the chewing gum, pens, and other coveted scarcities to elicit envy, so that everyone, everyone, everyone—children, teachers, neighbors—would want to be their friends. And no one would ever spit in their faces or taunt them from behind: "Dumb, dumb Fritz, foul fascist: Hitler, Hitler, dirty Kraut, looked around, his eyes popped out."

Maria and Petro Lischke would not have been Fink's first choice. Aside from the last name, there was nothing German about them: no memories, no sense of order, no bloodline. Maria wasn't even German at all. Fink had made it a point to check her file. Petro also, by the way, marked himself as Russian in his official documents. Well, and Fink himself, Heinrich Fink, also recorded himself as Russian and went by the name Gennady. But it couldn't go on like this any longer. If Fink had had children, he wouldn't have told them about the Beer Hall Putsch. He would have told them about Goethe or Thomas Mann; at first, he would have forbidden them from reading Remarque, but later would definitely have allowed it; he would have explained that, before Martin Luther King, there was the real Martin Luther, not precisely a revolutionary, but a fighter. Definitely a fighter. But Fink didn't have children. Petro Lischke, however, who drove a trolley and was in good standing at work, was expecting a child right on time. Just in time for the centenary.

As the Vice Chairman of the District Executive Party Committee, Fink called Petro and Maria into his office and suggested they consider it. Maria was huge and hoping for twins. All the better. You really couldn't wish for more. But the doctors weren't convinced it was twins and the Lischkes declined an ultrasound due to the "risks from radiation."

Despite a touch of fear, Fink took the risk of calling the district newspaper to send out a photographer. And when the Lischkes had a baby girl rather than twins—an enormous little girl at thirteen pounds—it was too late and humiliating to cancel. The apparatus that Fink had set in motion, though creaky, was already at work. And so the Regional Party Committee had approved the initiative and agreed to donate a television and a rug; the Soviet-German Friendship Club were preparing to welcome a delegation from Germany; and, at the regional administration offices, there was talk of contributing a one-time financial gift or maybe even an apartment.

One bed stood empty in Maria Lischke's ward. Mama Korniyenko had died during the night from a hemorrhage. She didn't know how to complain, didn't know it was possible and even necessary to let someone know she felt ill. She didn't really know anything about what was possible or what was supposed to happen, she didn't want to be a bother, she didn't want to get yelled at by the night nurse, so she got weaker and, most likely, fell asleep. At twelve, she fed the baby. Everyone knew that because they all nursed the babies at that time. By one, they were lazily finishing up with pumping. And then they went to sleep. A person can hemorrhage to death right in front of everyone. If they're under a blanket, say, or fully dressed, or maybe in a car or office, then you won't see it happening. You can't expect people to know just by looking that the person next to them is bleeding out. Especially if that person doesn't say anything. If she'd said something—well, sure. Of course, in that case—I mean we're decent people, because solidarity, because who, if not us? But she didn't say anything. So it's her own fault.

There could have been an awful scandal if the Korniyenko girl had had anyone other than her boy-husband. If there had been someone who knew how to shout, how to make demands and threats. But there wasn't anyone like that. Her bed was empty. The ward was anticipating investigations and reprimands, so Fink's idea suited them, too.

Any death can be hidden behind a big, beautiful idea—even more than one death.

Baby boy Korniyenko—7 pounds 4 ounces, 19.7 inches—wasn't German, but the apartment, rug, and color television certainly wouldn't hurt. They couldn't replace his mother, but still, it would be fair. Baby boy Korniyenko and baby boy Nefyodov would make a good pair, a good story. A triangle of Russo-Ukrainian-German friendship forms a solid, stable figure.

The mother of baby boy Nefyodov—6 pounds 4 ounces, 18.1 inches—glanced sideways toward the empty bed with its stripped mattress and asked, "Are you out of your mind?"

Fink promised to find out. It was a joke. A bad joke that no one even noticed because at that moment, the mother of baby girl Pahutiak—6 pounds 12 ounces, 20.5 inches—demanded to know, "Why only boys? Who decided to leave girls out of it? I need a rug, too!" The Lischke baby's mother said that they already had a rug, but they really wanted a television because Petro likes to watch soccer and, after a hard day of work, he certainly has every right to do so—in living color and not at the stadium, seeing as how he's now a young father and needs to sit at home.

The new mothers suddenly got louder and more wound up, unanimously agreeing that a rug, a television, and an apartment weren't nearly enough, and, if someone wanted this to happen, then they needed to be more serious and offer something substantial. They even started making a list: a garden plot, a fence, a Zhiguli, two more carpets, two televisions, another plot of land, a seaside vacation in Hurzuf, access to the specialty goods store, a Finnish down jacket, four strollers, four cribs, another rug. All these rugs were making Fink's head spin. He stepped out of the room, where Lischke and Nefyodov looked at him disapprovingly shaking their heads.

"Not happening," said Petro.

"That's right," agreed Nefyodov. "No one is going to make a mockery of my son."

In the picture, Fink was smiling. He stood on the bottom step, front and center. As he stood there, smiling and waiting for the flash, he just wanted to cry. He was thinking about the fact that he could give them Germany. Not Fascists, but Germans, who are definitely worth something. It could be an excellent gift. Excellent. But instead of a gift, it came out as coercion. And he felt like a fascist, the last fascist in the world, who had promised "never again" and supposedly had changed for the better.

The Pahutiak mama was standing behind him. She was smiling, too, because she knew the rules everywhere and liked to pretend that she was following them. She was thinking that now she could sleep on her stomach again. Maria and Petro Lischke smiled tensely. They'd already argued due to strongly differing opinions regarding the potential television. The Nefyodov parents looked sternly into the lens. The corners of their mouths turned upwards, but their eyes expressed something entirely different. Papa Nefyodov was thinking that he could have bought a tape player for the Zhiguli, but now everything would be spent on baby supplies, and he'd have to drive in silence. Mama Nefyodova was thinking that, now that the baby was no longer inside her, she could get a haircut without worrying that it might cause the baby to lose a finger, an arm, or even a leg. Papa Korniyenko didn't look into the lens at all. He looked at his baby and was terrified. Just terrified and nothing else. Papa Korniyenko thought, "Just don't let him die. Just don't let him die."

You couldn't see the babies' faces. But they definitely weren't smiling. The two little girls and two little boys were experiencing their last moment of omniscience and universal connection, that moment of transition when they were far wiser and greater than their parents and grandparents and the entire world, which would soon enough make them stupid, vulnerable, and not very happy, banging into the sharp edges which characterize not only objects, but other people, as well. Fink was sure that the Korniyenko boy could see his own mother who would someday end up being younger than him. And all of them, these human bundles, could definitely see Babá because she would never miss a circus like this, the type of absurd, tense situation that she liked to come up with herself, forcing other people to spend a long time trying to sort it out, before she would appear— as the camera flash, a health inspector, a heavy rainstorm, a brilliant thought in the mind of a fool, a raid on the bottle recycling center—and victoriously resolve everything.

"In honor of the 100th anniversary of the birth of Ernst Thälmann, new mothers in the Lenin District have chosen to name their children after that heroic German Communist viciously murdered by the Fascists in Buchenwald." Indeed, this caption to the photograph in the local paper contained little specificity, some untruths, and the bright spot of the overexposed corner. The bosses were not pleased. Fink promised to correct his error and offered journalists the opportunity to visit with the families at home. The offerings were made: a color television, a rug, two strollers, two cribs, membership cards for the Soviet-German Friendship Club, and an apartment in a brand-new building slated to be opened in the coming year.

One untruth lay in the fact that no one had seen Thälmann's dead body. It was never found. According to the official version, all that remained were ashes and the villainy of the Fascists who didn't allow Ernst to rest in peace. But that had never prevented Fink from believing that miraculous escapes are possible—that a person could disappear, dissolve, transform themselves, leave behind a life that had proved alien along with the memories you can't get rid of, and start over again. Much later, Fink formulated it for himself thus: "You don't only turn to ashes. You can also be born of ashes."

Another bit of untruth lay in the fact that the mothers hadn't made any decisions. Especially not Mama Korniyenko. Fink made the decision for her and didn't know whether he would be tormented by it for the rest of his life or whether the pangs would pass, as they had in the past, whether it would be forgotten and heal over, only to occasionally make itself known in a sudden wrenching of the gut, shortness of breath, or unexpected flush of shame.

They named the Korniyenko boy Ernest. With an extra "e," which really didn't belong.

And they named the Pahutiak girl Thelma, which was close enough to Thälmann.

Nothing could be done about the overexposed corner. The bright spot in the upper left area of the photograph showed up in every frame taken by the local photographer. It sometimes touched the parents' heads, sometimes merged with the sky, and sometimes shone like a chunk of the sun in a lackadaisical child's drawing. The photographer retouched the photo by hand, but somehow it still showed up in the typeset paper. At the newspaper, they spent a long time trying to determine who was actually at fault: the typesetter or the photographer. They ultimately arrived at the conclusion that outdated equipment was to blame.

After the dust settled, Papa Nefyodov bought himself a foreign car. Of course, in this matter, nothing was ever entirely settled; dusty remnants continued to float in the air, a mix of mites, specks, and contaminants. Any foreign-made car would be better than a Zhiguli, even at the most advanced age. He didn't buy it right away, but six years later. Until then, he drove without music. Mama Pahutiak slept on her stomach from the day she left the hospital. The Lischkes hated her because she embodied the opportunity that they had foolishly bungled and delivered into her hands. Even the color television they ended up buying couldn't change that. Because she, Thelma's mother, got her television for free, and they didn't. "But at least they hadn't sold their daughter." And plenty of people agreed with that. Little Ernest was healthy. But a year later, three years later, and even six years on, his dad was still terrified. Apparently, it couldn't be avoided.

Those remnants also included delegations from Dresden and Berlin, who brought washing machines and Siemens meat grinders for the families. The heads of the delegations lamented the fact that the children lived in broken homes. Fink felt that such stupidity was the effect of Communism, not the German character.

Also, and here the remnants were exceptionally dusty, three years after this photograph, in the place for which Fink's heart yearned so much, people tore down the wall separating them. However, Fink couldn't immediately uncover any connection between what had happened and what he had intended in the beginning.

PAPA KORNIYENKO
THE FIRST SEVEN YEARS

"One good thing," Bohdan said to Alla, "is that I have an apartment and you don't have to meet my parents."

She shrugged.

"Another good thing," said Bohdan to Alla, "is that I'm not going into the army because my mother bought me a 'white card' as a parting gift, so I'm exempt from military service and you won't have to wait for me. And one more good thing is that I'm smart. I figure things out quickly, I can study for the both of us. I cook, do laundry, clean, and take out the trash. And I've been offered a job at Intercomputer, by the way. I'm polite, Alla. Smart, polite, and handsome. What more could you want?"

She shrugged her shoulders again. Naked shoulders. Then she sighed, tucked her nose into his neck, sniffed, kissed him...

The archive Bohdan carried around in his head and didn't go through for a long time was certainly not a child's archive. For instance, you might come across Alla's navel with thin white fuzz "along the lower edge of the ravine," or the map of blue rivers on her legs wistfully seeking the sea, or the mole on her left breast nicknamed the "ladybug." "Ladybug, ladybug, Fly away home, your house is on fire, and your children are gone..." Fly away home... Fly away.

Music is math. Billiards is math. Dutch oil painting is also math. According to Birkhoff's aesthetic measure formula, the measure of beauty is the measure of order, divided by the amount of effort expended on comprehending the essence of the object.

In the Bohdan-Birkhoff formula, division by zero is prohibited. Which means that whoever doesn't make an effort will never see and appreciate beauty. Bohdan tried. He always tried. In mathematics, the ideal nation for lost and forgotten children, you can arrogantly invent numbers, believing that they never existed before. You can invent formulas and be amazed that, in theory, the world is solvable. Though never entirely.

Diapers are math and Ernest's fingers are Fibonacci numbers; a baby bottle corresponds to the baby's weight just as the baby himself does to the projection of his own future.

Bohdan didn't remember Alla's funeral, or how he and Fink had for some reason baptized the baby, agreeing to Heorhii for his baptismal name. He didn't remember how he'd arranged for flexible attendance in college, how he'd completed one semester and then a second, or how he'd tested the Intercomputer software. He only saw the clock: six, nine, twelve, three, six, nine, twelve. And the iron, the two buckets of boiled water for bathing, and the Maliutka washing machine, which got fed up with constant use and then flooded dirty water all over the bathroom and a bit into the corridor. He remembered that the infant health nurse was named Mila, and the doctor was Aleksandra Yakovlevna. He remembered the inhale-hatred for the words and phrases "*status epilepticus*," "umbilical hernia," "dysplasia," and "hydrocele." And exhale-love for the irritated "diagnosis not confirmed."

He didn't complain because there was no one to complain to. And no one had told him that he could complain.

He didn't think about Alla because there wasn't any time. And because he was very upset with her.

He didn't call anyone for help because there wasn't anyone to call. And because he didn't believe anyone would come.

He never thought about things getting better because he just really wanted to sleep. And because the most important thing was for the baby not to die.

He didn't stop for even a minute because he had to live and work. And because, when he did stop, all the horrors he didn't want to know about himself would come crowding in.

For example, a certain logic of arrivals and departures would emerge. His grandmother raised him, then left him at the doors of the Polytechnic Institute. Alla gave birth to his son, then left him at the steps to the maternity ward. So it turns out that his mother is alive only because she's not with him. Follow this thought to its logical conclusion while, say, standing in line at the doctor's office, ironing diapers, or in that moment when the result finally matched the target value... In short, at that basically normal moment when life would settle down for a moment and become almost sweet, he would tumble into the abyss of thoughts about baby Heorhii, also known as Ernest. According to the logic of arrivals and departures, the baby would also have to depart, leaving Bohdan at the entrance to some new and different life. "Aaaagh," screamed Bohdan in a loud inner voice and banged against an internal concrete wall until he bled. "Aaaagh."

Alla's mother visited from Alma-Ata. Twice. The first time, she brought honey and nuts. The second time, she said that the little boy needed to be officially registered. Alla's mother was beautiful, like a simplified expression in which the variety of fractions, variables, squares, and square roots added up to -b. At their wedding, she'd said, "Don't count on me!" Bohdan's mother visited from Damascus. Also twice. But only as far as Moscow. So baby Ernest had zero chance of rescue.

However, it was possible not to love him. Not to love him as Bohdan had loved his grandmother and had loved Alla.

Not to love him in order to prevent his pointless, premature death. Moreover, it was very easy not to love Ernest. He screamed, shat, peed his diapers, belched, got his hands or feet stuck in the bars of the crib, squirmed when Bohdan tried to dress him, twisted away at the sight of kefir, spat out his vegetable broth, sucked on Bohdan's shirt, splashed water all over the bathroom, mixed up day and night, demanded food out of schedule, smiled twice at Alla's mother, rubbed his eyes and got them infected, and broke out in red spots that could have been measles, scarlet fever, or syphilis, but they always turned out to be just prickly heat. He wanted to sleep in Bohdan's bed, learned to crawl and to climb out of the stroller, didn't share his toys, fell down the hill, scraped his nose on the asphalt four times. His first word was "Baba," his second was "more-more-more," and the third was "kookoo." Then Ernest said, "Sweeteeee!"? Bohdan decided that this was unimaginable self-absorption. Entirely unacceptable. He should be ashamed.

Much later, Bohdan read that "the joy of mathematics lies in the fact that we create certain objects and then discover that they possess any number of remarkable properties that we didn't intend to inculcate in them."

And this turned out to relate directly to Ernest and his "Sweeteee," which led to at least two deductions. First: no one but Bohdan himself could have taught the child that idiotic word. Second: "Sweeteee" wasn't a name for himself but a way of addressing someone else. And, since there was no one but Bohdan in the room or in Ernest's life, then the appearance of "Sweeteee" provided an exact answer for when the child had first called Bohdan "Papa."

There was no answer to the question of when Bohdan called himself a dad. For the first year, a downcast Fink pointlessly checked on them once a week insisting that Bohdan should "feel it." Though Fink proposed feeling something different every time: from the correspondence between a name and fate, to responsibility for the fate of the world, to fatherhood as a sign of being chosen, and to fresh air to be drawn in through the nose and released out through the mouth for two hours while Ernest slept and Fink "watched" him.

Inhaling the "fresh air" near the metallurgical plant, instead of feeling, Bohdan took it easy: he'd nap on a bench, ride his skateboard, meet up with classmates—mostly girls. Three times he drank beer, twice it was vodka. And one night he didn't come home at all: he wound up at the dorms instead. He woke up at six next to a girl he either didn't know or didn't remember, with no pants, no conscience, and, according to the social standards of the time, no right to raise a child.

"I thought you'd been murdered," said Fink. "But since that's not the case, I'll do it myself."

"I won't let it happen again! I swear!"

"Whatever. Let it happen again! Definitely! You just have to let me know. I have no idea what to do with children. All I can do is sit next to them or sleep nearby. You left us in an awkward situation. I gave him a piece of pickle so he wouldn't miss you, and now he has diarrhea..." Fink gestured toward a mountain of diapers by the sofa.

"Sweeteee!" shouted Ernest enthusiastically. "Koo-koo!"

"You need to start reading him books. He's not a bird, after all," frowned Fink and said that he'd come back to check.

At first, when he was still growing up himself, and later, when he was starting to grow old a bit, Bohdan would look back at Ernest's first year, and even the first seven, to find himself there and try to understand who he was. But the archive, which was definitely not for children, didn't offer special access, insisting instead that, in that string of monotonous days, there was nothing special or unique that distinguished Bohdan from other young mothers, except, maybe, for his lack of overfull breasts, mastitis or stretch marks. Bohdan insisted on his right to see his own case and threw out what he considered his trump card: "Everything was different for me. I saw him for the first time in the photo. The one where Thelma made bunny ears behind his head. Until then, I'm sorry, but no. Is that really normal? Is it really like that for everyone?" The archive didn't respond. Consultations were not offered when the archive was closed. And when it was open, Bohdan was generally drunk and the following morning he couldn't remember whether he'd worked with documents or whether Alla's navel still occupied all his memory files and was still the navel of the Earth for him—an omphalos flanked by two golden eagles.

Fink proposed a first day of school photo for the children born in the year of Thälmann's centenary. Ernest appeared in that photo, took form, and suddenly became visible to Bohdan. Fully visible—separate, pale, with small ears and a big mouth missing a lower tooth—that priceless tooth which had emerged along his first high fever. Ernest was thin, funny, and laughing. Thelma's bunny ears didn't ruin anything because nothing could ruin a little boy who looked that much like Alla. The words "my son" came easily to Bohdan. But "I'm a father" or "I'm a dad," no.

Fink took one group photo with a Polaroid and a second with one of the cheap automatic cameras that were just becoming popular and facilitated the development of large and small photography shops. Nefyodov had just opened his first photo shop and made free copies for everyone. Every picture had a bright spot in the corner. Nefyodov promised to discipline the machine operator and maybe the whole shift. Maria Lischke asked Nefyodov for a job. Thelma's mom proposed that they send the whole crew off to the same class. She was willing to pick the kids up after school and do lessons with them. A private afterschool group—what do you think? Thelma's mom was most likely a "C" student, but Bohdan thought it was a good idea. Convenient. Thelma's mom promised to give Bohdan a discount since he'd given up the apartment for her, although neither of them had actually gotten one. But it could still happen. Fink said that he could also collect the kids after school and do lessons with them, history for instance. "History of the Communist Party?" asked Tanya Nefyodova sarcastically. "That's over already—too late. You should have thought of it sooner."

In 1993, the Nefyodovs and Lischkes felt like the winners. It turned out that their choice and answer had been the correct ones: Thelma and Ernest were now just a belch of the totalitarian past. So now the families could amiably socialize, with only a hint of condescension and no nagging thoughts about dusty rugs. (One of those was still rolled up at Bohdan's apartment, and Thelma's mom had already cut hers up and sold it as eight smaller ones year before last at a market in the Hungarian town of Nyíregyháza.)

Fink had also baptized little Thelma, taking the name Elena from a book of saints.

"Henya, I've told you a hundred times that my Stefik doesn't like yellow chrysanthemums. I mean, I'm not even sure he should have flowers at all. The pollen's bad for his asthma. He'll be offended. Henya, did I ever tell you how he fought for every window when he was in the Ministry of Architecture? Every single little door? He was absolutely relentless. I barely convinced him to plant a nasturtium over there, in the corner by the porch. He grumbled that even our porch might have some sort of cultural layer underneath that should be studied. I didn't indulge him. I just didn't indulge him and that's that. So just pitch the chrysanthemums back where you got them."

"They're not for him..."

"Right, not for him. So then why does it say, 'To Stefan, from Heinrich?' Do you think I've forgotten how to read here, in Germany? Are you kidding? When I fight with my son, it's always only in Ukrainian. He already knows that if I switch to Ukrainian, it will go poorly for him. I talk to doctors and hairdressers in Russian. With Stefik, though, either was fine. He studied all the languages. Do you know how it was at his high school? They studied English, French, Italian... What kind of architect doesn't speak Italian? Take Giorgio Vasari, for instance. What language did he use for his architect biographies? That's right! Italian. He wrote them; Stefik read them. But, Henya, what do we care about Vasari? Am I right? Our Haska—now that's a book. The book of all books. And no need to learn a foreign language. Now drop the flowers and let's go..."

It was one and the same conversation every time—one and the same topic, one and the same people, one and the same details. These stories of their separate lives had been desiccated by the passage of time and resembled an herbarium: a large, beautiful album stuffed years ago with fragile, crumbling leaves, herbs, and flowers. Crumbling, but still fragrant with the scents of forest, trails, and steppe. Not without some hardening of the arteries and a touch of dementia. But whenever Fink would start up again for the 1,000th time denouncing his "bad Heinrich," Khrystyna always pretended to be hearing it for the first time. He did the same. He pretended it was the first time that he was hearing who Stefik was, what time he had to get up for work, and how he loved gambling—not here in Munich, but only in the States and only on the special machines where the coins jump straight into your hands or your bag, one after the other, one after the other...

"I was still young when he fell for me. Thirty-five. Well, let's say almost forty. I was plump then, not like now. The damn cancer ate over sixty pounds. But what cancer could live with me? Tell me that. Now my hair's grown out, my legs work, and I have plenty of wigs. I wear them to keep warm now, to keep the wind off my head... My Stefik came out to Ukraine alone—remember when it was first possible? It was 1989. He was looking for his father's grave. I said to him first thing, 'Death to Fascist Occupiers.' And he started crying, can you imagine?"

Once a week, Fink and Khrystyna have lunch together. Sometimes at her place, sometimes at his. Once a week, they go to a lecture at the university or to a concert. Khrystyna has a car, but they don't drive—no need to waste the gas. They take the bus. Once a week, Fink accompanies Khrystyna to the hospital for a Vitamin B12 shot, a physical exam and a prescription refill. A visit with the doctor, too, a woman from Kherson. She's so rude, says Khrystyna, but why not help the girl get ahead?

Fink's been here almost fifteen years and receives a pension. It's fine—there's enough money for what he needs. And he goes to Ukraine with whatever's left over. At least once a year. Sometimes twice.

Khrystyna's lived here for nearly thirty years. She owns property. A house. She rents one half of it out, but the renters never stay more than six months. They get tired of it. But that's fine: there are always new people. And new people have new stories. Khrystyna's stories are all old. Always the same ones. But Khrystyna is as relentless as a tank. She achieves what others consider impossible.

Three years ago, Fink came back from Ukraine with a book by Halyna Lischke. Halyna is the girl who could have been Thelma. But became Haska instead.

"Oh my God, my God... I cried my eyes out... I absolutely cried them out... Oh my God... I mean, Henya... Why didn't you warn me to have a stiff drink before I started reading it?! You can't do that to people. You just can't... Damned fascists. Damned Russian fascists and then... They can't get away with it. I'll get everyone to read our Haska. Her books will be in the libraries and schools here. By the way, have you seen the one built in 1926? Right at the end of my street? I keep thinking about what they used to learn there. 'Heil Hitler,' right? And now they're teaching something different... Just like at home. Who could've thought that I'd be getting ready to die in the very lair where all that plague started? And I'm sorry, Henya, but you're stupid—you're getting ready to go back over there, where it could all end... But we'll get Haska translated, just wait and see. I swear to you, we will... I swear..."

Once a week, Fink and Khrystyna bickered over flowers. Not just chrysanthemums. Depending on the day it might be asters, lilies, tulips, or daffodils. Once Fink even managed to bring dried cornflowers and daisies from home after a small fight with the authorities at Boryspil Airport for permission.

Fink would always make a bouquet and carefully cut out a ribbon of colored paper, meticulously writing the inscription in gold paint. Gold on blue. Beautiful. And time and again, Khrystyna complained about asthma and allergies and the possible resentment of the deceased, though Stefan had never been guilty of that sin. On the contrary, he was incredibly gentle, like a cross between a Finnish Santa and the long-haired John Lennon. Stefan had a small, firm hand and pale blue eyes, overwhelmed by the abundance of beauty under the heavens.

All the street names in Khrystyna's neighborhood started with the word *Wald*. Almost all. Many of them. Wald means "forest." Forest is a good, peaceful word, unthreatening and apolitical. Each little "wald" of lovely houses was a stream flowing into the sea—a forest sea, where the trees aren't trimmed into tidy rows, where the grasses and shrubs run wild, with just enough gravel on the paths, if any, to keep them from washing away into mud. The wind chases across in soft waves, and it's calm, solemn, and infinite. This is the big Waldfriedhof, sixty thousand graves.

In the Ostheim that was later renamed Velikokrasnoshchokovo, then Thälmannovo, and now Boikovskoe... In that Ostheim from which the Germans had been deported,

Krasnoshchokov erased, and the poor Boikos brought in from the Polish border—in that Ostheim, they had forgotten all about Thälmann. But then, coming full circle, the Russians remembered Thälmann and came back in 2014 to occupy it with tanks, just like Prague in 1968.

In that Ostheim where all of the Fink-Mennonites lived until 1940, there were originally only about three hundred people. And a little cemetery. Here, in the Bavarian Ostheim, there are a little more than three thousand. Not in the cemetery—living people.

Fink's mother had told him that they were Germans from Baden or Prussia. She was afraid to remember any more precisely. But why would Baden Germans give their settlement a Bavarian name? Why would they allow such confusion? It's stupid...

Fink had never lived in Ostheim. He never got to see what they said was the tallest spire, the 150-foot spire of the Sacred Heart of Jesus; he never walked on the Stone Graves searching for the fern flower that could transform dull and dreary Ostheim into a magical kingdom. He didn't go, didn't take the risk, and, therefore, never failed and was never changed into a frog, or bear, or dog; was never frozen into a petrified sculpture atop the Stone Graves. He never walked along the Stone Graves because he grew up in Kazakhstan, where the ethnic Germans were deported right before the war and he went to college in Zaporizhzhia because his father, as a frontline veteran, was pardoned and received the right to work hard to redeem himself once and for all. Fink learned from Stefan that he was supposed to have become a pacifist and been baptized as an adult, like all Mennonites. And from Khrystyna he learned that all sorts of people were buried in Waldfriedhof.

"Anyone and everyone. Even people who should have been thrown to the dogs. Hitler's pilot, for example. I even made myself a list, for the shock value. And then I thought, if our village had poured chlorine over the fascists and buried them in concrete like they did in the city, then I would never have found my Stefan, and he wouldn't have found his father. We didn't toss them out. It's true they were lying there without names... They didn't exactly introduce themselves to us. Particularly once they were dead. But the women decided: one per hole. And God have mercy on them. So, anyway... Leni Riefenstahl's still there, in Waldfriedhof. A whole section of Italians. Clean and cheerful. As for Ukrainians, there's Bandera. I have so many on my list... So many."

Khrystyna took a straightforward approach with the Lischke girl's book.

"I have a novel that everyone needs to read. Who do I contact?" she asked at the university after a lecture on management psychology. She looked gorgeous that evening with a white wig warming her head. People didn't even recognize her. She looked like an aging Marilyn Monroe. "Who do I need to contact? Are you humans or what?" she barked when no one answered her the first time.

"Are you humans or what" works. The farther west you go, the better it works. The desire to be human, or rather, a good human, makes some people do stupid things, and compels others to do a lot of good. An older lady whose son-in-law worked at a publishing house responded; so did a serious-looking guy of about fifty with dreadlocks and torn jeans, who was married to a Polish translator. And wherever you find Polish, you'll also find Croatian, Ukrainian, and even a little Russian. The wheels started turning, and Khrystyna only managed to follow where, who, how, and with whom. Connections stretched into Austria, reached Vienna, touched on German-speaking parts of Switzerland, and an answer arrived from Berlin.

"Brilliant," said Fink. "I never could have done that."

"That's why you're not a writer. I couldn't have done it either," Khrystyna responded with a shrug.

"You're brilliant..."

"Oh, come off it."

Once a week, Khrystyna and Fink went to visit the relatives. Stefan's mother and a bit of his father in the form of a small, stamped urn, which held dirt from each of the twenty German graves in the village of Boholyuby, Ukraine.

They always visited Stefan's sister, without fail. And Stefan himself—Stefan Reiner who had taught Fink to drink dark beer, to distinguish Corinthian columns from Doric, to read the Bible, to say Bosch instead of "Boskh," to gamble online in secret from Khrystyna, to listen to opera, and even go to the opera if the tickets were cheap, and also to talk about himself, to consider himself unique and allow himself to remember. Yes, Stefan, with his small, firm hand and development plans for cities he wanted to build.

But of course, Fink didn't bring the flowers for him.

TANYA NEFYODOVA
THE END OF THE MILLENNIUM

For many years, Tanya Nefyodova had a plot of land and knew other people's secrets. Tanya Nefyodova had never wanted her own apartment—not a cooperative Czech-style one, not a government one, not one purchased on a loan. No. She wanted to live in a house. Tanya Nefyodova wanted two children, a perfect picture: a boy and a girl. But the boy didn't arrive until she was nearly thirty, by which time she had joined her relatives in viewing herself with disapproval and she couldn't even bear to see pregnant women or other people's children at all. And while little Lyosha only turned up when she was almost thirty, the little girl never did arrive.

The land was an allotment from her job as doctor for the factory workers. The Khrushchev high-rises and the old, wooden houses, the rags and riches started right outside the gates. Well, the rags and riches of the high-rises began behind the door of each apartment. Their shared entryways were filled with spit and piss, the elevator knobs were always scorched, and burnt matches clung to the ceilings on the landings. Tanya Nefyodova wanted to try flicking a match up so that it would stick and cling to the ceiling. But she couldn't bring herself to do it. Tanya Nefyodova was a doctor, not a natural scientist. Climbing up to some thirteenth floor without an elevator, she would stop to catch her breath and read the graffiti scrawled on the blue or green walls. Vitya's a jerk, Lara's a bitch, Tsoi lives, AC/DC, Pink Floyd, I love Katya, Drop dead, you prick, Don't fight, girls... It's entirely possible that some of the graffiti was as old as she was. Vitya, who lived on the landing embellished with the words "Vitya's a jerk," already had grandchildren and had survived a minor heart attack. There wasn't any Lara in the building—neither a sweetheart nor a bitch. She may have moved or died a long time ago, but someone's resentment remained on the wall for many, many years, black at first, then fading to gray. Sometimes, the walls were repainted, but the old graffiti always made its way through.

"It's like 'mene, mene, tekel, upharsin,'" said one of her patients on the thirteenth floor (stomach ulcer, hypertension, rheumatoid arthritis, glaucoma). "It's a warning. It can't be erased."

"Though it can be written over," replied Tanya, embarrassed to ask what that "mene, mene" meant. In the pre-Google era, human ignorance was long-lived—compounded by shame, it could last for years, only to eventually be resolved by chance or until the question had been forgotten and disappeared on its own. And they did disappear: all sorts of clever, strange, beautiful, and, undoubtedly, largely unimportant questions. Stupid ones disappeared, too.

Nefyodov is both a person and a last name. (Tanya never called him by his first name, even in the heat of an argument. Neither did his parents, nor his employees. Even he had long since forgotten that his name was Andrey.) Nefyodov told her about Belshazzar's Feast in the year 2000. Not just anywhere, but in London. At the National Gallery. "Tanya, look at this Rembrandt and the writing on the wall. See the hand with no body? It's writing 'mene, mene, tekel, upharsin.' 'Weighed, measured, and found wanting.' And that's it—the end of Babylon. The end of Belshazzar. I never thought I'd get to see this... And here I am looking at it... Incredible!"

They came to London to "sniff it out." Tanya Nefyodov wasn't interested in either sniffing or in London itself. She already had a house, Lyosha, and a plot of land. London couldn't add anything to that and would actually take away her land. Nefyodov tried to take it away, too. He'd start up, "I make good money, I make good money... We don't need your three kopecks to survive. Why don't you stay home? Stay home, Tata, would that be so bad?" They would fight, make up and fight again.

"Papa, your shouting is going to give me computations," little Lyosha would say.

"Complications," corrected Tanya. "Not 'computations.' And the only way you can have complications is if you're sick. You don't want to get sick, do you?"

"No, I don't want to get sick. I also don't want to computate, okay?"

"He takes after his mama," Nefyodov would sum up, but still, a couple of times a year, usually in the winter, he'd start up again. And they would fight again, but less ferociously. And they would make up less ferociously, too.

And, while Nefyodov growled, "Don't humiliate me," Tanya Nefyodova would stubbornly put on her worn-out boots (or sandals in the summer) and make her way to the floors without working elevators or hide behind a fence waiting for someone to call off the dog or for the dog to get used to her and quit barking.

She still read the graffiti in the entryways. Viktor Tsoi wasn't so often alive. He went gray, along with all the "jerks," "bitches," and "lardasses." On the other hand, the "dicks" blazed there, along with "Holoborodko for Mayor of Mospyne," "Last one in is a rotten egg," "'Shakhtar is #1," and "Yanukovych is a Scumbag." Some were nice: the graffiti in the building across from the stadium declared, "We're all sisters" and "Mama says it's okay." Others were sad—like the one on the first floor, between the mailboxes and the elevator of a nine-story building: "What-do-you-know-about-hate?" The usual stars, swastikas, and bizarre spirals scribbled by a frightened shaking hand. Some not-so-usual poetry.

She continued reading the graffiti in the apartment buildings, but she liked houses better.

Her own house most of all, the one Nefyodov had built to replace the previous hovel on the plot. Her own two-story house with a veranda that Tanya embellished with different colored curtains from the thrift store stitched together like a rainbow or in "LSD-eye-gouging style," as Lyosha would say. She sewed them carelessly, to last a single season, so she could come up with something new for the next—maybe pastels or bright white with lace, but then she bought colorful ones again and again. The house with the veranda and "sails" always stood out.

"Love thy neighbor as thyself." Tanya couldn't manage that for the neighbors, but she could for the houses. After she fell in love with her own house, she learned to love other people's houses: houses which grew out of little shacks, or never grew at all; houses built of solid concrete block or red brick, with attics or stylish flat roofs, with summer kitchens, orchards, Japanese-style gardens, with dogs, cats, chickens and even a goat that Baba Stefa would take to pasture out by the number ten trolley stop. If Fink had lived in an apartment, Tanya Nefyodova would never have forgiven his arrogance, his toadying to a state that was already collapsing (not soon enough for both of them!), and his pathetic obsequiousness—toward whom? Whom?! She'd never have forgiven the bootlicking he was constantly pushing on them—successfully with some!

But he lived in a house—one with large windows, built long ago for engineers, and, thanks to its enormous windows, which were difficult to clean, she never asked him what it was like to fall off the ladder that turned out to never have actually led anywhere. What was it like to lose your secure berth, to bury your Party membership card, to go from working "full steam ahead" to being a minor clerk at the beck and call of the hard core and only provisionally "new" authorities? She was angry at Fink. At herself, too. At the fact that she'd agreed to put Lyosha in the same class with those children. Angry at Nefyodov who would respond to Lyosha's successes by mumbling, "Not an Ernest! Obviously not an Ernest." At Thelma who, in third grade, promised to give her a granddaughter someday. Mad at Thelma's mother, who never used some parts of her brain. Most of her brain.

Fink was healthy as an ox. He would call Tanya Nefyodova out for house calls on purpose, for a sore throat, or sciatica, or an asthmatic cough, which was all too common in Donbas. "Change your place of residence," Tanya Nefyodova would tell him through gritted teeth, instead of running away and bringing an end to these visits. Instead of ending them, she was drawn into strange relationships with these strangers, and they stopped being strangers, but never stopped being people she hadn't chosen and never would have chosen.

Given the option, she would never have chosen people at all. Just houses and dogs. And cats. Houses, dogs, and cats. Healthy, preferably purebred dogs and cats. That's it. "With that kind of attitude, you have no business being a doctor," Nefyodov would tell her. And Tanya would explode: "How dare he?! She'd pulled him out of the dump with his cheap VoTech diploma—maybe he didn't buy it on the black market, but he bought it nonetheless... Who was he, a proletarian in a cheap Turkish sweater... to tell her..."

"I haven't worn a Turkish sweater in a long time," Nefyodov growled in response. "You just haven't noticed!"

"Of course!" Tanya would scream back. "Of course, you're the one who's so attentive, who sees everything, notices everything. You're the one who knows exactly who can and can't be a doctor."

She would go on and on, and then, if he didn't apologize, she'd declare a boycott. Over the years, the boycotts became more frequent, because Tanya felt good in the silence.

"I can't get through to you," Nefyodov would sigh.

"Well, keep trying, don't stop" Tanya would reply in bitter silence.

"Are you getting a divorce?" Lyosha would ask. He wouldn't notice right away, but somewhere around days three to five, he'd realize something was wrong.

"No!" they would answer in unison.

"Do you know how I met your mother?" Nefyodov would ask, sucking up to Tanya. "She cured me!"

"Well, considering the fact that you married such a terrible person, you must not have been entirely cured," Tanya would grumble.

"Not entirely?" Nefyodov would guffaw.

"I know," Lyosha would say. "You had the bubonic plague brought to Donetsk by rats in the holds of ships. Back then, Donetsk was still on the sea. And then you drank the sea. Did I get it right?"

Lyosha always had a different version of Nefyodov's salvation. The serious illnesses Tanya had conquered included anthrax contracted from Surgut oil workers; crib death out of Chuck Palahniuk and F. Scott Fitzgerald ("and then she breastfed you, Papa, and you started to grow, mature and even, sorry, get old"); diabetes with an amputation and subsequent leg transplant, which turned out to be the wrong leg because the surgeon was drunk and mixed them up ("which is why you never played soccer with me, Papa"). In reality, the 22-year-old adult Nefyodov had caught chickenpox, which he mistook for syphilis, because, of all potential scary diseases, that was the only one he knew. He was so comical, so scared and unhappy, that Tanya made a couple of house calls to his apartment and swabbed his sores with antiseptic. Nefyodov's back reminded her of a house, a big, empty house which needed to be occupied. Nefyodov had a tiny scar below his shoulder blade where he'd ripped open an infected pustule, trying to stop Tanya's hand on his back. Tanya could find that scar with her eyes closed. Nefyodov promised that only the two of them would know about this "life scar."

She always wanted to show off the house. Thus, the curtains. And, undoubtedly, also thus, the strangers, those obligatory friends, the parents of her son's classmates. Nefyodov's subordinates didn't count. They were required to admire it. Tanya wanted non-obligatory delight. She was looking for genuine envy, a quiet sigh, resentment, she wanted the person who lived in an apartment purchased with her daughter's name to admit defeat. She wanted everyone to admit that defeat while she, Tanya, celebrated victory. She also wanted her beautiful plates, goblets, drinking glasses, wine glasses, and cordials to live, to fall, break and be washed, not just sit locked away in a cupboard waiting for a special occasion. She wanted things to be beautiful not for the 70th anniversary of catastrophe, but always. So all of it—the flowers, cushions, teacups, the old trunk bought for a song out in the country, the blue armchairs, cushy seats, cheerful tablecloths, lamps, and chandeliers—all of it could be mussed. Stained, ripped, drenched in red wine. Tanya allowed everything in the house. In return, she got the immense joy of the children and the longed-for envy of the adults.

Tanya Nefyodova loved her house and allowed it to love other people. She knew other people's secrets. But for a long time she didn't know her own.

THELMA
AROUND THE MILLENNIUM

Thelma didn't bring friends home. First, there were the three years her mom had provided afterschool care. She got thoroughly sick and tired of those "friends." Halya constantly whined and begged to be picked up. Ernie rolled around on Thelma's bed, colored her Barbie's hair red, and stitched his mittens as ears onto her bear for the school's "Golden Autumn" Festival. Lyosha was tolerable, of course. But he didn't eat vermicelli, soup with dill, barley, cream of wheat, syrnyky—the farmer's cheese pancakes—or macaroni casserole.

In fact, he really didn't eat any of the things her mother cooked trying to save money on the children's food in order to... steal it. Thelma called it stealing. Nothing of the sort. Her mother called her "Thelma-Hellion." And all the afterschool kids picked it up from her. And then when their teacher was out sick one time, a stupid substitute called her "Hellion" for an entire week, thinking it was her real name.

To keep her mother from complaining about Lyosha, Thelma would finish his food for him, and she got fat. No one had told her about the connection between food and a big belly. Her mom liked it all. "You're my round, little, puffy-cheeked plumperkins," Angelina would say in the growly voice she used before she'd start to nibble. Ernest just called her fat.

That's why Thelma didn't love Ernest for the second seven years—she loved Lyosha instead. She didn't love anyone for the first seven because she didn't know anyone suitable. The third seven, she loved Ernest. The fourth seven, Lyosha again. And then the alternation seemed stupid and pointless. "We grew up pretty late, didn't we?" Thelma said to Halya much later. "But then it was all at once and completely," Halya answered.

Thelma didn't bring friends home because no one but her mother would have let people into a home like that with wallpaper hanging randomly from the walls, covering up cracks from recent "settling," with its kitchen cupboards acquired at random, and the plastic shelves that were also considered cupboards and were coated in cooking grease. The bathroom featured mold-eaten paint instead of tile, and linoleum that was like a river: in some spots running along in light waves, in others worn through to the concrete below. "Children aren't people," her mother reassured her. "Children are better than people. They don't see the bad." Her mother had too high an opinion of children, despite Thelma providing no grounds for that belief.

Another reason Thelma didn't bring friends home was that they might steal something from her. Because Thelma herself stole things. At Lyosha's parent's house, where everything was allowed anyhow, she invariably found something unique and desirable. And took it without asking. Long matches with red heads in an enormous box, Aunt Tanya's almost finished perfume samples that had sat in the bathroom vanity for at least half a year, a couple of pieces of canned pineapple. She shared some things with her mother, saying they were gifts. She shared the perfume samples, and sausage, and grapes. Once Thelma stole a watermelon. It was early spring, and the watermelon was lying under Lyosha's tall bed. When Lyosha's father had brought home a carload of watermelons, every bed in the house became a refuge for them. So then all fall and even a bit into winter, they ate watermelons.

Thelma had crawled under the bed for her bra. The last year of the first cycle of her love, she wasn't fat anymore, she was average. And, unlike Halya, she had breasts and not pimples. And no, no sex. Just what Lyosha called a "tight squeeze." Panties on, but no top. Of course, the undies weren't reliable partners, especially not Lyosha's. But Thelma tried to keep hers on, like the Spanish kept Saragossa. Saragossa was also Lyosha's and sounded way better than Brest Fortress. She crawled under the bed for her bra and saw a watermelon. She could have asked. He, the not-Ernest, never denied her anything. Never. Pens, markers, stickers (from the popular French TV show *Hélène and Friends*), or Kinder Surprise Egg hippos. (For some reason, she stole the two lions from another set anyway.) He even gave her his Tamagotchi, which she starved to virtual death in ten days. But didn't throw away.

"Thanks to you," Thelma said to Lyosha when they were both 28, "I grew up as the only person in the country with a Tamagotchi corpse." The hippos, two lions, two booklets of stickers, ten red-tipped matches, seven empty perfume samples (with a bit of scent at the very bottom still), a pair of white Adidas socks, the empty box from some Polish cookies, a whole can of pineapples, two fresh sausages, spare jeans' buttons, a broken watch face (it was already broken), two hair ties, a small empty Baileys bottle... and twenty-seven more items (she always recorded her crimes)... Thelma returned it all to Lyosha when she left. She handed him the bag and said, "Look. Here's everything you gave me. And everything I stole from you. I'm a thief. You don't need me."

She couldn't return the watermelon. It was impossible to return the stolen one that she'd carried home in her gym bag and had cut open without waiting for her mother. It hadn't even been a watermelon anymore: just an anemic, white circulatory system. Anything red in it had dried up and vanished. Even the smell was gone. Where could Thelma find a watermelon like that to return to Lyosha?

Nowhere. The watermelon and the Tamagotchi. Thelma didn't return the Tamagotchi because she was too ashamed to return corpses.

"See what a thief I am," she said on the evening of January 1, 2000, after the party with all of them: the "after-school" kids and their progenitors. Where they'd taken pictures according to weird Grandpa Fink's chirpy directions. Lyosha's mother had looked at Fink just like Lyosha used to look at a piece of dill floating in his soup. "And you don't need someone like me in your life. You see?"

And he nodded. He nodded, damn it. He nodded, shit-shit-shit. He didn't say anything. At all. Nothing... and then for a long time... nothing. She would have left anyway because that's how it had to be. That's what she had to do. But he was supposed to say something, something funny and light, so it wouldn't hurt so much. At least he could have tried to talk, could have given her a little nudge in the chest, saying, "And what is that all about?"

She wouldn't have answered and would have left anyway. But she would have left thinking she could come back. To wait out the shame and come back. But no. He nodded, took the bag with his things, and slowly closed the gate that Aunt Tanya had decorated with tiny, shining, twinkly, yellow lights like little gnomes.

What have we got to lose? Thelma had heard those words from her mother her whole life and she didn't care for the construction at all. We've got nothing to lose was much more accurate. Much.

"Hi, Ernest," she said into the receiver that same evening. "I have a couple of hours, we could go for a walk..."

Instead of a couple of hours, it turned out to be a whole seven years. It didn't happen easily and not right away. But Thelma, unlike her mother, was never flighty. On the contrary, she was very focused.

"I stole a watermelon from him, almost a year ago—last March," Thelma told Ernest as they walked down Pushkin Boulevard kicking the snow that wasn't falling silently, instead making some sort of revolting crackling sound, and obnoxiously flying up your nose and under your collar. There was no making friends with that kind of snow. You just had to ruthlessly trample it. "I stole a watermelon from him, now he's discovered the shortfall and kicked me out in disgrace."

Ernest clicked his tongue and frowned.

"What?" asked Thelma.

"You know, my horse died. In a battle with a dragon. I'm thinking it died of fright. He was afraid of everything. If you slammed the door too hard or turned on the water in the bathroom too loud, there'd instantly be a pile on the ground. He'd shit himself. Can you imagine what it's like to constantly be picking up shit behind a horse?"

"What horse?!" asked Thelma, furiously spitting out snowflakes.

"The white one, Thelma, white with a white mane. The one I'm supposed to ride in on to save you." He tsked again. "It's just not meant to be."

He turned and walked quickly down the street toward Hospital Number Five to the number ten trolley stop.

"You're a stupid horse, Ernest! You are!" Thelma shouted after him and went the other way towards Artem Street.

Two horses, her idiotic mother and one millennium were too much for her. So much, in fact, that nothing had any meaning: not the snow; not March, which would eventually arrive; not the passport she could get and then go far, far away. "They can take their pictures without me next time," Thelma repeated to herself over and over.

But it's not actually that easy to kill yourself on January 1, when there are far fewer cars in the street than people, when the slow, hungover drivers don't want a problem and just want another drink, and then another... It's not that easy. But if you jump out of a dark corner onto a spot where the snow's been cleared and it's extra slippery, then you might manage it.

"I'll swear on whatever you want," Thelma told Halya many years later. "I swear to you that Babá saved me that night."

"Babá is a spirit in our part of the city, and you were in a different part," laughed Halya.

"I'm telling you. She grabbed my arm and pulled me out of the way. And she said..."

"Any normal old woman would have pulled you out of the road. Any one."

"She glowed!"

"Under the streetlight? That's not as hard as you think."

"Yes, yes, yes. It is hard to glow with an inner light. Yes, yes, yes. Come on, we learned this crap in the same class."

"Inner light is entirely impossible," Lyosha had explained logically to the teacher back then. "Inner light is a result of the combustion of static electricity and is no cause for celebration or for writing articles in the newspaper."

"She took my arm and pulled me so hard that sometimes I feel like it still hurts..."

"If I were her, I'd have given you a punch in the face, too."

"Thanks. But she didn't do that. I just felt warm. And good. And she said..."

"Bibbidy-bobbidy-boo!"

"No. She said, 'take care of your ovaries: you're going to need them.'"

LISCHKE
DONETSK
TROLLEY

There was this other time when a passenger started having a seizure. The trolley was jam-packed and it was literally impossible for him to fall down or hit his head on the railing. He was just flailing and banging into everyone around him. People would have been happy to move, but there was no space. It was rush hour. So what did they do? That's right. They started yelling. But not right away. First, they started shaming the passenger. Saying he was acting badly, that he was violating the rules of socialist communal living and spitting foam like a Malyutka washing machine, which normal people would never buy anyway, because they're impossible to repair.

We really have to teach people to start yelling straight away when something's wrong. Animals are a lot smarter about that than we are: if a dog gets its tail caught in the door, it starts whining. It whines so much that you can hear it at the end of the line, even if you're still riding past the university. It's not even whining—it yelps and howls. That's what people need to do. If they would shout louder, someone would pay attention right away, rather than later, at the funeral, when there's no point anymore.

Of course, a trolley driver is no doctor. That's for sure. But the manual does indicate first aid. Indicate how? On paper—that is, with no actual obligation. Iodine, bandages, tourniquets, gauze... What can the passenger expect? He'll have to blow on his scratch until the nice driver smears it with iodine? For instance, it's strictly forbidden to give birth on a trolley, but to die of a heart attack? By all means.

So there he is banging about on the heads and bags of his comrades. And now his comrades are shouting like they should. Loudly. So what does the driver do? He certainly can't rush off to the hospital with sirens blaring. He can't rush off anywhere at all. He—that's you, it's all of us. Because we're on the trolley wires and electricity. There's just one thing missing: the end of the line. Continue on foot from here. People don't want to go on foot. People want to believe that, if you don't raise any fuss, you'll get further. Follow the scheduled route with the familiar stops: birth, school, marriage, work—and done. The end of the line.

Generally, the driver will stop the trolley, fully aware of the problems he's now created for all the other drivers on his route and their passengers. But he stops anyway. He opens the door and lets out all the people who are shouting. Expels a few with some choice words. Then turns to whoever he's identified as the most morally grounded, and requests help to carry the epileptic man off of the bus and carefully lay him down on a flat surface. It's usually old women who will offer to help. But then you have to lay them down on a flat surface, too, and there aren't actually all that many flat surfaces along the route. "Wide Is My Motherland" is just a song after all, and not necessarily the best reflection of reality.

Never, under any circumstances, mess with someone's tongue when they're having a seizure. Absolutely not. Give the grannies, grandpas and all the medical "experts" a swift kick in the ass and point them to the nearest phone booth to call for help if they don't want to waste their own phone minutes. And if they dig out a pin and start poking around in the poor man's mouth, then you'll even have to shout: "Pin your own tongue—to your old fox fur collar." Because a person won't swallow their tongue and can't choke on it: stop pulling out pins.

Petro Lischke is always talking about real-life events. Other people's lives don't appear to be relevant. Unless, of course, they're on his route. So he talks about his own life. He doesn't like silence. Quiet he likes, but not silence. Silence is threatening. The pressure comes from inside, everyone has their own: it rises and rises, there's pressure, it strikes your head, and done. You've gone off your trolley, accept the consequences.

Petro isn't silent even with himself. He hums in the shower and when he's making something in the kitchen. He's not even quiet when he's watching soccer. He gives advice—mainly to the players. Because, when the game is in full swing, advising the coaches won't really help. Pass, offsides, penalty kick. Who'll take the kick? One time, a coach for Shakhtar rode Petro's trolley. Probably his car broke down. And he forgot to bring money for a taxi. It happens to people. Often even. Petro talked to him for the whole ride: who to cut, who to bench, something's got to be done about the goalie, he said. Of course, the coach didn't answer or even hear him. But he didn't object either. So that means they had a good chat. Petro loves to tell that story, too.

The children are racing around upstairs at the Nefyodovs', and the adults are downstairs in the living room. They sit there silent until everyone's thoroughly drunk. That "thoroughly" looks a little different for everyone. Nefyodov gets irritable and picks a fight, pestering the mathematician with questions about the meaning of life. His Maria laughs, and Tanya starts clearing the plates right away, even if there's still food on them, and then goes off to wash the dishes. She washes them vigorously, intensely. She brings them back to the table clean and starts looking at the windows. Petro's sure that the minute they all leave, drunk Tanya will pull out a stepladder and wash her windows. Pahutiak is drunk even without vodka. She's always flirtatious and kind of flushed, with a lot of perfume. Petro finds her attractive. He likes the fact that she's not quiet. If it's not him talking, it's her. "Two clowns," Maria says when they get home. "You're like two hired clowns. When will you ever learn to be quiet? To stop telling stories?"

If you only knew, thinks Petro. If only...

Petro chatters because silence is frightening. He talks to make noise to drown out his own shame and stupidity, along with the loathsome voice that still manages to whisper: "Everything will work out, you just need to try again." Petro Lischke plays the slots.

The fear and shame didn't come on quickly, not right away. He'd stop off after work for a half hour or so. He'd win some and lose some. Mostly he won some. Just a little, but, compared to his salary, which was no longer being paid regularly, it was actually quite a bit. He bought Bounty chocolate bars from America for Halya, slipped Maria some cash for boots, brought meat from the market, helped his parents buy some glass for the greenhouse, and brought Maria's parents a big jar of red caviar and a huge sturgeon as a New Year's gift in 1996. They'd never seen anything like it in the village. Maria would say, "My breadwinner." Seriously and affectionately. Compared to Nefyodov and Korniyenko, he was a pretty mediocre breadwinner, which ate at him. He went to his slots knowing almost everything about them: how they rumbled, whether they had money, how many seconds it took for the picture to change, how hard to press the button... Every day, and eventually every month, he was more confident that he'd stop someday. But before he stopped, he'd collect all the money in the world. Well, in the neighborhood. All the money that the local losers threw in. He still won sometimes, but he was afraid to tally up his balance. He took on extra shifts at work, although, according to the safety guidelines, he was unfit due to fatigue. But he took them anyway. And he borrowed money off an old buddy from driving school. Except his friend wasn't driving anymore: he'd "moved up" somehow on "metals," and was now something like a capo "overseeing" the Motodrome flea market. This buddy suggested that Petro make a change and "join the business" like everyone else: street hustling, collecting debts, beating up deadbeats. But what kind of "enforcer" would Petro make?

Yes, he was paying it down. But not enough. His pal let it ride for a while thanks to their old friendship, but eventually he put him on notice: "What's it gonna be? You can pay it off with interest or you can help us out. Work it off."

Later, running through the "replay," as his Maria would say, Petro thought that the gangsters must have had a severe staff shortage: they would take people right off the street, with no qualifications for beating and murdering. And it also occurred to him that gangsters operated like a cult or a pyramid scheme: it wasn't enough to bloody people's mugs yourself. To get a bigger cut, you had to bring in new people. More people means more income. Just like with Maria's Mary Kay. The most active girls—the ones who sold the most and recruited the most saleswomen—were promised a pink Mercedes or Cadillac. His pal already had a Mercedes, but, whether it's cults or business, you can never stop. Maria said the inventors of network marketing had been nominated for a Nobel Prize. Probably for that "you can never stop." Although, if that's the case, they should nominate someone for "life·is movement."

Because he owed so much interest, Petro decided to switch from the slots to cards. He also bought lottery tickets. At first, he attributed it to desperation, but then he got used to it. Once the casino and the slot machines were completely off the table, the lottery remained as a sort of methadone, a substitution therapy.

Two thoughts justified the gambling. The first was about the money and his girls, who should look good and not want for anything. He never kept anything for himself. He just took the wheel and followed the route without stops.

The second was the feeling. Supposedly bad. But that didn't matter compared to how he felt when he was waiting for the picture to change, when the coins were pouring out, when the rolling roulette ball was hitting the numbers, when it came to showdown and Petro Lischke revealed a royal flush. That was everything all at once: shrieks, groans, ecstasy, delight, justice—not higher justice, of course, just minor justice, but complete and comforting. In that moment, he understood that a miracle was not only possible, but present here and now: pouring, clanking, bouncing, and clicking across the table. Just this moment, this moment. Petro never got so far as imagining what he'd do if it were a million. An entire, enormous million… A Mercedes flitted through his mind; an apartment bigger than the old one that the transportation department had allotted them back when he'd started, before Halyuska was even born; another Mercedes; a trip to the beach or even the United Arab Emirates… But that was all insignificant compared to the anticipation of imminent victory he experienced only with the bets made in the utter despair of a worthless loser.

He owed a thousand dollars. You could get killed for five hundred in Donetsk in the '90s. One hundred was considered serious, big money. But a thousand was a terrifying pit he could never dig his way out of. If he didn't eat or drink, if he got paid in full and on time… If he admitted everything to Maria, if he told his parents…

He should have started yelling right away, instead of having a fit and beating against the heads of his comrades. But Petro was silent. So he chattered. His pal said: "Into the new millennium with no debts. Hear me? So, that means before the New Year. Otherwise, my people will pay a visit to your house."

The Nefyodovs were the only people Petro knew who might have a whole thousand dollars just lying around the house, piled up somewhere in the bedsheets or tucked between the books on a shelf. But Petro Lischke could not ask Nefyodov. He'd have to pay it back piecemeal, not all at once, so for many months, or even years, he would be the loser and a drunk, aggressive Nefyodov would lecture him on how to live his life and how not to. And all the kids, and all the wives would listen and agree. And he wouldn't be Halyuska's Daddy-magician anymore: "Let's sneak out and buy this doll, T-shirt, hair clip, skirt, and a little something else."

"It's not my money, don't you see?" said Tanya. "It's not mine, so I can't take it without asking. Don't you see that would be stealing?"

"I really need it. They said they'll come to my house. I really need it. And after this—I promise, never again. I promise. Tanya! I really, really need it. Nefyodov will laugh at me. I have a family. I need to be a man. Please... Tanya. I'm not going anywhere. It'll take a while, but I'll pay you back..."

She shook her head and didn't give it to him.

ANGELINA

BEFORE THELMA AND A BIT AFTER

Baba rode trains. She definitely had connections in the Transport Ministry or Department of Transportation. Because regular people didn't get the Kyiv-Warsaw route. Not even the Donetsk-Moscow route. Baba was a train conductor. Three days on the road, then three at home. Or two days on and one off. "The road keeps us fed," her grandma would tell Angelina. "Just so you know, the road will always feed us."

Hungarian pâtés, a pink Mickey Mouse pencil case, a black lace school apron, and a white cambric one, a hat with a huge multicolored pompom on top. The hat got stolen from the locker room during gym. And the fake cheetah coat right out of the school coatroom. But Baba brought home another coat, a rabbit fur. She brought it and said: "They're just things. Never cry over things...."

Angelina gave the Mickey Mouse pencil case to a girl whose dad died in the mine. If she'd still had the hat, she would have given her that, too, but it was already gone by then.

The road fed Baba everything: the boots that Angelina sold at a profit to her friends and their mothers in ninth and tenth grade; the Kholodok mints that would make the boys and girls form a herd and follow her around. They wouldn't follow her around for her chewing gum much anymore; they'd gotten older and were embarrassed. But gum could still strengthen a friendship. The road gave Baba the things that almost no one had: candies, Finnish raincoats, stockings, Italian shoes, jersey fabric, knitting yarn, canned pineapple, Pepsi, Schweppes, 7-Up, Christmas lights, bathroom

Angelina had already worked out the formula for miracles when she was little: a miracle is when something comes from nothing. Moreover, nothing wasn't simply the empty bag that Baba took on her trips. Nothing also meant the empty fridge, and eyes that slide past you, and Thelma. A miracle happens when maybe you're sad, maybe not, but something unexpectedly shows up out of nowhere that makes you laugh and surprises you, and beats out a rhythm in your chest or ears: "awesome, awesome, awesome." It doesn't even have to be something you need or that will be yours. A miracle always defies expectations and often isn't fated for you. When the Italian boots didn't fit Angelina's arch, Baba said, "Oh well, it wasn't meant to be." But the boots didn't stop being a miracle: they smelled, they were soft and bright red, they lay one on the other in a bag, or stood side-by-side on the dresser awaiting a buyer—defiant, fearless border crossers, and it didn't matter who got them. They were couriers of joy even when she encountered them on someone else's low-arched feet.

Because of Baba's bag, Angelina was confused about magic for a long time. Although it seemed to her that she wasn't confused and understood everything perfectly. Take Shubin, for example. A sorcerer and weirdo. He lived in the mines and coughed. Angelina understood there was no point in treating the cough, because it was useful. If Shubin started groaning and coughing, then that's it: you'd better run. Run to the cage and shout: "Ring the bell! Everyone out!" Because the cough meant either the mine was about to collapse or there was methane. If the gas explodes, then the mine will also collapse. Angelina didn't like Shubin: he was stingy and didn't cough for everyone. Shubin didn't cough for the daddy of the girl Angelina gave the pencil case. And not just him—for the whole shift that day in the Zasyadko Mine when fifty workers died. The children of the other dads just weren't in Angelina's class. And it's just as well, because she wouldn't have had enough gifts for everyone. Shubin coughed just fine for Angelina's dad. But still she worried and, at night, she'd come into the room where her parents slept, which for some reason they called the hall, and stand in the doorway to cough. Papa didn't wake up. And that was bad. But Angelina hoped Shubin would cough louder.

Shubin was the sorcerer for boys and miners. Babá was the sorceress for everyone else. For a long time, Angelina thought that her baba was the same as Babá. She'd get upset when the girls would say that Babá took naughty children away but let some of them go. "Take them where?" Angelina would grab hold of the ferociously-combed-out hair and pull, knowing full well how much it would hurt. "Take them where? To my room? To the conductor's compartment? That makes no sense, only employees are allowed there!"

Babá wasn't like Shubin. Shubin was born who knows where—people from every shaft or mining village would claim he "was from right here, the house just didn't survive." Babá was a local. Between Oleksandrivka and Lar'ïnka, or maybe just past Bosse, or, no, closer to the factory... Her house was somewhere nearby. It had been confiscated then spontaneously collapsed, or maybe it had been a whole estate, with horses in the stable and partridges and a light broth for lunch. But it turned out she was against the tsar, and then it turned out she was for him. She was arrested, and fled, was arrested again, but then she appeared again next to her house where her treasure was buried... People would look for the treasure now and then. Or, if Babá was in the mood, she might even slip something from her stash to someone she liked. Like one time a man saw Babá near a bar and when he got home, he checked the industrialization bonds from the time when they used to pay his father's salary with bonds and discovered they'd gained value. He bought a new car.

Another time, Babá patted a woman's head at the hairdresser's—and then, when the woman was going through her attic, she found some drawing in her mother's trunk that turned out to be by Burliuk. It didn't turn out right away to be a Burliuk—the woman traveled all over first. In Sumy, they told her it was definitely by him, and then they confirmed it in Kyiv, too. And, while she was taking it around to show everyone, she learned all about that stuff—Cubists, Futurists, "the slap in the face of public taste"—and fell so in love with it that she opened a gallery. In New York. Not in the Donbas New York, the one that's near Horlivka, no—the actual, real one in America. Angelina didn't know who Burliuk and Futurism were, but the words were simple and beautiful. So she easily memorized the story and always retold it accurately.

Once she figured out that her baba and the sorceress Babá were different babas, Angelina was a bit upset and very frustrated that everyone else already knew and she was the only hopeless idiot. Then she realized that Shubin and Babá were actually very similar. They both acted like real people instead of like magical beings. Which probably explains why so many people believed in them, even though they couldn't quite believe in God. God was too good, whereas those two were ordinary, sometimes petty, and sometimes really unfair. That is, like everyone else. No one could say exactly why Babá would choose certain people, not always the best, for her good deeds, and would attack other, good people, with nasty tricks. She regularly attacked school kids, for example: the minute you started copying an answer, she'd knock something off the desk, so your cheat sheet or your legs covered in formulas from knees to panties were seen not just by the kid at the next desk but by the whole exam committee. But then she burned down a shop for a couple of jerks. Angelina was already grown up then, it was after Thelma was born... Two college students had decided to make a little extra money moonlighting. They'd drink some of the shop liquor themselves and treat their friends to some. In brief, there was a shortfall. Most likely they would have been killed. In the early 90s, murder was the highest disciplinary measure separating the "wise guys" from the "losers."

And? Well, there were people who actually saw Babá set the shop on fire. One night, when the students weren't there—they were working night shift in the oncology department. The owner never paid them for the last month's work but, compared to having your skull bashed in with a baseball bat, you can't really count that as a tragedy.

Why did she choose them? Why them in particular? Why didn't she choose someone who was actually good, instead of these petty thieves? Why? It's a mystery...

"Because she doesn't have a good head on her shoulders..." Fink told her one day. Angelina was indignant. "Without a head—that's the Horseman. Mayne Reid's. No one ever saw our Babá on a horse."

Without a good head on her shoulders... Brainless, so to speak. You could say the same for Angelina's choices: Thelma's father, who joined the army and then married his unit commander's daughter; she chose her daughter's name for the sake of an apartment, but also because it was pretty; she got a job that would be fun, not just for the money. Even though money was always short. Her parents had moved north, to Surgut, Siberia, in the early 80s. Angelina's own baba's parting words were: "Geniuses. You've exiled your own selves." After which she never answered their calls or read their letters and never sent them a thing. It must have been dull in the North. They got divorced and both remarried there. They even had more kids. They would fight through Angelina, threatening to take the Donetsk apartment away from each other. But they had no intention of taking Angelina away from each other. At least her dad didn't work in the mine anymore, which meant he couldn't be crushed down there.

Angelina's own baba approved of her keeping the baby and giving birth to Thelma, but she didn't seem to approve of the machinations with the name. She didn't approve, but she did understand that the apartment was necessary. "When the North is over. It always ends, one way or another," said baba. "They'll bring their families back for sure. You'll have a real barracks here, sweetheart."

She died at the train station. She used to miss it terribly and would walk there and back every day. Petro Lischke kept saying, "Tell her to turn off onto Universytetska Street, and either I'll see her or I'll tell the other drivers to pick her up. Tell her not to be shy." She wasn't shy; she just wanted to walk.

Thelma was ten then. "They" didn't come, sealed up in their Surgut, with their children and their money problems. Without Fink, Angelina couldn't have managed all the paperwork, the morgue, the transport, and a cemetery plot. But Fink was there. And, if she'd had a good head on her shoulders, Angelina would have chosen him. If she'd had a brain, she certainly could have and really should have. Eighteen years is a fine age difference, definitely unlikely to lead to the army or the unit commander's daughter. Fink was always fussing over Thelma and positively shone when he looked at Angelina. He was always right there. Reliable, sensible, dull.

"He fusses over Ernest, too," Papa Korniyenko told her. "He's weird…"

"Why weird? He just wants to give our children his German last name."

"Well, that's not likely to work out for mine," Bohdan grinned.

Thelma was ten when Angelina found out that baba was Polish. In her passport, which was required for the death certificate, without which they wouldn't dig a hole or release her body from the morgue, the box for "place of birth" showed "Hrevt Village, Lublin Voivodeship, Poland."

Thelma was twenty-one when she told Angelina, "Not Polish. Ukrainian. A Boiko. The Soviets and Poles swapped land and swapped people. How old was she in 1951?"

"She was born in 1926."

"That means she was twenty-five when they were deported. So your dad was born there. Who was my great-grandfather anyway?"

"Who is anybody with us?" smiled Angelina. And laughed. Not that she thought it was funny; it was just a habit.

He set up his clinic, the aid station, in a house where no one was living anymore. The old lady had gone out to the garden to water her nasturtiums—and got hit. Just her, the nasturtiums were fine. And, as it turned out, they didn't actually need watering: just some sun and a little rain. The house was also fine. It was so old that it no longer had any intention of dying. It was shriveling up little by little, its doors and windows slowly slumping lower and lower toward the ground as it started to lean; at night, it crackled, creaked, and moaned. It got warmer once they put in new windows. It creaked even more once they started heating it for winter, but it also laughed looking out at the old woman's fresh grave in the garden. That house probably thought that it would outlive them all, that it would find itself some new owners who would gladly tear everything down and build a villa, or maybe a little Finnish cottage, like the one that used to be across the street a year ago but had now perished in a flash.

"Who are you?" asked the commander.

"A dentist."

"Hey guys, who wants some new fillings to show off to the sniper?"

They all cracked up.

One held up his hand, introduced himself as Hryts, snickered again, and said he was in school the last time he'd seen a dentist: "This whole brigade of sadists came in, caught us in the hallways, put us in chairs, and they didn't even tie us down... I still wonder why we put up with it. Why didn't we run away? What do you call that machine you use?

A drill? A drill in your mouth is way scarier than Buryats on the Ukrainian steppe. Man, we could just throw you behind enemy lines. Pull out the bitches' teeth with no drugs. Greetings from Hryts."

"A dentist." The commander shook his head in disgust. "A dentist."

"Well, I'm really here as a field medic."

"Well, then, a field marshal," snickered Hryts. "That's completely different."

"Alright then, Marshal, show me what you do and don't have. Anything for headaches?"

"You've already got that covered," Marshal said, with a nod toward the machine guns.

"Those pharmaceuticals are for export only," growled Hryts. "So our 'brothers' don't get headaches."

"Something for headaches? Diarrhea? Blood pressure? You got alcohol? Tourniquets? Droppers? Saline, glucose, antibiotics? Celox? Surgical needles? Come on, pal, whatever you need—give me a list. Just be thorough. Think."

Marshal nodded, "First, firewood. It's got to be warm in here."

"Get on it," the commander ordered Hryts and Wolf, who hadn't taken part in the conversation. After they brought the wood, Wolf quietly asked Marshal to look at his "damned tooth. During battle, it's fine, like the motherfucker's not even there. But the minute there's a break in the shelling, it jumps out like a damn jack-in-the-box and cranks up: 'Go ahead and kill yourself, 'cause I will never leave you!'"

It would be ridiculous to add dental tools to the list. Conventional wisdom says that there can't be any toothaches when legs are getting blown to bits, skin blistered, or eyes and hair burned off. Marshal drove out and got some equipment. It wasn't his, but still not bad at all. He got hold of a mobile dental engine that unfolded into an almost full-fledged clinic with spit-sink, air and water pistols, a saliva suction hose, fan, work light, and a compartment for warming medications. It didn't function entirely as designed due to the issues with running water and the generator's habit of failing intermittently, plunging the "office" into total darkness. There was also an issue with painkillers, because, although there were enough, he hated to use them and had decided to ration them because what if there was a fire, a mine, a sniper, powerful shelling—then what?

Marshal pulled Wolf's wisdom tooth even before he got the equipment. That wasn't difficult.

Operating on a goat—now that was difficult. Also bizarre, idiotic, and painful.

Some guy had driven up and said, "Guys, I've brought you some meat! Help me unload it."

"So, I'm thinking, exactly how much meat does this guy have that he needs help unloading," chuckled Hryts. "I'm thinking right away how to distribute it, so it doesn't go bad... And it turns out he's got a live goat in the trunk. And the guy looks at me and asks, 'Should I butcher it for you, or can you do it yourselves?' Well, what do you mean can we butcher it? What are we, little girls? What, we've never butchered a pig?"

"Well, I haven't," confessed Wolf. "Only time I've ever seen a live pig is on TV."

"What show? Text me the name, and I'll watch it, too," says Hryts. "I'll get my mother-in-law to record it."

"I haven't either," said Marshal. "I couldn't do it."

"You doctors are all the same. Cut people open—absolutely, with pleasure. But a pig—oh my god, no way. Live and learn."

Oh, yeah. They learned alright. Absolutely everyone. The whole company mastered the lesson and never walked past Hryts without a comment about his love for the goat they'd named Dzyga. But everyone also took selfies with Dzyga. Marshal, too—he couldn't help it.

"We should have slaughtered him straight away," Hryts would ruminate from time to time. "While our adrenaline was going, right, Marshal? Because look now. I left him tied up in the yard for one night. By that morning he'd got free and was already the alpha dog. Now look: 'Dzyga, come! Dzyga, sit!' What a good boy! See? He was supposed to be a goat just for the meat. And he turned into a real dog."

Not entirely a dog. For instance, he didn't master the command for "Speak." And, if he heard "Come!", he'd give a lazy little shake of his beard and amble on over without enthusiasm. Alma the half-shepherd and the little mutt Brecht beat him every time. They would dash ahead with mocking barks, running back to him two or even three times, eagerly checking to see if he was running or if he'd turned back into a goat. Even the cats beat him, although they always pretended they were just going about their business without noticing the command.

They'd come to check whether there was anything good in the bowl, or just to be petted. Then they'd purr like out-of-sync engines on a couple of T-70 tanks.

No one knew how Dzyga had managed to muster such authority in just half a day. He couldn't do any amazing tricks. Well, he would batter his horns against the gate until it either flew off its hinges or opened with an offended creak. And he did follow the guys wherever they went, while Alma and Brecht just lay around the yard. He could also freeze on the spot, staring straight ahead, boring his eyes into anything he didn't like. His eyes were small but expressive and generally dissatisfied. He could see mines with those eyes, or maybe with his beard or horns. It's impossible to say whether he had this skill from birth, or if it had developed during the war. But if Dzyga froze still as a statue and then started bleating ("Poor Greeks, how many Dzygas did they have to listen to, for them to call their plays 'goat songs,'" joked Wolf)... If he started bleating, then you could confidently mark that spot on the map as "mined." First on the map, and then in the field—as long as you could safely get there without risk of getting blown up. Marshal would write the inscriptions on the lids of big pots and pans taken from abandoned or destroyed houses: "Danger! Mines!" Then Wolf, Hryts, and the other guys would fasten the lids to the ground. The landscape started to look like the kitchen of a madwoman cooking her delicacies in underground burrows among the roots, coal, and Scythian gold.

Danger. Mines.

Dzyga could watch for danger and be affectionate. He'd learned from sneaky Brecht how to lean in and coax petting from any hand; from Alma, he learned to growl. It came out a bit falsetto, but the sound was like nothing else. It scared off strangers.

Of course, not the strangers sitting out past the field, who would occasionally start shelling or shooting lazily, as if hinting that they could see everyone through their rifle sights and do as they pleased at any moment. You couldn't scare those strangers off any more than you could scare the dead.

"Watch out for them," Hryts would say when Dzyga came out to the toilet to say good morning. Alma would come out first and stick her face in the crack between the wooden wall and the door. While Hryts was squatting and huffing, Alma would manage to lick his entire face. "Okay, okay, it's enough, good job," Hryts would say, pushing her away. Next came Brecht, who would jump up and lick his hands. By the time he left the crapper, Hryts would be clean.

Dzyga didn't lick him. Dzyga would swing the door wide open, then freeze, occasionally swinging his head from one side to the other. Dzyga came out to chat. And Hryts would say, "Watch out for them. They're real goats—like you used to be. Get it? They're already in the trunk. Meat. You hear me? They think they're the only ones with rifle sights. But I can see every hair in their noses through mine. And that hair, Dzyga, needs to be trimmed. It won't hurt. I'll show you when we get home. You too, Alma. I'll show you all…"

Hryts was still conscious when the guys brought him to Marshal. A leg wound. The blood was bright red and gushing out like a fountain. Even a dentist could see that he'd hit a femoral artery, and it was just a matter of time before he bled out. They were two hours away from a surgeon and a hospital. Maybe an hour and a half. Tourniquet, IV, warm blanket. Two warm blankets.

Marshal ignored Hryts's yells, as he called out for the goat instead of his mother, "Dzyga! Dzyga! Where's Dzyga?" Marshal didn't pay any attention to Wolf, who carried the injured animal in with back and stomach wounds. At least not until he'd done everything he could for Hryts and called in a transfer to the hospital.

He turned around. One look was enough to tell him that Dzyga was done for. Wolf had laid him on a plaid blanket on the floor.

"Please, doctor, save my brother. He's the one… He jumped on me. Like an eagle, I swear to God. He spread his wings and covered me. Like my mom, if you want. If you can't believe in the eagle. With his whole black, woolly, stinky body… He jumped up, slammed into me and knocked me down… Please, Marshal, man, I'm begging you…"

There's a scene just like this in a Jim Belushi movie. It was Marshal's favorite: the dog seems dead, but he's actually listening while his owner is apologizing and saying he loves him and promises to get him anything he wants. Even a female poodle.

Dzyga's small, expressive eyes were going glassy, but still Marshal methodically removed mine fragments through incisions on his back and stomach, carefully placing them in the spit-bowl that worked without running water. Two, three, four, six... The blood wasn't spurting out anymore. Not Dzyga's or Hryts's. And it's not a movie. Maybe someday...

The two guys who came for Hryts were in good spirits. Injured isn't dead. A leg isn't a head. Even without a leg, God forbid, prostheses these days—oh man! People run marathons.

"You've got some bad timing, man," one of them joked as he lifted Hryts. "Why such bad timing? Huh? You've got this nice goat here, all ready for shashlyk. Were you getting ready for a party? Me personally, I don't like goat. Do you? Hey, calm down, they'll feed you at the hospital. You hear me? We'll get you there just fine. You hear me?"

"You're a damn goat. You're a goat. This here's Dzyga. Our dog," howled Hryts.

"Hey, did you give him opioids?" checked the driver. "Does he have a concussion? Any brain swelling? Did you check his head?"

"It's all in here," said Marshal, handing them the papers in a plastic folder. "His head is fine."

"Then why's he raving?"

"You're the one who's raving," snapped Wolf.

"That's right. Exactly. You and your buddy are both raving. Because this is no shashlyk, pal. This is Dzyga. Our dog."

They buried Dzyga in the garden, next to the old lady and the nasturtiums that hadn't been watered in a long time. On the pot lid they used as a tombstone Marshal wrote: "Minesweeper. Too well loved to ever be forgotten."

MARIA
LIFE AS WAR

The light pink is a factory color. It's a special factory color Cadillac makes for cars ordered by Mary Kay. You have to be able to dream of Cadillacs. You have to learn how. You have to want to dream. A Cadillac can be a dream.

The training sessions completely knocked Maria out. Everything they talked about seemed disconnected from reality. Like a movie. *Rocky, Pretty Woman, Nightmare on Elm Street*. The bizarre sound of the word "trening" in Russian, the otherworldly voice of the trainer, the group meals, the "appreciations," the applause for highest sales...

The success stories and the recognition board. Utter tedium. Maria looked terrible in her photo. She had to lower her sales numbers to get the bad picture taken down, and then swiftly increase them, to get a new one taken. And she still didn't want a Cadillac. Much less a pink one.

Maria didn't want any of it. But, as if out of spite, it all worked for her. The girls at the Tech School where she studied bookkeeping were just starting to wear makeup, starting the lifelong routine. They didn't have the hang of it yet, their hands trembled and jerked; their cat eyes came out like cursive *M*s; their lip liner plotted the cosine function with errors and discontinuities, with intervals of sign constancy, monotonicity, and extremes. Eyeshadow transformed their eyes into maps of rivers and seas. The girls mostly chose blue eyeshadows. But the ones who chose brown were no different; their eyes became mountains and ridges. Maria would pull out her magical brushes, the whole collection: the one with the dandelion top, thin ones like little braids,

the substantial ones you could probably use to apply wallpaper... Maria would pull out her magical brushes and dive
into the light blue valleys or climb the dark heights of Fuji-
yama... She would remove the excess, add a shadow or two,
tidy up the pencil rebellion around the mouth. Two or three
strokes, or sometimes a whole hour of work, and the girls
could totally, absolutely have appeared on the pages of *Burda*
or *Otto*. Maria didn't set out to make them beautiful, she just
needed to sell product: brushes, applicators, creams, shadow, facemasks, "foundation" (which everyone called "tone
cream"), and mascara, to be eternally called "brasmatik"
from the exotic French term *brosse automatique*. The demo
lesson lured them in, following the prescribed routine. Once
she was transformed into a princess, any frog would believe
that the magic was in her skin. Or in the kiss. But never in
herself. And the frogs happily buy skincare, collect kisses,
and fear wearing their own faces at night with their husbands or boyfriends. So a frog will set her alarm for six in
the morning, so she can greet her beloved's first yawn of the
day with eggs on a plate and brasmatik on her lashes.

Girls were practicing their makeup not only at the business school but also at the vocational school, the trade institute, the hairdresser's across from the stadium, the beauty
salon near the Opera, the grocery store on University Street
and the White Swan department store. Wherever Maria set
foot they were learning to do makeup, as the magic brushes in
her hands smoothed skin, hid pimples, defined cheekbones,
minimized noses, and expressively emphasized brows. Everyone also got a square mirror in a pink plastic frame.

Maria made money herself and brought in more people.

"Into the cult," her husband Petro liked to say. "The
Church of Cadillac Witnesses."

"It's not like that," she said. "Relax. It's called multilev-
el marketing. The technique of direct sales. The colossal

savings achieved by eliminating rental expenses make our goods accessible to the middle class."

"And do you have to take exams? So you can use those exact words in that obnoxious tone of voice?"

Petro was annoyed. And Maria was annoyed, too.

Because... war. The usefulness of any job was measured by its usefulness in wartime. Healing people—yes. Sewing them up, bandaging, giving injections, putting on casts—yes. Bread—yes. You have to eat when there's war, because, even if it is your last day on earth, how will you know? You just eat because you have to eat. Bread, potatoes, easy vegetables, so yes to greenhouses, too. Shooting is good. Shooting well from any type of weapon. And barrels, bullets, and shells for the weapon. Basically, the whole military-industrial complex. Sewing was fine: not clothing for style, but things that are waterproof and warm. If shoes, make them boots. If coats—then they should be waterproof and warm. Underwear and socks are useful. Songs are fine. But not necessarily as a profession. Songs could be a hobby between shifts at the military factory. Petro, for instance, with his trolley didn't have one of the proper professions for war. But driver, yes. Driver is good anyway. Deliver, take out, evacuate, mobilize. The one behind the wheel decides everything.

By the standards of war, Maria was a useless human being. They don't need bookkeepers or painters of pimpled faces at the front. Sometimes Maria would convince herself that making people beautiful for their burial was something, but what burials will there be if nuclear winter destroys everyone: made-up or not very? How will anyone be buried if the whole Earth becomes one mass grave, and beauty is forgotten, an impossibility? Although there were certainly worse jobs. Sculptor, for instance. Or film director. But Maria's job was definitely among the bottom three and sometimes even sank to the very bottom. Because an excavated Venus de

Milo could tell us something important about what existed before... And a director who happened to avoid sinking into the earth could also describe some of what came before... Maria's brushes, and pomades, skin tonics, soap, and acetone-free nail polish removers could only describe stupidity. Massive, universal human stupidity with a thin layer of ivory foundation. And a Cadillac... Well, if it were repainted in dull, inconspicuous colors, it could help in a war.

Three times a week Maria went to the shooting range. When Halyuska turned three, Maria was testing for her Master of Sport certification in shooting. In the mid '90s, she got into sport shooting. Skeet, trap, double trap, Nordic Trap, English Sporting, lateral and vertical flight paths, crossing or looping trajectories, doubles—she could talk about it for hours. Which is why she had no more business drinking than Petro. Sober, Maria was a sweet, elegant woman with perfect makeup, but one bottle of beer turned her into a bloodthirsty space pirate, eager to bring down an American missile with a single shot from a smoothbore rifle. Or not an American one. Because Mary Kay was actually American, and neither she nor her successors would be adding thousands of independent consultants and paying them "percentages" if their leaders were preparing for a missile attack against us. So it turned out that all this fuss with the glamorous, the convenient, and occasionally waterproof was actually a story of nuclear deterrence. Which didn't comfort Maria nor improve her status.

Her parents were embarrassed to tell their neighbors what she did for a living. Her mother-in-law would purse her lips disapprovingly whenever Maria brought her a gift: "So you got this with a discount, right? Or maybe even for free? I get your cast-offs?" It seemed like all the relatives were waiting for her to stop frittering away her time, "knocking on doors," "pestering people," and to finally settle into an office job like a normal person. "Office"—compared to "factory"—the word itself sounded like jazz, or even The Beatles. Meanwhile, Petro, even without an office and with all his unpaid salary, was considered the breadwinner and foundation of the family. Maria was ashamed to say how much she earned. Because even at home the value of a profession was assessed on its usefulness for war and on what people would say.

The girls said "thank you" to Maria, and Petro never went to the market.

There was no opportunity for Maria to jump up and say: "We live on my paycheck! I'm the breadwinner! I hate all this, but I'm feeding my family!"

Petro never went to the market; he didn't know the cost of meat or milk. He was firmly convinced that half a pig from the village would last for the entire year—until the next half a pig. And he was good. Genuinely good. He was warm and funny, and hers. Maria never got up at six, to offer herself to him with lashes, cheekbones, and perfect hair. Petro was also burly, even large. Maria saw herself as a flat, poorly drawn sketch. A girl in panties, who needed some cut-out paper clothes to cover up the fragility and precariousness of her composition.

Petro was different. Fearless, easygoing, and kind. "As kind as an elephant," said Maria who'd never seen a real elephant.

When Fink told Maria that Petro was gambling, she believed him right away.

When Fink demanded that she "make him stop this by threatening to divorce him," she was ready to murder Fink.

When Fink informed her at the dawn of the millennium that Petro had gambled his way to the gangsters, Maria didn't even consider crying. Halyuska cried. And Fink, damn him, said, "What's a big girl like you doing crying like that? Stop right now!" "And when should I start, when is it okay? After the gangsters kill my papa? Is that when?" wailed Halyuska.

The world Maria saw through her rifle scope was clear, defined, and comprehensible. The other world, the one without the "frame" of a scope, was never comprehensible. It wasn't that the city seemed too big to her. It didn't seem any way at all. And it wasn't about the times, which people called "hard," but if you talked to the old folks there had never been any other kind, only this blurry kind. Always. The time itself didn't shoot; the disc flew on a random trajectory and didn't even look like a target. You couldn't shoot at what people said, at the tears that weren't allowed to grown-ups, at the husband whose salary was the foundation of the family, even when it didn't exist. You couldn't shoot at yourself—a nice paper doll from the last page of *Pioneer* magazine.

"Do you hear voices?" asked the psychiatrist. She seemed annoyed.

"Of America?"

"Why America? *Voice of America* isn't forbidden anymore." The psychiatrist was still annoyed. Normally, people just buy the certificate of sanity—there's no need to drag doctors away from their work. Maria didn't know. Of course, she would have paid for it. Why create a hassle for herself and everyone else?

"What is forbidden?"

"That's the problem, everything's allowed," the doctor sounded angry and depressed. "Everything is allowed! And there's no compulsory treatment. You can be a Napoleon or a Bonaparte. Hearing voices? Insomnia? Panic attacks? Anxiety? Are you alone in the mirror? Do you have obsessive thoughts? And why do you need a rifle? Are you a hunter? It's not normal. A woman shouldn't go hunting. She's the keeper of the hearth!"

"Would you like me to do your makeup?" Maria asked her. "I have everything with me. Smoky eyes? Chanel style? Vamp? Shall I?"

Maria wasn't always alone in the mirror. There was always something looming in the background: the wall, a nightstand, a wardrobe, the client's closed eyes, Petro coming up from behind to hug her. Panic attacks—yes. Insomnia—rarely. Obsessive thoughts—plenty. Maria just didn't know they were a sign of illness. She thought everyone had them. Well, and voices: coughs, sniffles, even breathing. Maria had grown accustomed to hearing Halyuska from the moment they met. Is she breathing, not breathing—a state of constant anxiety.

The psychiatrist chose smoky eyes and declared Maria healthy.

Healthy Maria bought herself a smoothbore rifle.

"It's just for birdshot" she bragged to Bohdan because she had to tell someone. Someone polite, but not curious. "It's not scary. Just birdshot—but in a fraction of a second."

"How big a fraction?" asked Bohdan.

"If the target's close, maybe zero."

NEFYODOV
BORDERS OF TIME

Nefyodov's earliest memory was from when he was two years and four months old. From two to eleven is clear. After that, nothing. After that, it's just like everyone else. He vividly remembers images, landscapes, weather, smells, and voices. The town of Yevpatoriya, the sea, the mud, sick children, and him. The diagnosis of pediatric cerebral palsy was highly dubious, but, to be on the safe side, treatment with mud therapy was recommended. His mother packed him T-shirts, shorts, and socks. Toys weren't allowed. But his T-shirts, white, ironed and smelling of home, were labeled. The embroidered letters "A" and "N" made fine toys. The raised threads were the forest. The flat ones were the road. If you bit off a fingernail it could be a car, or even two. You could cause a crash, call the police, and run away to hide behind the top of the letter "A."

He remembered one time when he got hysterical, refusing to put on someone else's gray underwear that Alla Stepanovna had dumped out of her giant bag right onto the sand, saying: "Everyone take one!" He screamed like he'd been knifed and went back inside naked. Went—more like ran. He was healthy. He didn't drag one leg, didn't limp, confidently held a spoon, didn't drool, and only bit his nails to expand his automobile collection: a taxi, a truck, a Volga, a Zhiguli, and a jeep. He felt ill in "the mud." But not like the other children, whose beds were often wet or soiled. Not like the others who wailed or quietly whimpered. Alla Stepanovna gave him candies for good behavior ("lie there quietly"). But Nefyodov liked sausages and he hated bad smells.

He would go to the nurses' station and stand there until someone would follow him down to the ward and change his neighbors' sheets. By the time he was six or seven, he already knew where the head nurse sat, which shift would yell, which shift hit, and which one drank. He knew the cook, the medical director's driver, and the two guards who would catch him after his escape attempts. He was healthy, so he was at the top. Whenever there was an inspection, they showed him off as proof of the effectiveness of mud healing. He was the only one in his ward who didn't wet the bed. But the only reason he didn't was because he was healthy, so he could get up and run to the toilet at the far end of the hall.

He saved Alla Stepanovna's candies in his nightstand. He would bring them to the drinking shift as a tasty treat to share. The nurses were nicer once they got a bit tipsy: they'd wash the floors and his neighbors' bottoms. They'd take the children out for walks and even tell stories. The cook would give Nefyodov bread. Bread also made a fine offering. Mitya the security guard let him pick flowers from the flower beds. The flowers were for the hitters. He would bring bouquets and lay them at the door—like at Lenin's Mausoleum. The whole shift was charmed. "What a sweet boy," they'd say and soften up a bit. They didn't wash the floors, but they would give him clean sheets and let Nefyodov clean up the other kids himself. He didn't like bad smells, but he wasn't afraid of shit. He cleaned them. And for the yelling shift, Nefyodov yelled, memorizing and repeating words you won't find in any book.

By the time he was eight, or a bit older, he began his education. Half a year at normal school, half a year in the mud. Nefyodov didn't like studying. Only reading. Everyone on the ward read. Beyond that, "What can you get from cripples other than blood samples?" An excellent, hilarious, and affectionate joke that led to Nefyodov's seizures. The seizures were the only moments when he was weak and dependent on whoever was watching. He had a safety pin for the seizures. Mitya the guard had suggested it. Mitya said that, if you get a cramp swimming in the sea, stick yourself immediately, and it will stop. He said, "You won't drown with a pin." Nefyodov had no intention of drowning. Only running away: his tendency for flight was recorded on his medical chart just below his diagnosis, which was extremely questionable. Twice they caught him at the gates. Twice at the bus stop and once at the train station in Yevpatoriya. That was his most successful escape, which Alla Stepanovna called his most heinous.

When Nefyodov was eleven, they got a phone installed in their apartment in Donetsk. The first two digits were "66." In those few short months that Nefyodov attended normal school, someone would call and then not say anything. Nefyodov would say, "Hello," but only hear quiet breathing at the other end. He imagined a girl like Cosette, the Lark who never sang. He looked for her among his classmates. But their gazes never rested on him. They didn't even remember him: not the girls from his block or from the next block over. No one remembered Nefyodov, no one made friends with him, missed him, or waited for him to come back. But someone called and breathed into the phone.

"It was Babá. I'm telling you," said Angelina laughing. "She was casting a spell on you because she decided to save you. I'm telling you, that's who it was."

"No," said Nefyodov and shook his head. His head resting on the pillow.

His imaginary Cosette looked like Tata. He'd recognized her right away. The minute she set foot in his apartment, took off her hat and shook out her hair. Just like Cosette, she didn't sing. No, she had never knit socks for Aunt Thenardier's daughters. She never even suspected the existence of such an aunt... But he recognized her right away.

It would have been stupid to tell Angelina that. Angelina, spontaneous, bold, direct and lively Angelina, who talked about herself readily, who laughed at herself and, when she did, it was as though she was inviting him to dive into the Crimean sea of his childhood, promising to be his safety pin in case of sudden cramps.

First, Nefyodov took off his armor ("of shit and sticks," as Lyosha would say). First, he took off his armor, then his pants. He didn't know you could just be friends. He'd never developed the skill, and there was no need to learn it.

Nefyodov knew what a deal was and how it worked. He thought he understood how it worked with women who were not Tata. He slipped extra food to Angelina for the afterschool so that "the children wouldn't starve"; he bought supplies for "the group": pencils, notebooks, mittens, plates, lamps, glue, colored paper. He installed a proper toilet and proper faucets. But Angelina rejected tile: "Let them get used to real life!" And he stumbled over that "real life." He saw it all, the whole forgotten, boarded-up mess he thought had been buried forever. He saw it all—with its crutches, yellowing sheets, rusty sinks, thin watery soups, wretched dry grass, Mitya the guard, and Alla Stepanovna who let him go. In the end, she let him go, forcing the commission to declare him healthy. Successfully cured.

Angelina still didn't allow the tile, but Nefyodov managed to yell at her about barbarians, sanitation, about his mother and father for whom it was simply more convenient. Convenient. Convenient. Six months away, three months at home. Convenient. Only a little scary because it was convenient. Under the supervision of doctors and with physical therapy. And with the mud.

He managed to yell that it wasn't about the tile, but about the fact that things shouldn't be damp, shouldn't be bad, and that the boy in the next cot over was named Hosha, and that he knew how to talk, but howled instead. Howled and howled. Because it was either howl or run.

"How many children were there in all?" asked Angelina.

"Twelve," answered Nefyodov. "Eight in the ward for the older kids."

"No, that's a lot. Four is the maximum. Even then they'll manage to fight, quarrel, and wipe their hands on the wallpaper."

If Angelina had acted shocked and drowned him in pity, Nefyodov would have run away immediately. The sign "Forgotten and buried," the dusty, inconspicuous door, the deep underground storage for excess baggage guaranteed that neither Alla Stepanovna nor the other officials would ever surface. But they did surface. They came out to take a look at the dirty wallpaper in Angelina's new apartment, the two sofas laid out for naps, the porridge that Angelina considered healthy and essential.

He told Angelina the things he should have told Tanya. But he couldn't talk to Tata about his weaknesses. He couldn't tell her that the chicken pox had scared him to death, that it took him back to a place that smelled of sulfur, sauerkraut, and bleach. He couldn't tell her that her house was also his house, and that there always had to be candy available to bribe anyone, anytime. Candy and money. He couldn't tell her that, on New Year's, he wrote a wish on a piece of paper, that he hid packets of dollars under his shirt so that they would cross the time border with him and multiply, that he obediently took twelve sips of champagne, one at each stroke of the clock. He made wishes about everything for every one of them, strengthening his spells with all possible charms for wealth, which meant freedom. He couldn't talk to Tata about his weaknesses. Or to Angelina about Tata.

There is not and never was any reasonable answer to the question of why Nefyodov removed his pants when they could have just been friends. Even if it had been awkward, breaking the rules, so what? They could have just talked, without worrying that the pretext, the children's extended day, would end. He could have told Angelina right away that he was just a random passenger in her life. But she wasn't a conductor and didn't ask for his ticket. She chattered on and never created pointless drama—even when she had a point. Though sometimes Nefyodov wanted drama. Yes, he wanted passion. He wanted to see that he was desperately needed, that someone couldn't live without him. But Angelina definitely could. And apparently Tata could, too.

There was a dull feeling of guilt and a vivid sensation of omnipotence, explosions and their craters, mortar fire and shell-shocked silence, almost fireworks and almost a wasteland. Nefyodov was elated one moment and terrified the next. And he constantly yelled, hiding behind the noise that he produced in quantities large enough for him to concentrate on sales.

Forty. His time was flying by. Flying toward death, helplessness, beds with metal springs and reeking floor rags. And nothing—not his Fuji studios all over the city, not the packing paper factory he was building, not the crazy but perfect house, could change that. The smell of therapeutic mud caught up with him, pinned him to the ground and urged him—if not to lie down now, then at least to scope out a spot that would be convenient for his relatives to visit. As he planned his own funeral, Nefyodov realized that he didn't want to see Angelina there.

"Don't come," he told her.

"Alright, I understand," she said. "But I'll still be reflected in your mirror."

"Where do you get these asinine ideas?"

"In *Natalie*," she answered, unoffended. "It has articles about the art of breaking up. And certain special phrases.

I really liked that one. I thought that I could be reflected in your mirror and stick my tongue out at you. It would be funny for you, and I wouldn't mind."

"And what does it say about actual art?" asked Nefyodov, feeling relieved and a bit repulsed for some reason.

The bathroom of his fine house was definitely not the place to start this conversation, or to be alone with Angelina at all.

"Call everyone to the table," Tata had said. "Angelina's already sprayed all of my perfumes in the bathroom and is moving on to yours..."

"The millennium will start without her," Nefyodov smiled.

"And we'll be in it," Tata assured him.

Angelina was holding a gold bar of Paco Rabanne and smelled just like Nefyodov. He frowned and uttered lightly "Don't come," picturing the vulgar image of "wife and lover fighting for the right to put him in the ground." Angelina couldn't have guessed what it was about. Couldn't have guessed and didn't ask. It was almost like a gift, a small, unnecessary, ordinary gift, wrapped up in 150 layers of the colorful tissue paper that sold so well at New Year's.

"They say you should hug for a good break-up," Angelina said.

"Well, then let's have a bad one," proposed Nefyodov. But too late, Angelina was already melting into him. And the bathroom door, that no one had locked, because nothing secret or shameful was supposed to happen, could happen, was planned to happen... The door suddenly flew wide open with a creak.

I need to oil those hinges, thought Nefyodov.

ERNEST
DONETSK
CARTOONS

Not every child can get lost in Kensington Gardens or be abandoned in the jungle. Not everyone is so lucky as to learn to fly, never lose their baby teeth, befriend fairies, or be raised by wolves and Baloo the Bear. Ernest was raised by chipmunks and ducks. Abandoned on the couch, he was happy to lose himself in Central Park, in a big tree not far from the police station, where Chip let him try on his hat and Dale would retell scary stories. He slept in the embrace of Roquefort, whose real name was actually Monterey Jack. He never could forgive the Russian dubbing that made that petty change, cheapening his love and devotion with falsehood.

Monterey Jack is a cheese, too. And just as inaccessible in the 1990s as Roquefort. But someone had to spoil the affectionate American diminutive, Monty, with the moldy green French Roquefort.

"I'm sorry, I'm so sorry," Ernest often says.

"It's okay," Babá answers, "it's okay. He doesn't mind. Not everyone who gets redone even knows about it. Just don't tell him again, and you're fine."

"It's not fine," worries Ernest. "I'm the dummy who said, 'Roquefort, don't go. Roquefort, help me...' It's me..."

Chipmunks, ducks, and Babá. Even better than Mowgli and Peter Pan had it. Donald Duck and Uncle Scrooge, and Gadget and, of course, Babá—they all talked with Ernest, ate and drank with him, pulled up his tights... Especially the tights: heel over the heel, onto the legs, two seams up the back and one in front. They stood in the corner with him, unseen by the teacher, and took him along—to save the Statue of Liberty, hide Scrooge's dimes, make umbrellas, search for uranium in Borneo, or wash Dale's Hawaiian shirt. Sometimes they spent whole days in the corner because their invisibility and Ernest's abandonment were connected. "Such a good boy," said the guilty teachers to his father or to Grandpa Fink. "You old giraffe nags, you lying hens," Babá would mutter in a temper, shaking her fist at them. "Such a good boy" Ernest giggled and sometimes, when he couldn't hold it back anymore, laughed out loud. The next day they'd put him in the corner again. For yesterday's laughter and tomorrow's potential laughter, which the hens never forgive anyone.

Ernest wanted to be Chip, Lyosha could be Dale, and Thelma would be Gadget. "But who will I be?" asked Halya, hurt. "How about Zipper?" offered Ernest magnanimously, considering the funny green fly a fine gift for a girl from a respectable family. But Halya wanted to be Gadget, too. And, if it weren't for Babá who always showed up when she felt like it but was never late, Halya and Thelma would have clawed each other's faces at every family gathering, and at school, and afterschool. They would have fought not just over Gadget, but over everything. Later, once they'd all matured a bit, it stopped, and neither of them held a grudge. There was nothing to begrudge.

Babá always threw out a trump in time: maybe Simba, or later *A Nightmare on Elm Street*, or even a bootleg Helloween tape left behind after one of the parents' parties. Babá's invisibility made her different from the chipmunks and ducks. For instance, Ernest didn't quite know the color of her hair, whether she wore a fur coat and boots, or went around barefoot. He couldn't find out how old she was, where she lived, or where she went when she wasn't with him.

"Don't worry, sunshine," she said. "I'll be here as long as you need me."

"And when the wind's in the east? When the wind's in the east, will you fly in like Mary Poppins?"

"Oh, Lord, spare us the east wind. We don't need that grief. You just tell your Mary Poppins that we didn't invite her here, you hear me?"

"I hear you."

He could hear and smell her. Sometimes she smelled like an old lady: of bread, Easter cakes, garlic, and borscht. Sometimes like wet wooden boards, artemisia, chamomile, and dry earth. And sometimes she didn't smell at all but just thundered in his ear, raging, laughing, threatening someone, and breathing fire. She warned him:

"Don't tell anyone about me, or they'll decide you're not right in the head."

Ernest shrugged. He didn't say anything. He wanted them to know her. Like Karlsson or Wendy.

"When I grow up I'm going to write a story about you!"

"Is that a threat or a promise?" laughed Babá.

He would have liked to hug her. To snuggle up, give her a smooch on the cheek, give her a kitty or a puppy, and make sure she settled down nearby... He knew that Babá might not actually exist. Particularly not in that world where everything was... hazy. Things that were hazy included whether there was a God; whether he was being watched over by his Mama, who was both in the cemetery and in a frame on the wall at the same time; whether you could eat snow; whether forgotten or lost wishes came true; whether you needed to listen to your elders who didn't listen to anyone themselves... Babá came for him, on the first day of kindergarten, when his father was pulling him and he was resisting, dragging his good sneakers across the asphalt. He clenched his teeth and didn't say a single word; he closed his eyes and didn't shed a single tear.

"Don't be scared, sweet dove, don't be scared. We'll have fun together. I promise! You hear me?"

"I hear you…"

At about thirteen, Ernest decided that Babá was a problem. The chipmunks and ducks, the cartoon theme songs he hummed to comfort himself, the drawing of Chip under the glass on the table where he studied, ate, and played, his ability to "watch cartoons by heart" for the one hundredth, or one thousandth, time—none of that was a problem. But Babá—maybe.

"Are you embarrassed by me?" she asked.

"I'm not embarrassed. I'm scared… I don't want to go to the hospital. I don't want to be a psycho," he answered.

"Well, okay," drawled Babá, using the words and intonation of a Hollywood star that she definitely didn't get from him.

"Is there someone else?" asked Ernest nervously.

"Don't get upset, but, for better or for worse, you're definitely not my only one."

It got quiet without her. One day, two, three, a week… Ernest wanted to be her only one, the one and only, but there was no one to talk to about it. His dad had room in his life for math, "the ladies from work," and the family Fink had created. And Fink also had others besides Ernest: Thelma and her mother, Halyuska's parents, Dale-Lyosha, and the Nefyodov house that had to be coveted. His mama on the wall didn't fix anything: Ernest was rapidly catching up to her in size and, soon, in age. And, catching up, for some reason, he didn't feel anything for her but sadness, a shattering sadness, like the gray sky of a stifling gray evening that would suddenly fall, gradually dissipating into night. On the other hand, if he wasn't Babá's one and only, at least the psych ward wouldn't be dull. And Lyosha got a cat right about then. A tiny, fluffy little moron who chased candy wrappers and his own tail, a dry linden leaf, and later—the giant snowflakes that would land on his nose, his paws and his withers—if a cat even has those. They named the cat Tiny. Ernest started visiting Lyosha of his own volition, not just to secure the bonds of the bizarre parental friendship, which had continued for some reason, making their casual childhood relationships into sometime overly confining and excessive. There were occasional explosions caused by Halyuska's attacks on Thelma, or Thelma's threats to marry one of them, or Lyosha's snobbery—a generous snobbery indifferent to wealth or poverty, the snobbery of the heir to the "Photography Empire" whose plastic showrooms were now more common in the city than bakeries.

They named the cat Tiny. He had blue eyes. Ernest pretended that he was going to play video games, although he actually had the same system at home. Ernest's father might not have an "Empire," but his salary—plus bonuses, awards, and benefits—was fit for a king.

Lyosha was Dale, but Ernest assigned him to be the mad scientist Nimnul who catches cats to feed his "giant generator" with their energy. Chip-Ernest couldn't allow Tiny—a white cat with dark markings on his back—to be fed to anything. In short, Ernest went to corrupt someone else's cat. Very stupid. Very.

Because Tiny didn't give a damn about Ernest, or Lyosha, or the crunchy, now completely black, linden leaf. The cat assiduously stashed the leaves under the porch so he could gracefully leap out in front of Lyosha's mother, scattering the leaves at her feet. His saucy blue eyes were glassy and a bit sleepy. The world beyond Lyosha's mother held no interest for him—not even in the form of sausages. She, Aunt Tanya, even if not an actual aunt, not his aunt, not Thelma's, not Halyuska's, but still... All the women were aunts, and all the men were uncles: that's how it was in that tribe at that time, in which Tiny delivered a twine mouse or a paper butterfly-airplane that Ernest made for him, straight to Tanya's lap. Aunt Tanya was Tiny the Cat's one and only. And that was a beautiful thing. Frustrating, but beautiful.

Then one day he was gone. Tiny wasn't sitting at the door, or lying on the stool by the mirror, or lounging in the armchair, or hiding in the bathroom, or attacking from behind the toilet. It was March. Ernest had come back from the Emirates with a real toy mouse, not a homemade one, with a light-up belly. The glasses for Lyosha were a pretext. "Kuch-kuch," whispered Ernest, who'd listened to how the Arabs called cats. "Ku-kuch, kys-kys..."

It was March. A possible time for cat love.

"Where's the cat? Did he take off?" asked Ernest.

"He gave my mom ringworm," Lyosha answered with a shrug.

"And?"

"Ringworm! She has a spot right on her chest, where he liked to sleep. She's worried it'll get into her hair and she'll have bald spots. She's treating it like mad. You'll have to give her the mouse."

"And?"

"They set him up. Don't worry. In the cafeteria of the loony bin on Petrivka. Mom has a friend there," said Lyosha gloomily.

Gloomily. With a sadness like the gray sky of a stifling gray evening that never turns to night.

"Probably no one would have taken him. He's got ringworm. Bald spots on his back. He must have picked it up outside somewhere. It's a bad case. He's in the cafeteria. There's food…"

There were plenty of normal people in the loony bin on Petrivka.

More among the sick than among the healthy.

"What do you mean, a cat? What cat? This is a mental hospital, not a vet clinic!" the healthy people said—that is to say, the orderlies, doctor, and admissions nurse.

"They usually sit out by the trash, but not for long," said a quiet man in an old gown that looked like a school janitor's rag. "Come with me. I'm allowed to walk outside here."

"You see, he's a house pet. No one taught him to hunt— the only thing he can catch is snowflakes. And only if there are a lot of them. He's never seen a mouse in his life. And he's afraid of cockroaches. You see?"

"I'm scared of them, too," agreed the man.

Tiny wasn't by the trash.

"I'll call you if I see him. They let me make calls. I'm really just having a rest here. I'll call you if I see him. I'm Jean. Jean isn't a disease. Jean Igorevich," he said with a smile.

"Ernest. Also not a disease."

"Look harder. Don't leave. What was it your chipmunk used to say? If at first you don't succeed, try, try again," Babá suddenly interjected. She showed up and butted in like she'd never left.

"That was Donald Duck, not a chipmunk."

"The cannibal duck? The one who devours other ducks for Christmas?" Babá laughed. "Alright then… Although, I like the chipmunks better. Don't leave, sweetheart, don't leave… Look for him, call louder."

"Ernest. Also not a disease. And the cat is Tiny. I'll just call him for a bit here, alright? Maybe you could call, too? If you can."

The man turned out to have a magical voice. Rich and velvety, promising all the sausages in the world. And Ernest's voice was still breaking then; on the high notes he still sounded like a kid or a girl. "Tiny... Teeny... Little bit... Tiny... Itty bitty..."

He appeared out of nowhere, emerging in response to the random femininity of Ernest's call. He sat down next to Ernest and sighed heavily.

"Well, I'm not Tanya. What now? That's not a good reason not to go home," said Babá. "Beggars can't be choosers, kitty."

"Ee-oo," said Tiny in a pitiful voice and looked up at Ernest with deep blue eyes.

Ernest left his number with Jean Igorevich. The ringworm was improving, but there was still one bald spot on his back. Babá called the cat Baby instead of Tiny. He growled and agreed. He always agreed with her. And if you count Ernest, that makes two of them.

The cat died in February of 2014, right before the war. Fifteen happy years. True, without eggs, with no street, no snow, and no blackened linden leaf. Lyosha was the only one at Baby's funeral. He quickly got drunk, and, instead of a decent eulogy about how the dearly departed had always peed into his sneakers, he started asking stupid questions.

"I don't understand why I didn't tell them that he could be treated, needed to be cured? Why didn't I tell them? What kind of a monster am I? Am I even human?"

Ernest didn't have an answer.

BOHDAN KORNIYENKO
JANUARY 2000

The first time Bohdan tried to find himself, Ernest was finishing sixth grade. But he found nothing: nothing whole or broken, or even appropriated. Just a giant, boring hole. An abyss you could peer into with no fear that it might look back at you. There was something hanging around at the bottom. Bicycles, skates, a couple of skateboards, tennis rackets, and a diving suit glinted in the sun; heaps of condoms reluctantly rotted; bits of broken tile were scattered around, as were old wooden window frames, Zhiguli tires, a couple of Nokias, a leather jacket, stacks of popcorn buckets, and plane tickets in tattered plastic folders... The trash heap at the bottom of the abyss must have been huge. But it was hard to make out and hardly memorable. A heap of large trinkets, devalued desires, and tiny scales covering a thin skin, probably protecting it from something.

Alla had been gone for a long time. Alla, previously associated with pain but also comfort and a sense of rightness. Her portrait hung on the wall promising that things would always stay that way. In reality, that was just a form now, a memory, but not Alla herself. Math—that pure, merciless, ideal mathematics, whose beauty could explain everything—was gone, too. What remained were talents and skills, a flair for software trends, and the ability to find other people's errors. Bohdan still found it interesting, but now he was testing programs rather than writing them: plunging into mystery stories without corpses or robberies.

"I'm a boring person," Bohdan told Halyuska. "I don't meet the criteria for your essay. Write about your dad instead."

"He doesn't 'break stone,' like in the Ivan Franko poem. He just 'turns the wheel.' It's a Franko journalistic essay, with a free choice of topics on contemporaries. Anyway, they're going to kill him soon for his debts. Papa, not Franko. Ivan Franko died a long time ago. If I get hold of some money, could you give it to him? Like it's you giving it to him, not me. It's called 'laundering.'"

"Of stolen money?"

"I have no choice. You're not going to give me a thousand bucks to write an essay about you, right? And I'm too young to earn it through prostitution. The client could get locked up for molesting a minor. And I don't have anything to blackmail you with. Or, maybe, there is something? Is there?"

"Halya!!" shouted Bohdan. "Halya!! What are you even saying?"

"I'm saying it's a little late. It should have been sooner. I've been tracking everything. I eavesdropped and spied on him. I hoped Aunt Tanya would give dad the money and then he would give it back to her. What's the word in Ukrainian? Oh, right! Lend! Lend him the money. But she said no. So I got really mad at her and stole it. I know where they keep their money because Les told us all one time when he was showing off.

"Les—is that Lyosha?"

"That's what you call him. I don't. In Ukrainian, it's Les. When we were over there for New Year's, I stole it. Les thinks Thelma stole it, Aunt Tanya thinks Les stole it, and Nefyodov thinks it was Aunt Tanya—mainly because that's what she told him. But now it's already January 5. They beat

Dad up, you should see him, and now they want two grand. Two grand for punitive damages."

"Halya!!" Bohdan shouted again. "I'm not asking why me or why it's so mysterious. I'm asking about you! Seeing as you've come here in the end, why didn't you come earlier to ask me for the money?"

"You're not going to like my answer."

"That's fine," said Bohdan. "Taking everything into account, it seems we're pretty much family. Let's have some tea or coffee, and go over everything calmly, in order. With pauses."

"Sure, however you want. Absolutely," said Galya morosely. "We've got time for pauses. They broke Papa's leg, so he won't be racking up any new debts himself. But if those... gangsters... still have their meter running..."

"My family," thought Bohdan. Holidays, feasts, group photos. Not frequently, but regularly. Diets; vacations to Turkey, or better yet—to the Emirates; a first trip to Europe—and not to buy cheap stuff and schlep it here for selling, Angelina, but as a tourist. Feel the difference? Renovations—where the big winner is always Tanya and her House with a capital H. A family whose father is hardly acknowledged, embarrassed by the source of their kinship, but, as though under a spell, they get together again and again to discover "Cousin Mary's" strange obsession with guns and the hole in the firstborn's, Nefyodov's, strategic business plan. There didn't seem to be any love lost, no obligations to old friendship, no common interests, no shared passion for hunting or crochet, and yet, no one wanted to escape; even the kids didn't try to slip away, having been foisted upon one another by Grandpa Fink's turbulent political fantasy.

"I no longer think about it the way I thought about it yesterday. And especially not the day before yesterday. Keep that in mind," Halyuska says, blushing deeply.

"She finally blushes deeply," thought Bohdan and smiled silently.

"First of all, the reason I didn't come to you is because you're poor and greedy. Because only a poor, greedy person would sell his own child and the child's name."

"Alright then," sighed Bohdan.

"Second of all, the Nefyodovs are rich. And, in the current social structure, wealth can be achieved only through criminal activity. Good people don't get rich. So they should share. It's only fair. And third... Ernest. Not a great third. Not so pleasant. Would you, for example, want a daughter-in-law whose father gambles? It might be hereditary, according to your logic."

"What might be hereditary?!" shouted Bohdan.

Out of fear. Out of stupidity. Out of his own idiocy, which isn't a diagnosis but at this rate will definitely become one. He shouts because he's scared and doesn't know what to do. There's no explaining to Halyuska that thirteen never passes—or fourteen, or twenty... No age passes or departs forming the hummus substrate for the mineral deposits of some promised adult life. Thirteen freezes in a stalactite of snot, twenty as a bloody lollipop, twenty-five towers as the wooden fence Ernest fell off. It only seems like every year behaves better than the last. In reality, each successive year just gets shorter, leaving behind not something magnificent reaching for the heavens but something brief, inconsequential, and sometimes very fragile. Each successive age and year became more like splinters lodged under the skin. Splinters, not stalactites. Maybe that's why each year seemed to actually pass.

"What might be hereditary?!" shouts Bohdan.

"Well, you know... My tendency to steal. You don't think so?"

"No. Definitely not."

Every time Bohdan was about to talk about himself... Not with Halyuska, that just happened... Whenever he was about to have a talk with himself, something inevitably came up: Ernest's measles, a high-profile murder at the stadium, a cellphone software project, a visit from his mother who always carefully checked that he'd been paying the utilities, a snowy winter, or one with no snow at all...

Everyone around him talked and talked, and he didn't have the strength to squeeze in between the words. So he talked, too, worried, flared up, and thought that one day he'd die without even noticing it himself because the general flow of life around him would absorb and dissolve him. Although Ernest wasn't exactly "the general flow," of course.

Bohdan had a thousand dollars. He could lend the money, but not gift it. And Halyuska was at an impasse, which revealed all manner of other impasses hidden under plaid blankets, buried in broken pencils, tucked into notebooks with torn pages... The impasse of childhood, in which you can't solve anything on your own. And there are no good options.

It was impossible to return the money without saying who stole it. It was impossible not to return the money, leaving little Lyosha under suspicion. It was impossible to tell Petro, at least right now. Maria—also impossible. Angelina definitely didn't need to know: she was the type to drag Halyuska's disgrace through the years and then pass it on as an inheritance to her children. What about Fink?

"I have good news," said Bohdan. "They rarely kill for that amount anymore. They've become more or less civilized. Trust me."

"No." She shook her head. "No. Next you'll say 'let's go to the police.'"

Bohdan sighed and smiled ruefully. The idea of the police really was ridiculous.

"I'm afraid they're going to add on more than those two thousand while we're sitting here hoping for the best. And I don't have anywhere else to steal more."

"And?"

"You'll give Papa the money. As if it was from you. As if Aunt Tanya told you to, okay?"

"And he'll gamble that away, too?"

"I'll pay you back. I have a plan—a little at a time, from my earnings. It'll probably take me three years, but we can peg the payments to the exchange rate of the dollar. No one loses anything. And I won't even look in Ernest's direction. I promise."

"Maybe you shouldn't be in such a hurry regarding Ernest?" said Bohdan.

"Once a thief, always a thief," Halya sighed sorrowfully. "There are no guarantees of decent behavior. The crooked daughter of a crooked father."

A mature, responsible person would never have gone along with such a scheme. But Bohdan felt like a mother hen. A teenage mother hen. All of his cynicism, pragmatism and boastfulness, his ability to vacation in the Mediterranean in late October, all his survival skills in a world that strikes first and asks questions later, all of that evaporated next to these children that he sometimes felt he'd given birth to himself.

Bohdan went to the pharmacy across from the ER and bought crutches. Three of them.

"I do have my own," said Petro Lischke in a hurt tone. "But thank you, of course. Why three?"

"One to break over your head! Come on, get dressed. Don't sit here jabbering."

"And what am I going to do dressed?" Petro clarified dully.

"We're going to pay them back."

"I'll manage without you!"

"I should have brought four," said Bohdan, raising the crutch over Petro's head. Raised it and brought it down with a deafening crash onto a chair. The chair shuddered. Once, twice, three times... It shook, groaned, let out a final creak, then folded its legs and collapsed into oblivion.

"Oh wow..." said Petro, respectfully.

His extortionist benefactor wasn't particularly pleased. He preferred the version with compound interest increasing Petro's debt. A thousand wasn't enough for him. Because one thousand was the amount for the first of the month. On the ninth, "as in, today, guys," he needed two.

"Count it," said Bohdan.

The pal slowly counted the money and then invited them to dinner. To celebrate. No hard feelings. To old and new friendships.

"You should have brought four," Petro whispered to Bohdan. "Crutches, I mean. Crutches."

"Maybe another time," Bohdan said loudly.

"Well, then I'll see you later," agreed the extortionist.

And he wasn't lying. Within a year, his snout was plastered all over the bus stops, lamp posts and fences. His smile flashed from the windows of high-end stores and was an "insert" in laundry detergent samples. His flyers read "Leninist longevity for the Lenin District." It's entirely possible that he had a sense of humor. With which he became a deputy of the district council.

TANYA NEFYODOVA IS FIFTY

Tanya Nefyodova is fifty. And she is no longer Nefyodova and no longer practicing family medicine. "There should probably only be one doctor in the family," she says. "And that's Lyosha now that he's in dental school."

"Well, he'll never go hungry," Angelina gushed. "And when we get old, we'll still have our teeth."

Angelina fawns on Tanya because she's remorseful. She's not actually ashamed, and she doesn't want to be blamed.

She doesn't like it.

Tanya Nefyodova is now Tanya Shvets. She got married two years ago and changed both her name and profession. She's a designer now. She says, "It's so odd: I'm still going around to different entryways and climbing stairs with no elevators. They don't turn on the elevators right away in the new buildings. The walls are as clean as a hospital. It's kind of disturbing. Sometimes you want to read a little something on them."

Shvets is a cardiologist at the regional medical center. A cardiac surgeon. Vitya. The soft "tya" dangles from his name like washing on a line. But Viktor would sound even worse. Vitya and Tanya were classmates and are the same age. Vitya is known for his beard and his diagnostic skills. He operates worse than he diagnoses. But the fees for both are high. "You get what you pay for." But sometimes he goes a little nuts and doesn't accept payment for the initial exam. There were even times, plenty of them, when he spent his own money on medicines, devices, and bandages for his patients.

Tanya showed up at Vitya's office with angina after Nefyodov took off. Nefyodov just blurted out, "I can't do this anymore." Tanya wanted to ask, "Can't do what anymore? Why can't you?" But she didn't know how to talk with Nefyodov and didn't know what she was supposed to do: fall at his feet, clutch at the hem of his jacket, cry, or run after him. Nefyodov said, "I'll come by for my things." And she packed up his things. It took six large suitcases—two of which they'd bought in Paris when they couldn't fit all the souvenirs into the one they'd brought with them. It was a shame about the new suitcases, but it felt somehow indecent to wrap his suits, jeans, and sweaters up in sheets. Tacky.

Tanya wanted to ask someone, "Will he come back?" But she was too embarrassed.

Tanya's mother exploded. "I knew it! You were always useless. Now deal with it!"

Mama was already over seventy, but Tanya still got on her last nerve. When Tanya was young, that inflamed nerve led mama to beat Tanya with a belt and put her in the corner, rip pages out of her notebooks and force her to rewrite her "scribble-scrabbles." Mama went to Tanya's school demanding they be stricter with her, not to let her get away with anything. Now there was no corner, no belt, no school, and so none of the usual mechanisms to make her "deal with it." But it turned out that no one other than her mother wanted to delve into it.

"You're hopeless. It's your own damn fault. You couldn't keep a husband! What a disgrace you are—a disgrace, an embarrassment, and a piece of shit, Tanya. Why am I being tortured like this? What are we going to live on? Your salary? Just don't count on my pension! And you're not even entitled to alimony. You should have listened to me and divorced him sooner. Remember: at your age, a decent woman needs to be married. But who's going to fall for you? Huh?"

"What do I do, Mama?" asked Tanya.

"What do you do?! I'll tell you what you do. You chase after him, humiliate yourself, you stupid little doormat. Beg him to come back. I don't know... Get sick and die. He's sure to come to your funeral... Although I didn't go to your father's. I wouldn't give him the respect. Think, if you're capable of it. Spy on him, find out who he's in bed with. Just write an anonymous letter. I did—didn't think I was too good for that. It worked twice, but then you all destroyed the Soviet Union, and he ran off right away."

"Who ran off?" asked Tanya.

She couldn't think. Or breathe. Or eat and drink. She couldn't walk. Or look.

Lyosha dragged Nefyodov home.

"Parents, come on, talk... Papa, what's the problem? Mama, you go first. Who did what wrong and who promises never to do it again? Come on, make up, make up, make up, alright?"

"Can I take this ashtray, too?" asked Nefyodov.

"Papa, have you lost your fucking mind?"

Tanya flared up and wanted to scream at her son, "How dare you talk like that, you snotty little brat?" She flared up as if she were still alive and furious. As if there was no burn, as if there was still life where she was the "gendarme," punishing, keeping track of everything, encouraging—Nefyodov with the search for the "chickenpox" scar and Lyosha with permission to "go poison himself at McDonald's."

The ashtray Nefyodov wanted to take was a gift from Tanya. She'd bought it for him at the antique market in Milan. Nothing special, blue glass with a gilded rim, about the size of a tray. Maybe it actually was a tray. Who can say for sure at this point? But the seller had said, in English, "ashtray," and Nefyodov's gaze had fixated on it. A ravenous gaze. Tanya couldn't remember a time he'd looked at something that way. They continued on toward the chairs, chandeliers, and mirrors. Then Tanya left Nefyodov in a cafe and went back for the blue glass. She wanted to buy the ashtray in secret and sneak it home to surprise Nefyodov. But she couldn't hide it in her bag or under her raincoat. It was too big and fragile. Tanya brought it back to the cafe and put it on the table, next to the pizza and the *vino de la casa* that Nefyodov had ordered so he wouldn't have to choose.

Children understand little about the secret language of their parents: their signs, secrets, significant words, and signals that supposedly adult people exchange because they have no idea how to talk. Lyosha raised the ashtray high over his head and smashed it on the marble floor of the kitchen. The shards were small, even tiny, and, for some reason, white. Like freshly fallen snow. Although it was summer. A desperately hot summer.

"The house is mine," said Tanya. "You'll buy Alyosha an apartment. I make no claims on the business."

"Yes," said Nefyodov. "I'll help."

"My mother will be pleased," Tanya said for some reason.

"Well, what if I'm a drug addict? How about gay? A gay, gambling drug addict. A card shark... at the casino. Would that stop you?" asked Lyosha.

Nefyodov and Tanya simultaneously asked about different things. Tanya screamed menacingly, "You're a drug addict?!"

And Nefyodov, plaintively: "Are you definitely gay?"

"So, no problem with the cards and casino?" asked Lyosha.

"So, it was you after all... You... You stole the money from me? It wasn't your mother? So, Tata, you covered for the child? You knew everything and enabled him? And now look what it's come to. See?" exploded Nefyodov.

So, Lyosha failed. But it could have worked. Nefyodov shouted as usual, and Tanya looked out the window. The

○

curtains that summer were white and beige, made of old lace, tulle, a bit of linen, organza, and cotton. The veranda, and the whole house resembled a ship. *The Flying Dutchman* at the very instant it turned into a phantom. That very last instant when everything was still good.

Nefyodov slammed the door. Tanya looked out the window. Nefyodov's back promised a return: it moved uncertainly, unwillingly, following the legs that were also walking, most likely out of habit.

Then, a couple of days later, Angelina came. She said, "Tanya, I'm sorry. We already broke it off four years ago. Remember the first time Thelma ran away from home? That's when we split up. She caught us in the bathroom. We were actually breaking up, but she thought the opposite. And I was so surprised, thinking, 'Where's that draft coming from?' You always keep the house closed up in the winter, so you're not heating the street. You're so sensible and thrifty. Just good—you do everything right. Please forgive me."

"Breaking up with who?" asked Tanya.

It wasn't often that the words came out before she could think. But out they flew. And she thought that it was so stupid and helpless, that there'd be no way to rewrite that "scribble-scrabble." Because four years ago, and probably longer, they'd settled into the word "always" and ripped out whole chunks of goodness from her life, that she could no longer think of as good. Because Nefyodov "always" had that.

The toad arrived right then. It hopped in, slimy and warty, with legs like a folding table. It pressed against her ribs, spat into her diaphragm, hopped around in her shoulder and even somewhere around her back, paused for a moment, and then began choking her until everything went dark.

Angelina was the one who called the paramedics. And the one who took her to the hospital. Pureed soups, white chicken meat pate, and her viscous, fruity *kissel*... Oh, God, kissel... Baked apples, juices with and without pulp, filtered through sterile gauze. "You don't have to worry, it's sterile," Angelina said.

"It's angina," said Vitya Shvets. "And no one's going to die today. Or tomorrow."

"I didn't recognize you with that beard," said Tanya.

She actually had been preparing to die. It wasn't the worst solution—to just stop thinking, stop shaking Nefyodov out of herself, stop crossing out days and entire months which were now packed with lies and a life that hadn't existed. At first, Tanya and Vitya weren't a match. Tanya didn't want to be a sleeping beauty or a rescued princess. And Vitya built himself up as a hero, macho man, and lover of classical music. Then it turned out that he really did love music.

He loved everything that Tanya knew nothing about. Viennese opera, billiards, frittatas rather than omelets, trips to the mountains and a bit of amateur alpinism, skiing, of course, Masonic conspiracy theories, cypresses, MRI-confirmed diagnoses, fantasy novels, headphones that grew smaller with each passing year, colorful socks, yoga, and German. He hadn't managed to marry on time because there had always been cute nurses, one better than the next, cute colleagues with family problems, cute patients. "I couldn't get by without it, Tanya, not without that. What happened, happened." He was categorically opposed to breeding. He had a principled, panicked, and persuasive stance.

"Every day, I see how we die. Birth is the first step to death, and frequently—death under poor conditions."

"Girls call it 'childfree,'" said Tanya. "For boys it's just 'Where's your tree, blockhead?'"

Vitya wasn't touching or funny. Except maybe for his feral gnome beard. And his life was filled to the brim. Cheese selection, hotel reservations, hiking itineraries, sports equipment and pool cues, a diving mask, an exhibition of cat drawings, a lecture on esotericism, sauerkraut rolls. Vitya Shvets took hold of Tanya and dragged her into a different world, where there was lots of everything. Even too much. But that "too much" didn't leave any time for chopping the past into pieces, running it through the meat grinder a hundred times, and leaving it to putrify.

Oddly enough, this other world allowed Tanya to put her own world to rest. And to become a designer, whose initial clientele consisted of post-stroke or bypass patients. Vitya gave Tanya a small, used but peppy Mercedes and proposed that they "formalize their relationship."

"Why?" asked Tanya.

"Well, it's probably time for me to settle down," said Vitya. "And I like your house. I don't have the energy or time to build one like it for myself."

They got married and flew to Vienna for the opening of the season. They saw *Tosca*. But no matter how she tried, Tanya couldn't get the stress right—either in the name of the opera or in her new life. Everything was fine. Almost the way she liked it.

They celebrated her fiftieth birthday with new friends and clients. But she invited the "family" to the house. The veranda had been glassed in, so it was now transparent like an aquarium. With no curtains. The two ovens had moved from under the stove to the center shelves of a special cabinet. Vitya called it "cooking at eye level." They put a glass floor in the kitchen and lined the bottom with flowers and grass. A bit tacky, but you could always change the "filler." Vitya promised to consider corals for the next renovation. The doors now had stained glass. Including the bathroom.

The house had changed. But it was still recognizable. Like Tanya, who was no longer Tata, but still wanted "them" to be sure to admire the floors, the new dishes, the parquet with different types of wood, the well they'd dug so that "you'd always have your own water." Nefyodov came, too. Alone. Although they said that he wasn't single anymore, that he was seeing someone and would be getting married again soon. To Tanya's surprise, all the kids came, too.

The birthday party was supposed to be a celebration of victory. A counterattack to escape encirclement. A celebration of new possibilities, an opportunity for Tanya to shine in front of Angelina, in front of Nefyodov, and in front of Thelma who shouldn't have run away from home because of some Tanya. But run she had.

"She's really a good girl," Tanya said to Lyosha.

"Alas, no longer mine," he agreed.

But there were no fireworks. No discernible envy or solemn speeches to hide it. They ate well, chatted about the fact that they'd unexpectedly grown up, but still hadn't figured out what that meant, about how there used to be house phones and you could eavesdrop on the children, about the fact that potatoes supposedly weren't food anymore, but it was not yet clear what actually was food.

Fink said, "Let's get a picture. The kids are already twenty after all."

"Yes, and some of them are still Ernest and Thelma," chuckled Bohdan.

They lined up on the porch and started smiling. Maria and Petro, Angelina, Bohdan, Tanya and Nefyodov. The children. Separate children with completely incomprehensible lives. Thelma, Lyosha, Ernest, and Haska, who'd decided to leave the "babyish" name Halyuska behind.

Vitya took the picture. And so he wasn't in the frame.

"So you're the husband of this grandma?" the teacher asked Fink.

"No, I've been without a woman my whole life," he answered.

"Well, like I said, a very strange family. Suspiciously strange. The mother isn't a mother, a grandfather with no wife. Is she even her grandmother?" Her penciled-in eyebrows converged at the bridge of her nose, where it became clear that the right was wider than the left. "Do you have any documentation?"

"Here's my passport."

"We don't give out children on the basis of a passport."

"I have a notarized consent form. Here," said Fink, passing her the piece of paper in a plastic folder, and thought how smart Haska was. Prudent Haska. Almost like Clever Gretel, but actually clever. "Can I take her home now? We still have homework to do."

"No," said the teacher. "We're going to talk right now about what you're teaching the child. And how you're teaching her. And who allowed it. You'll answer for this! Answer to the principal, and maybe to our entire teaching staff and the district!"

Fink had come to Kyiv because Haska needed to go first to the East and then to the West. She had to "tour the world a bit" with the book. With both the original and the German translation, which was already on sale and needed her presence in those places where Frau Kristina asked, "Are you human?" For now, that meant bookstores, but visits to

German state parliaments were in the works, too. Bavaria was first on the list.

Someone had to stay with the child: drive her to school, do homework, feed her, supervise the cleaning of teeth and ears, the washing of hands and hair. Then the hair had to be brushed and braided. Lately he's been considering a haircut, seriously short, "like a boy," just a couple of inches long... But the idea of going that radical all at once was scary. The women might kill him over that missing hair. On the one hand, Fink was already eighty and every single day for the last ten years he'd been amazed that he was still alive and well. He was genuinely amazed and grateful, but he was also somehow ready to die. He already had loved ones on the other side and he was not at all afraid to lie there with them—or walk, fly, be a cat, parrot, or ghost—whatever they actually do over there. On the other hand, to die during such horrific and uncertain times from women's rage and a bad haircut would be embarrassing and stupid. Lately, he frequently imagined himself achieving some great feat, just as he'd imagined in his distant and not-so-beautiful childhood. But what? Well, the plan hasn't changed much. Fink saw himself, his body strapped with grenades, slowly moving towards the front line and maybe, just to set the trap, he even walks with his hands up, so they can see—it's just a kid, no, an old man—completely harmless and not quite right in the head. He's just walking, letting the enemy get closer and closer; he promises them secrets and military intelligence, maps and the name of the most important commander, and then he pulls the pin and takes three, or four, or more of them with him into a fiery hell.

But for now he's braiding hair and cooking cornmeal porridge (which is called polenta now), macaroni (now called pasta), and chicken soup. He's getting entangled in the declension of adjectives, the measurement of segment lengths and the reading of topographic maps, which, he assures Dina, will come in handy during the zombie apocalypse, when there won't be any electricity or Google employees. "Will we hide in ravines and drink water from rivers?" Dina asks in delight. "And the zombies won't get us?"

"It depends on which zombies we get," Fink mutters to himself, but not out loud. Out loud they have natural science and Khrystyna who is managing not only the Bavarian government, the book, and the bookish Haska, but also a music group near the front line in Avdiïvka. It's hard for Fink to understand how she found it. For a long time, she was taking her extra clothes to her native village, because things were "falling off her, since she'd gotten as thin as a model," then she started taking a couple of bags a month from neighbors and other concerned people to the refugees, and then at some point she switched to guitars, synthesizers, and microphones, because—culture! Occasionally, a driver from the International Transport Agency or the car sharing site will call Fink rather than Khrystyna to collect the next round of theater costumes, drums of various sizes and sounds, or vitamins "for voice and brain function". "Keep some for yourself, Henya. You need to feed your brain, because sometimes it's completely empty." Recently, Khrystyna came up with the idea of bringing the Munich Opera to Avdiïvka. "Well, at least a part of it. Well, at least three musicians. Or, two... Or the war's going to end without these Germans even getting a whiff of gunpowder."

Fink has his doubts. Both that the war is about to end, and that the opera is what everyone wants.

He's ashamed, but thoughts aren't actions. Although, he's a little ashamed of his actions, too. For the first time in his life, he lives in the Obolon neighborhood. It's not really about the nice neighborhood, it's the fact that he's living as he wants. As he always wanted. It's unfortunate that his age makes him slow, clumsy, and forgetful. But happy that his health is decent. "Happy—without ifs or buts. Fink lives with Dina. She's eight and in third grade. Together they (mostly) conscientiously do her homework. Dina crosses out her mistakes with a beautiful wavy line, adding a knot or a flower at the end. She assures him that the notebook will "be like an ocean someday. All the pages will flow together."

"All the rivers run into the sea, / Yet the sea is not full; / To the place from which the rivers come, / there they return again," pronounces Fink, who has been reading up on the Bible for a while, so he can grasp what it will be like on the other side.

Dina writes "flow" with a silent "e"—"floe"—insisting that it makes more sense, and should be spelled the way one hears it. Her teacher disagrees. Dina brings home a wide range of grades. The spontaneous silent *e*'s usually result in something lower than a "6." Poor Fink can't get used to that. He consults the table he's created for himself and determines that a "6" is essentially a "satisfactory" that could be a "good," if the teacher was nice.

But the teacher is not nice. She's young, tall, and striking. Brimming with anger like a full keg of beer. She spits when she talks to Fink.

"Have you seen her essay? Have you read this nightmare? Is anyone even keeping tabs on what this child thinks? This was homework and you should not have allowed it! Should have forbidden such shamelessness! What's more, this was for March 8, International Women's Day, a day for celebrating spring, beauty, and femininity! Here, read it!" The teacher sticks the notebook under Fink's nose. She's hanging over him, glowing red, just like the bright red of the Communist Party and its Lenin District Committee once hung over everything.

"I don't feel right about reading someone's private writings," mutters Fink.

"It's not private! It's an assignment!"

Fink got frightened. The fear was sticky, it erupted somewhere in his gut and slowly spread first to his arms, then his shoulders, and reached his head in a final wave, beating out the words: "run, run, run." Fear of the stones his classmates had thrown at him. Fear of the line on the forms where he had to write "German" while senior comrades laughed: they explained that he was a statistical error, the "ethnic minority" who proved the rule of internationalism, and the fact that he was unmarried was yet another error that must prove something, and that it was great when all of the errors are in just one person—it's easier to eliminate them if the order comes down. Eliminate them...

"Why did you push your way in there in the first place?" asked Khrystyna. "Why didn't you just settle into some quiet spot?"

"I wanted to be good. I was tired of having rocks thrown at me, I wanted to throw some myself."

"Well, there you go."

MY GRANDMA IS A SNIPER

My grandma is beautiful. She has big pink ears, big blue eyes, and hands. My grandma smells like smoke. She loves shashlyk. She also has beautiful boots. They're called combat boots. She has two rifles. One is named Motya and the other is Kytsya. My grandma doesn't bring the rifles on vacation because it's not allowed. You can shoot the rifles when the commander gives the command. If you calculate the wind correctly, you can kill a lot of Ruscists with them. Ruscists are the ones invading our land to kill us all. My grandma is a sniper. She won't let them kill us all. She also has a beautiful dress that we bought at Zara. I love my grandma and all my other grandmas.

"My Grandma Is a Sniper"— that was the title of Dina's essay.

"What's the problem?" asks Fink, his fear suddenly turning to rage.

"This is war propaganda. We want peace. Russia is our neighbor. We're practically one people. We're brothers! " the teacher rages, spitting out the words. Her mouth smells sour.

"Sisters," says Fink. "If you're anything, it's sisters."

MY TEACHER IS *VATA*.

My teacher is beautiful. She has gray ears, hair in her nose, and not a single day of living in the Soviet past. She smells like sauerkraut. She loves to eat cabbage soup. She has beautiful boots called hoof boots. She has only two brain cells to rub together. One is called "forpeace." The other is "butwe'rebrothers." She does have other brain cells, but she doesn't use them without a direct order from her commander. If you calculate the wind correctly, she'll turn up in Moscow. My teacher is *vata*. She'll let them kill us all and eat us. The zombies have already eaten her.

"You do understand that this is unacceptable? You understand that Dina is a bad example for the others? Something has to be done about this!"

Fink nods. His rage doesn't pass. However, the title of the essay he has just hastily composed is flashing before his eyes. The word "vata" won't mean anything in twenty years.

There will be a few dinosaurs who still remember, just as he himself remembers a time when certain empty words seemed funny or absurd. "Economics must be economical." "Lenin even now is more alive than all the living." These words can't be translated into German without going into lengthy, tiresome explanations. "Vata" in German would be *Watte*. Cotton wool... And nothing more. Not the padding of the jacket Soviet prisoners wore, stitched through with poverty and despair; or the idiocy of non-entities who do nothing more than binge and shit; not hopelessness, nor filth, nor crowds of zombified lunatics ready to bite and kill for the sake of Stalin, to be dug out from the Kremlin wall.

"Vata" won't mean anything. But "sniper" will. Fink isn't sure whether that's good or bad. Although maybe drones... Drones will protect people from direct murder.

"So, my dear, would you like for her grandma to come and explain it all to you herself?" asks Fink, as gently as his anger allows.

"What?" The teacher jumps back. "What? Are you threatening me? I'm going to... I'm going straight to the principal! What is this?! I won't allow it!"

Fink goes to the principal. Dina is waiting for him in the classroom. She's worried that no one will pick her up; she'll be abandoned and left forever at this "stupid school where they put children in the *ugol*." And Dina doesn't know what that "ugol" is or what happens there. No, she does know that ugol is the Russian word for corner, but why you have to stand there, and how it's supposed to be a punishment when it gets you out of writing or listening to the teacher—no. She doesn't understand that.

"I won't allow it" is no longer a drop, not the last drop, it's a flood after which no one will ever be dry again. Fink is silent in the office; so is the principal. Only the teacher squawks on like a frightened hen. Although rather than

a funny "cluck-cluck," Fink hears the threatening and humiliating "won't allow." "If someone promises to kill you,
believe him." Fink has no intention of "freezing," and he
won't let them "freeze" Dina. He can't fight. Not just because
he's old: he was afraid for a very long time, and that never
goes away. But flight is an option. Not in the physical sense.
Although he could. It's a normal reaction: run away to save
yourself. Although maybe it's better to fight.

Dina has already changed nurseries three times. In Mariupol, Vinnytsia, and Kyiv. Two in Kyiv. The first was a sweet
little private school, but it eventually got too expensive.
Three nurseries and two schools. This was the third. So Fink
hopes Haska won't object. And Khrystyna. And Grandma
Sniper. And Dina's father. And her mother.

He notifies the district that they are switching to home-
schooling. It's no one's business what they'll do with Dina
next. Most likely, they'll find a school where there's a war
going on instead of "butwe'rebrothers."

THELMA
2004–2006
ESCAPES

The "Negrobank" was near the dorm of the Polytechnical Institute on Khmelnytskyi Street. They always had a good exchange rate and always had money. As much as you needed, not like at the exchange booths: "Oh, hang on, I don't have anything left in the till." The "bank" was reliable, despite the fact that the traders didn't always look presentable and somehow even appeared dull. Especially in the winter, when they would wear strange faux fur hats and plaid coats, probably picked up for the occasion in the kids' department store. The money changers' faces were dark and dour, especially in the winter, which they didn't like and could never get used to.

Whoever was "on duty" that day would go up to the car and ask: "How much?" Then he'd go inside and come back out with an envelope. Always with the correct amount, without miscalculating or shortchanging anyone. Ever. Sure, a couple of times someone tried to "put the squeeze" on them. But the way it worked was that other people—tough, angry people—would find the "squeezer." It might be the police, who provided cover for the "bank," or it might be clients who were committed to "the maintenance of financial order." The "bank" operated on the honor system. And, strangely enough, it was far more reliable than all the others, which would collapse, disappearing with their depositors' money, or brazenly go bankrupt, leaving their owners with cars, apartments, land, and shares in good, promising enterprises. Fortunately or unfortunately, "Negrobank" did not offer loans. It operated as a large, round-the-clock, always fully stocked money exchange.

Thelma learns later that the word "Negrobank" is insulting. It's a slur for these dour people who don't like winter but never cheat anyone, because business can't tolerate that. Thelma learns later that the word "Negros" is like the slur "*khokhols*" for Ukrainians, or like "Injuns," or "ragheads"—that it's a word people use to exhibit their "greatness," to separate the worthy from the worthless. But that winter, the first time she ran away from home, the supposedly funny Russian song was bouncing off of every corner: "They killed a Negro, killed a Negro, the bastards wiped him out..." And "Zombie-Negro" sounded funny and cool.

She came and told them that she didn't mind the cold or the winter, so she could be the one standing in the street, as long as they'd look out for her, of course, and not let anyone harass her, and not harass her themselves.

"Get out of here," said the gloomy not-a-Negro, an Arab, but who could tell the difference?

"My name's Thelma," she said, sticking out her hand.

"Mustafa. And get out of here. I'll call the police right now."

"And then what?"

"Then nothing," Mustafa acknowledged.

"I'm asking you for work. I'm not cold, but you are. See? I ran away from home."

"You can't run away from home," he said.

"But I already did," said Thelma, shrugging. "If you don't give me work, I'll sell my body. And you'll be responsible."

"Your mother will be responsible." Mustafa was getting irritated.

"Is that what you would say to your sister?" asked Thelma. "To your daughter?"

"No," said Mustafa. "But you have to go home. Do you want me to take you? I could say I found you somewhere?"

"My mother beats me and my father's a drunk. And he beats me, too," Thelma wailed dramatically. "I'm a poor, frightened little girl..."

Thelma got the job, Mustafa, and his sister Maryam. She got lucky with the sister. She got exactly what she needed. In all senses, it turned out. Maryam taught her how to make couscous and didn't let her accept the fried herring that the Vietnamese students generously shared with the entire seventh floor. Maryam braided Thelma's hair and called Angelina every day to let her know that the child was alright. She would call from her cell phone to the house phone—which wasn't very cheap then, not cheap at all. But very awesome. It's too bad Thelma only found out about it much later.

Mustafa and Maryam agreed to let her stand at the entrance to the dorm, watch for clients, and pretend to hide from the police, but, if anything happened, warn them about raids or "police crackdowns on lawlessness," tell people the exchange rate, deliver the envelopes to the right customers with their contents intact. They were both studying to become geodetic surveying engineers. Syria already had oil, phosphates, manganese, and iron ore. And salt. The salt surprised Thelma the most. She thought only Ukraine had salt, in the caves of Artemivsk where you could lick the walls. Mustafa and Maryam planned to conduct gas deposit surveys. Mustafa dreamed of another geodesy—astronomical—that would allow people to create and describe maps of black holes, other universes, and various interactions between cosmic bodies. But gas was more important and far more expensive. Maryam said her father wouldn't approve of their participation in the "bank" on Khmelnytskyi. But what your parents don't know they can't disapprove of.

Thelma spent her break and half of winter term with Maryam, Mustafa, Karim, Peter, Astauna, and Samuel.

"You're all so different," she told them. "You have different noses, hair, even eye color, if you take a good look." "Mm-hmm" they replied, some softly, some gutturally, some nasally. "That's right, you all look the same to us at first, too. With the same face."

In March, Thelma went back home and to school. At school, they thought she'd been sick. Fink got her a doctor's note. So what? It's always possible. Lyosha hadn't looked for her. He hadn't come, hadn't called, nothing of the sort. Her mother couldn't even meet her eyes because she felt so guilty. But Thelma couldn't hate her anymore. Ernest hadn't looked for her either, but he sat silently next to her now, which meant something that Thelma didn't care to figure out.

Seeing them all every day meant seeing her mother frozen in the arms of Lyosha's father, and Lyosha who hadn't even asked why she was leaving and considered her a recidivist thief. Which, of course, she was. A little bit.

And Ernest was right there. With his horse jokes, turning away from her in the snow and fog.

It was unbearable with all of them.

Thelma wanted to go back to Maryam. Thelma had stolen a barrette from Maryam on Valentine's Day to make sure she'd have an excuse to come back. She actually decided that the barrette was a gift from her beloved. Never mind that the beloved didn't know about it.

It wasn't Maryam's best clip, but it did have rhinestones, two of which had fallen out a long time before, not while Thelma had it, but in Maryam's own life.

"Here," said Thelma. "I'm returning this. Maybe you were looking for it. Here it is..."

"Keep it," Maryam said sternly. "If you stole it, you must need it. But don't come here again."

"But Lyosha didn't say anything when I gave him everything back. He didn't say anything at all."

"Don't steal. It's simple. No one wants a thief."

"I never took a cent, not a kopeck, not an apple from you without asking. Nothing you actually needed," said Thelma, distraught. "And I still haven't. I want to come back."

"No," said Maryam, shaking her head. "It was too much already."

Thelma left the barrette on the sidewalk, like flowers at a monument to Maryam. She was distraught. She went to Fink to cry, because sometimes you need a grandfather, a clucking old grandfather who's getting ready to move to Germany, abandoning all of them, those who were and weren't named in honor of the beloved German Communist and prisoner of Buchenwald.

"You're not stealing," Fink said. "I'm certain of it. You're scoping out a different life for yourself. But don't take anything more. Just scope it out... Visually. On television, for example. Watch movies on video. Oh my little *Vogel*, sweet *Hase*."

Fink wasn't sure whether the German *Vogel* took feminine adjectives or whether *Hase* took masculine as these words did in Russian. But this way would do for now. A little bird. A bunny. What else could he call this girl whose wanderlust took the shape of things she couldn't have?

"Visually?" sobbed Thelma. "Like, just peek in people's windows?"

"No, no, not into windows... Just look. Some people eat well and beautifully. Others read books. Some people go places. Thomas Mann, for instance, went to Switzerland when Hitler came to power. But Kant never went anywhere. Although, one day Russia came to him in Königsberg. With the Seven Years' War."

"And then they left?" asked Thelma.

"Yes, then Russia left and gave everything back to Friedrich."

"I don't know who Friedrich is... And what would I scope out with them? What do they have to steal other than paper? Think up something else for me to scope out. I don't understand that!"

That summer Thelma ran away to Alushta in Crimea and found a job as a waitress. She learned to make pilaf, chebureky, and baklava, for which she lacked the patience but she tried. She was almost fifteen, but looked a couple of years older, which was enough for her to work as a waitress. In the fall, she went back to school and, on Sundays, she sold batteries at the Mayak electronics market. Halyuska's dad drove the trolley on that route. Not always, but a lot of the time. "Hi, Uncle Petro," Thelma would say. "Just like your grandmother. The apple doesn't fall far from the tree," Petro Lischke would answer and buy her a bus pass once a month.

"Actually, my great-grandmother," Thelma would mutter quietly. She'd sit in the back, turned away from everyone, looking out the window. Sometimes she'd breathe on the window and write an elaborate "f" in the moist cloud on the glass. It turned out that her great-grandmother had also been running away. And not to look at the trains. Running away from them. From the extended day group, which was hard for a healthy person to tolerate, and from Lyosha's father, who didn't show up all the time "just because." Her great-grandmother was running away out of shame or out of feminine solidarity, leaving the apartment so that they— the children and the adults—could do whatever they wanted. Thelma felt sorry for her great-grandmother, who'd run away from home at the only distance accessible to her, equal to the length of the electrical wires of Uncle Petro's trolley. Sometimes, especially in the winter or in the rain, it drove her to tears. Thelma quietly wept as she rode past the park, the university, the railway hospital, and then got off at Donchanka, leaving her completed inscription of "f" with a few more letters on the glass, which would evaporate before the next passengers could see them.

One good thing is that Thelma was never once raped, beaten, robbed of her earnings, kicked out of school, picked up during a raid on the market, or placed under court supervision.

Another good thing is that Thelma bought CDs, pirated ones, because there weren't any others and, in fact, people didn't even know there was any other kind...Pirated CDs with the first and second seasons of *SpongeBob*, a cartoon about life at the bottom. About a city at the bottom of the ocean called Bikini Bottom. An idiotic squid; the scientist-squirrel Sandy; and Eugene H. Krabs, SpongeBob's boss, and everyone's boss except for Sandy. A boss with a house that looked like an anchor.

Thelma gave the CDs to Ernest. Neither Thelma nor Ernest considered themselves too grown-up for *SpongeBob*. And even later, neither Tarantino, nor the Coen Brothers, nor Guy Ritchie could change that. "I wonder," Thelma would say, "will *SpongeBob* last until we're forty? Or fifty? What do you think?"

NEFYODOV
2004–2011
WATERCOLOR

Once Tata remarried and everything was final and irrevocable, Nefyodov checked into the hospital. It was like lying in the grave but longer, and it involved more pain. He was alone in the room, with a television, refrigerator, toilet, and even a shower. Instead of seeing someone else's gray underwear and torn pajamas, he had his tracksuit there. Instead of the scary Alla Stepanovna, he had the kind doctor Hryhorenko who was the department chief and had no beard. And that was almost enough, since Nefyodov brought his own candies. All different kinds: candy in boxes and bags, as well as several pounds of bulk candy. Under the bed, there were three full boxes of candy with wrappers made at his factory. Every day, the cleaning staff pulled them out to mop the floor, and they never left empty-handed, at first choosing the most expensive ones and later—their children's favorites. Whenever he was running low on candy, Nefyodov felt the approach of death—its sour, sanatorium breath, which, actually, was what initially led him to check into the hospital. He called it the principle of "like cures like." He also wondered whether, if he managed to do the one thing he feared most, he might somehow catch the hands of the clock, hang from them, and turn back time—as far back as possible.

Whenever he offered samples, Nefyodov perfectly understood every self-flagellant, every cutting teenager, every whale that beached itself on the shore. Nefyodov wanted to be afraid of something other than Tata. And he was. So his blood pressure spiked. But his leukocytes and thrombocytes were normal; his cholesterol was good; his joints had no rheumatoid formations; his heart had all its valves and atria; his spine showed no visible deformities; there was no sign of kidney stones; all cancer markers were negative; perhaps his adenoids and glands could be removed—but why?

"Basically, you just need to stabilize your blood pressure. You're healthy enough to have babies still," said Dr. Hryhorenko.

"Is that so?" said a surprised Nefyodov. "That's an interesting turn of phrase."

And then he thought that he should probably get his ears checked, too. Deaf whales who lose acoustic control over their environment are first to throw themselves on the beach. And there are ear parasites. Whales go deaf. And in such cases, should you really push them back into the water, helpless, without the will to swim?

Be that as it may, Nefyodov left the hospital as an officially healthy, though slightly deaf, whale. Alla Stepanovna, Mitya the guard, and the sensation of barbed wire surrounding any hint of physical weakness: those all stayed with him.

So he started building a house. Not like Tata's, no, not like Tata's, not at all like Tata's. It was in a different neighborhood, in Smolyanka, with a different veranda, different stairs, different furniture, a different glass floor in the kitchen, and different stoves at eye level.

"I want to hire you as my designer."

"No."

"Are you afraid? Your husband won't let you? Ambivalence? Memories? What precisely does 'no' mean?"

Or:

"Lyosha, please ask your mom to call me. I want to help her earn some money. I need my own designer, a good one. Tell her I have confidence in her."

Or:

"Tata, I sent you some pictures of tile. I can't choose. Could you help me?"

And a couple of times, when it was a matter of being drunk, Nefyodov was truly awful: aggressive, stupid, and ridiculous.

"Do you pay your taxes? Maybe you're keeping two sets of books? What if I send over an auditor? Huh? And then your whole business is down the tubes. What kind of doctor are you if you won't show the patient the schematics? What if the patient treats himself and drops a beam on his head? Or poisons himself with paint fumes? Did you take the Hippocratic oath or not? Who's responsible for all this? Huh? I'm asking you for the last time. And then that's it—I'm sending them over."

"Go ahead! Send the damn wind over! Or a thunderstorm. What are you, Zeus the Thundergod?!"

Yes, he wanted to send over the wind, thunderstorms, the tax inspector, the police, the prosecutor's office, "brothers," the town council, the fire inspector, a hurricane, a mudflow, overdue loans, default, inflation: Nefyodov wanted to send every disaster he could imagine. Every disaster but disease. Nefyodov needed even vile, bearded Vitya Shvets alive. So that, if he did kill him, it would be without pity or compassion.

When Lyosha told Nefyodov that his mother now listened to opera and went to the mountains, it became clear that Tata was no more. And if there's no Tata, then there's no Nefyodov.

"Do you know what this is like?" Nefyodov said to his son. "It's like the pigeons in the Piazza San Marco. We arrived really early in the morning on a train from Rome. There was no one in the city, all the shops were closed, it was quiet. I had a roll and some dry, flavorless, half-eaten, packaged croissants with me. I would never have bought them, but they were lying on the table in our compartment. I couldn't just leave them there. I love it when something useless comes in handy. I fed the pigeons. And they were all mine. Wherever I went, they went. I swear, they were just like trained circus pigeons. I go, they go. When I ran out of bread, they abandoned me. Then some loser came out with a full bag of crumbs and that was it. I was left standing there alone, calling them back with empty hands, but they didn't give a damn about me. One of them even shit on me. Well, but that's good luck—it brings money. Works every time. But I didn't want money right then; I wanted to be chosen. But they ran off in all directions like chickens. Scattered..."

"This is all so hard," sighed Lyosha. "Everything with you is so hard."

"And for you it's so easy!" shouted Nefyodov. "For you it's so easy. That's why you've gotten fat. You eat a little something everywhere, right?"

"I can understand the pigeons, Papa," said Lyosha and disappeared.

Every month, Nefyodov would wrap up the money he wanted to give his son and lock the envelope in a safe. He occasionally counted it, to understand how long it had been since Lyosha had answered the phone, or a text, or even an email. Nefyodov didn't like emails but had to write them.

Like didn't cure like because homeopathy can't treat amputation. Nefyodov agreed to sponsor the Miss Ukraine beauty contest. He sat on the judges' panel hoping that his missing leg could be reattached with this simple method. It turned out later that, even if the leg had been reattached successfully, it would have been a third leg—inconvenient and useless, just hanging there like a broken tail. But that was later.

In the beginning, it was actually fun. Weird, but nice. The girls were sweet and not heavy. When they sat on Nefyodov's lap, he hardly felt their weight and was very surprised by the ease with which all kinds of relationships could be started up and then wrapped up here behind the podium. There was red-headed Dasha—"Miss Charm"; Maryna with the belly button ring—"Miss Elegance"—though Nefyodov would have given her the award for acrobatics and ingenuity; and Olha – "Miss Intelligence." She could read and write and wanted to become a journalist. There was also Katia without a memorable trait because she quickly married one of the producers, though it seems she miscalculated there, as the producers in the city weren't what they seemed. To tell the truth, they were nobodies.

It was fun for a couple of years, but also expensive and pointless. None of Nefyodov's girlfriends became the all-round winner, and you couldn't really claim that the company particularly benefited from the advertising investment: sure it increased awareness. But it would have increased anyway, because the factory was the first, and for a time, the only, manufacturer who could wrap bank cards or plasticware in clear film, or chocolates, or napkins and oddly shaped toys in film with printed graphics.

A cosmetics firm was a sponsor for the third contest. The jury included the firm's regional representative, on whose lap the girls did not sit. It would have been awkward for them, and she, Maria Lischke, in a playful pink business suit, had no need for it.

"Oh!" said Maria, extending her hand to Nefyodov. "So you're here now. How is it?"

"Financially—that's your topic."

"How about non-financially?"

"Let's have a drink," proposed Nefyodov.

"Sure," she said.

A pink suit. A little girl color, revolting and trivializing. But it looked good on Maria and suited the frozen face not of a woman, but the regional representative of a major firm.

Nefyodov wouldn't want it for himself: not the firm, or the woman, or the suit. He didn't even consider Maria one of the pigeons who'd flown away from him in the square. All the rest, yes, and he even missed them sometimes, but not her. He couldn't even remember her clearly. Blonde? Brunette? Fat? Short? How did she smell? How did she laugh? Did she laugh at all?

She sat stony-faced on the judging panel, but then smiled, applauded, and nodded encouragingly at the appropriate moments. She always voted "no." Against every contestant. It turned out she'd only invested money. "People like that are capable of anything," thought Nefyodov.

"I'm recruiting losers here. So yes, that's my field," said Maria. "Not everyone wins. Some of them aim for people like you and not the crown. But the crown means nothing either. I represent the victory of the losers. Both in the room and on the stage. Grab a trolley cart with lipstick, foundation, powder, and off you go. By the way, we have a men's line, too. Interested?"

"Let Petro pull the cart around," Nefyodov growls.

"Petro drives an actual trolley. If you recall."

Nefyodov turned out to be right. As always. That Lischke woman was capable of anything, anything at all.

She dragged Angelina along. Or else Angelina dragged herself along, because they had all just continued their life without Nefyodov, visiting each other, annoying each other, talking about nothing because, just like Nefyodov, they didn't have anyone else for conversations that started with the words, "How have you been?"

"How have you been?" asked Angelina, the ban on whom had been voluntary, simple, and entirely easy for a prolonged period of two, or even three years already. She actually topped the list of those who'd been crossed out, who he could definitely do without.

"Can you imagine," said Nefyodov. "You can't even imagine these twits... Especially one of them, in the intelligence contest for the brainless—you know what she came up with? They asked her what style she would use to paint the judges..."

"And?"

"I was expecting Caravaggio. Michelangelo at the very least... They all know Michelangelo—the ninja turtle. So I was just counting on her memory, not her brains—see?"

"Your mistake," said Angelina and shrugged. "The only artist I know is Aivazovsky."

"Alright... But this idiot said she saw me as a watercolor. A watercolor! And I even got lucky with that: she was going to draw Maria here in charcoal..."

PETRO

OFF THE TROLLEY AT THE START OF THE MILLENIUM

The psychiatrist frowned at Petro. Her frown was a professional deformation that doctors mastered within the first month or two of working. Not just psychiatrists—all doctors. It was like a lab coat, but for the face. A natural mask of disgust, fatigue, hopelessness, and X-ray. If the X-ray was installed into the head, the facial expression sometimes improved.

Some patients could count on sympathy, smiles, and even jokes. That is, if they had funds. Private funds, the receipt of which is hardly a sin, considering that the rescuers need to survive no less than the sufferers.

Petro thought that, if you could die without doctors, you should do it quickly and efficiently. All his colleagues, and friends, and relatives—in fact, everyone he knew—thought the same. Every year, the whole trolley depot got a full physical. And, every day, a minor one. Not a check-up, rather a sobriety test.

"Why are you all here at once?" joked the doctor. "Come on, one at a time, or I can't tell which one of you isn't drunk."

Their own little daily comic routine, but it was still unpleasant and awkward every time.

"Any concerns?"

"Nope," Petro would reply cheerfully.

"Healthy." The doctor would nod and stamp the paper. "Call in the next person."

And every next person also had no concerns. Not about the salary, the lack of parts for the vehicles, rude passengers, or the management who had somehow contrived to renew the fleet by buying old trolleys that fell apart the first time they left the depot.

Never whining, or complaining, or naming your pain in vain signified "healthy." Something like that.

"What's the trouble?" asked the psychiatrist.

"Well, I play..."

"For Shakhtar? How is it you're so pale then? And you're a bit old, aren't you? For professional soccer, I mean," she said with a smile.

It wasn't much of a joke, but Petro was afraid to comment.

"Voluntary admission then?" the doctor asked.

On the one hand, it was obvious to Petro that this was just a professional figure of speech. On the other hand, his trolley poles weren't long enough to get him around this "voluntary admission" without flying off the wires, so to speak.

Sure, he was willing to admit to anything, but he couldn't see how that would help at this point.

"Can't you like implant something? Put in some kind of 'spiral'? So that I never want to play for money again? Do you have something like that?"

"Esperal. It's called Esperal. And if you're not an alcoholic, that's not the right approach. And I have some reservations about that method in any case. For you, I recommend the in-patient neurosis clinic. For a month. Maybe two. Get an IV drip, attend some group therapy, go for walks on the grounds. The food... Well, it's nothing to write home about, but losing a bit of weight wouldn't hurt anyway."

"But will I still gamble?"

"Yes," said the psychiatrist. "You'll always be at risk now. You can only hope for remission, without any hope for a full recovery. But remission can be lasting and even lifelong."

"A life sentence," said Petro sadly.

"Depression, regret, lack of motivation, low mood—all that's for a psychotherapist to manage. What I can offer you is the clinic and pharmacology. Are you ready for that?"

He had promised Maria to do "everything," so yes, he was ready. His wife's "Operation Open Eyes" had left no room for refusal.

"These here are our expenses, and here's your salary. You do the math for what day of the month your salary runs out and we start spending mine. And make sure to include household needs, utilities, some clothes, and gifts for your and my folks in the village."

"How long have you been the man of the house?" asked Petro.

"What do you think? Thank God for your broken leg. But now that you're walking again, I want one more month of peace to finish building out my team and be guaranteed a profit from my consultants, even if I don't sell a single tube of lipstick myself. I need a month where I'm not thinking about whether you've lost your shirt, who you owe money and who's punched you in the head over your debts. I'm asking you for just one month..."

"And after that?"

"I don't know. You could be my driver. I can handcuff you to the steering wheel, wrap the seatbelt right up to your neck, sew a movement tracker under your skin, hire a security guard to watch you, lock you up in the house... I don't know. I have to think about it."

Petro thought, too. In the psychiatric clinic, which turned out to be just a regular psychiatric hospital, Lischke wasn't considered dangerous or even potentially aggressive. He tried not to burden anyone, never complained, and agreed to a broad-acting IV drip of sedatives and soporifics, and even group therapy where people gathered together to feel ashamed together and sit silently together.

His own shame was red hot. It boiled up starting in the morning, making its way from his stomach to his head, pouring out in sweat from his forehead and spots on his cheeks. Petro spoke kindly to it, but it was taciturn and unfriendly, like the chief of the morning shift who had always withheld Petro's bonus without giving any reason.

"Psycho, psycho, slipped his trolley," Petro repeated over and over, recognizing that he had hit rock bottom and that nothing worse could happen from here, because the disgrace would last for his entire life. True, Maria promised to get a certificate stating that he had had severe pneumonia—a serious life-threatening case with a high risk of lung failure.

"My mom buys me a new certificate every time. First, my liver seems to be giving out; then it's suspected tuberculosis, later—angina. Everyone at the theater knows I come here to hide from the shadows, but they pretend I'm actually sick," said Petro's new friend from the fifth ward.

His name was Jean. He was an opera singer, but not a star, no solos. When they were cutting people from the troupe, he'd started working as a lighting technician part-time.

"That's when it all started. I started seeing the shadows. If there's more than just the sun or a single lantern, when you direct multiple spotlights at someone, then more shadows appear. However many sources of light there are—that many shadows. And the reverse: however many shadows, that many lights. Shadows give birth to us and shadows devour us. Whenever I see it, I'm afraid. I go hide in the corner and cry. Then Mama gets me a doctor's certificate about my liver and puts me in here. While the shadows go on devouring everyone on the stage without me. Have you ever been to our opera theater? It's strange but they all think it's better to die of silicosis than despair. Despair is like syphilis—a disgrace. But we have to be like samurai. Never disappointed or exhausted. It's more important to seem healthy than to be healthy. More important to seem brave and decisive than to actually be either one. You know what it says in the Haga-kure? 'A samurai will use a toothpick even if he hasn't eaten. Inside the skin of a dog, outside the hide of a tiger.'"

Petro didn't know what the Hagakure was, but he thought a samurai was something like Bruce Lee and was very surprised when Jean told him that true samurai have to live as if they're already dead.

"That won't work for me," said Petro.

"Me either, apparently. If it did, would I cry backstage? Would I be afraid? But the shadows move in and the sun is just a fake mirage someone puts there to fool us. Just look. The shadows give birth to us and will devour us."

Lischke taught Jean to play poker. He couldn't help it. He made the cards out of paper, which meant the marks showed through and revealed the other player's options. Cards at the top of the deck were also nearly transparent. Petro closed his eyes so he couldn't cheat, but he cheated anyway—in Jean's favor who was so delighted by every win that he forgot about the fake sun. They played outside, and whenever it was windy, the cards would blow around. Petro and Jean would chase them all down so the doctors or orderlies wouldn't catch them, but two or three always got away, flying off somewhere beyond the fence. It was usually the aces.

"I don't want her to tie me up with a seatbelt."

"Oh, you have a mom, too?"

"A wife."

"With a seatbelt? To herself? She loves you like a mother. I don't know if that's good. You would know better than me."

"Loves me? You call that love? Make me her personal driver? Hire a guard? Deprive me of my freedom of move-ment? Stick me in here? You call that love?"

"And you don't? What do you call it then?"

Jean was discharged first. As he was leaving, he said, "Don't worry, I'll be back in six months to a year. Or at the theater. Come by the theater. I may be better at lighting than at singing. And you can play cards on your own. If you need a convenient partner, let me know. I don't mind."

"I'll think about it."

They shook hands and even wanted to hug but felt embarrassed. Petro was left alone, though he shared a room with three other people. The other patients didn't interest him, and he didn't interest them.

"I won't be your driver," Lischke said to Maria when he came home. "I don't want to. But my remission is stable. I'll play by myself on the computer. Can we do that? Or do you want a divorce?"

"No," Maria answered. "I want to kill you."

"I want to kill you sometimes, too," admitted Petro.

He went back to the depot, and for a full week, maybe even two, his colleagues didn't smoke around him or, if someone happened to forget, they would wave the smoke away with their hands and guiltily stub out their unfinished cigarettes. Pneumonia's no joke. One wrong move and you've got TB or something worse.

The first run of the morning was half empty. Some retirees and a bit of sun peeking out. He squinted and thought that they were all going nowhere, and that they really didn't have anywhere they needed to go. Everything was still closed, the only things open were insomnia and loneliness. But they were going, because it's not the goal that matters, but the journey. It turned out that Lischke and his old folks at the crack of dawn didn't follow the warrior code of the samurai at all. They were simple, intuitive Buddhists. Spontaneous – like the market around Shakhtar Stadium.

ANGELINA PREGNANCY

He says, "You smell like candy."

She laughs, "Pastries. Cookies. Some with chocolate, orange jam, vanilla; Lenten cookies, puff pastry, cookies with crisp or crumbly dough, even Bizet cake..."

"Like the composer?" he asks.

"I don't know, but definitely like music."

"Quit it!" shouts Babá. "Enough! No more! Now it'll start all over again: the intestines ask the ass what it had for breakfast. Halt! Halt!"

She just laughs and asks, "Why don't we ever see the Virgin Mary? Why do we just see crazy wild Babá, and Shubin, and not Jesus?

He says, "I don't see anyone at all."

"Now it's the Virgin Mary you're after?" snaps Babá. "Gone crazy with your blaspheming mouths. Do you need to drag the Virgin into your whoring? Do you want to give her a heart attack? You wicked, abominable children! Didn't you hear me say 'enough'!?"

He says again, "I don't see anyone. I don't even see you, I can only smell you, and feel how you've gained some weight and gotten softer now..."

"You're about to be out on the street! Anyone who says I've gained weight has a death wish. I'll get incredibly offended. Incredibly... And then my cookies will have tears in them. I'll cry into every batch, and they'll turn out salty... Wait, that's it—salty... Salty! To go with beer. Why hasn't anyone invented salty cookies? This is it—my million-dollar idea. Would you buy salty cookies from me?"

"Buddy, do you hear me?! Take your hands off her right now! Get off her, you old goat!" shrieks Babá. But he doesn't hear her. He just hears a ringing in his ears; his blood pressure spikes; he's a bit short of breath. He's fifty-four. It's not old, not time for Viagra, but still—there are issues. He moves his hands away but not far. He strokes her head. Sniffs her hair.

"Tenderness... That's even worse," whispers Babá. "Run, child, run..."

But she already sees how it is. No one's going to run anywhere. This asshole will get his adventure, and then whatever happens—happens. But this bastard is going to see her. He is definitely going to see and hear Babá when the time comes.

Babá doesn't like Shubin. Shubin doesn't like Babá. But sometimes they have a chat. Shubin says, "What do we do about the fact that we're the only miracle they deserve?"

A short-winded, rasping old man and a disheveled, crazy crone. Both of them from nowhere, neither ours nor theirs, and there aren't even any drawings of them.

"I've figured out a way," brags Babá. "I overexpose their photos. I show up as a sunspot."

"Give me one," scoffs Shubin.

"Then you give me some methane. Because sometimes I just want to blow them up, but I don't have what I need."

"They say you're pretty good at setting fires."

"Could be," she says, blushing. "It's nice to hear that you're paying attention."

"Sometimes I want something light and warm, or even hot, too," he says.

"Is this about milk or fires?"

They haven't been joking much lately. There's too much grief with more on the way. Their ability to see into the future doesn't go far. They're used to the fact that they can't see the

grand design and never will. Babá and Shubin are sad miracles. Miracles of the last resort, that final leap to overcome
the darkness that doesn't always work out. They're not really
arsonists. Babá just does it out of despair, only sometimes.
They're actually wildland firefighters. Guardians that some
people don't hear and others don't understand.

But it won't come to fire—not yet. Yes, Angelina's shop
could be set on fire with its two convection ovens (one bought
on credit), two proofing cabinets, three double bowl sinks,
work tables, a granite surface for the chocolate that leaves its
scent on Angelina's hands, with its tile, light, temperature
control—her shop that some people find irresistible and
others find intolerable, because they want something other
than all this sweet, sticky, maybe cream-filled unhealthi-
ness. It could be set on fire.

But he'd just buy her a new one. He'd save her business
and then be her hero. But now he's just shit and scum, supposedly "better," but actually not. Not better, not good, not
needed. "Just be friends, children, just friends, no one's
dragging you by your privates," groans Babá. "How about
we just do this like in Bollywood, alright? 'Jimmy jimmy,
aaja aaja'—and then you run away without even kissing…"

But nothing useful comes of her sighs. Their bodies are
greedy—and smart, too. They already know how to share
the warmth, simple as a blanket in the winter. Their bodies
grow warm and sweaty, granting them the illusion of fear-
lessness and immortality, which their silly minds mistake
for happiness.

"Former lovers," thinks Angelina. "It's like coming back
to an old house that's familiar, but you haven't been there in
a long time. Sure, there are some creaks and drips, a cupboard door falls on your head, the ratty sofa, dust, forgotten things, but there's the same tree peeking in the window
that's always been there and the same little birds or their

descendants—doesn't matter which—on the windowsill, and sunbeams cross the room just like they did before. The creaking is fine—and the stabbing back pain, too. After all, you're home. Nothing to learn, nothing to worry about: not my baba whose train has crossed the rainbow bridge, or the children who've already grown up and are now blaming us for everything, and holding a permanent grudge."

"You smell like despair," says Angelina. "And don't lie, and don't tell me you don't. I won't believe you. You smell like you always have."

"Are you reading *Natalie* again?" he asks.

Babá leaves them. She doesn't spy on them, she's not a voyeur, and she's not going to try and put an end to this because she's no kamikaze. It's always the same damn thing: Nefyodov brings Angelina his childhood sorrows and fears, she mishandles them, catastrophe follows. It's stupid—doing the same thing over and over and expecting different results. Then again, Babá doesn't visit the wise.

"Year of birth?" asks the pretty young doctor.

"1968," Angelina answers.

"Age of first menstruation?" she asks again.

"Twelve, I think."

"Children?"

"One daughter. She's twenty-two now."

"Abortions?"

"God spared me that."

"Maybe not," says the doctor. "At least not this time."

"What does that mean—'not this time'?" Angelina snaps. She's sure. Sure, it's pretty early, but not extremely: one of the girls in her shop was thirty-seven when everything just stopped and disappeared completely... She's sure that she's arrived with early menopause. She has some slight nausea, sweating, sudden mood swings—honestly, there are moments when she could kill someone, kill them with her bare hands and then eat some garlic cookies. It's just a shame that she's already made the salted ones but didn't think of garlic earlier. They can't manage anything without her: not recipes, or loans, or discounts on the wrappers. And just try to get that discount out of Nefyodov: he clamps down on those prices like a total shit. Like the shit that he is. "I keep work separate. Discounts are only for bulk orders. And you're an exclusive buyer for me, with small volumes." Well, thanks for the exclusivity and small volumes, of course. With a job like hers, the gym has to be like a second home. Angelina goes every day for either a "booty burn" or fifteen miles on the elliptical, after which she has to practically crawl out of the gym. But she has the will power and character.

Her thoughts are stupid, fast, trivial, and terrifying. She lets them trickle in, hoping to hide and get lost in unnecessary, interrupted, soothingly ordinary thoughts. Angelina hopes to escape. But where now? Where to?

"Ten weeks," says the doctor. "You still have a little time, but you'll need to be quick."

"No, I don't," responds Angelina firmly. "I don't need to be quick."

"At forty-two?"

The doctor is young and serious. Her glasses have blue rims and yellow temples. Stylish. To her, Angelina is a woolly mammoth who's mistakenly crawled out of a mine shaft and is trying to pass herself off as an elephant, when she really should be dragging herself off to a mammoth cemetery in the permafrost—in Surgut, for instance.

"Forty-two. I'm not telling you what to do. Just think about it. When the child is twenty, you'll be sixty-two. When it's thirty, you'll be seventy-two. You have an apartment? With what—two rooms? Your eldest is going to need a place to live. Or are you expecting her to move in with her husband? What if he moves in with her? That is, with you?

That's four. Four people in two rooms. Plus, grandchildren. You'll have grandchildren, and this child will be a teenager, wanting to listen to music, play games, go on dates—not babysit your grandchildren and drag you around to doctors' offices!" The doctor starts out calmly, but she almost bursts into tears towards the end.

"Poor girl," thinks Angelina. Then asks aloud, "And if I manage to buy everyone housing, would that be alright?"

"And will you also purchase a guarantee that you won't get sick or die before you're eighty-nine?"

"Uh-huh. So, when the child is forty-seven, then, in your opinion, it will be okay for me to die?"

"Do what you want," pouts the doctor. She has small, beautiful, delicate hands, red cheeks, and a small nose. Her eyes are almost invisible behind her glasses, but you can see her freckles.

Angelina thinks it's going to be another girl. And freckles are cute. But she won't have freckles. She'll have clear, slightly olive skin; a full, hungry mouth like Nefyodov; curls... And dimples closer to her lips than to the middle of her cheeks—like Angelina. And Thelma.

"You need to know the risks. Unfortunately, they are real. But if you've already decided, then don't get on the Internet. Do the recommended testing, eat well, walk regularly. Register the pregnancy, monitor your blood pressure... But you do still have two weeks—no more."

"There it is—catastrophe," said Babá. Not to Angelina because there would be no point. For two weeks, Angelina hides behind her cookies, biscuits, cakes, orders, and flour purchases, and she rents a storage space: a more or less long-term strategy in case of her absence. Just in case.

Three weeks. And one more—just to be sure.

Angelina never had a moment's doubt. She just didn't want to hear from all the "well-wishers," "experts," and know-it-alls. They usually shut up once they realize that it's too late. Then they stop talking, give in, and wait for the worst to happen so then they can go around with long faces telling the world—which is mainly their neighbors—"Well, we tried to tell her."

During those four "underground" weeks, Angelina knew for sure that she wouldn't marry Nefyodov. Not because he wouldn't propose, but because she didn't want to. That train had already left the station. Back when she was watching the kids after school, when she mistook stupidity and baseness for love, there was just one time, for a couple of months, when it seemed like they might get married, because it had already happened, because it seemed like they were good together, because life was still ahead—a life that could be different for them. Definitely different for her.

But even then, even with her short-sighted reasoning that tended more toward rhinestones and cocktails than synapses and gray matter, she recognized that Tanya was his only possible wife and, conversely, that Nefyodov couldn't be a husband to anyone but Tata. She recognized it, learned to live with it, then let it go and just lived her life.

She's going to tell him. She's definitely going to tell him, and she'll be fine with whatever, and she won't get upset at all. Whether he wants to be the baby's father or just a bank account, whether he wants to keep it a secret or decides to give the baby his name, if he rejects it, runs away, curses her, and disappears forever... It's up to him. She'll respect his choice.

"This time I want to do everything right," Angelina tells Thelma.

"Well, you've lost your fucking minds," Thelma responds, a little too calmly. "Do everything right? At my expense? At Lyosha's? Hey, here's your little brother or sister—they'll be your responsibility now."

"The doctor already tried to bury me in advance. You don't have to bother," protested Angelina.

"Well, it's a shame she failed. Because I don't plan to," snapped Thelma.

"That's fine. No one needs you to. We don't leave corpses to rot in the street, thank God."

"Have you picked a name yet? I suggest you look to the Americans for something: don't humiliate the child with Communism. Bill, George, even Ronald. Girls' names are harder. But you can do it. I believe in you. Maybe Bella? Or Georgina? So we can match. So you can 'Do everything right.' Great job, Mom…"

MARIA SHOT AT THE DIVAN

Maria shot at the *divan*. She didn't have to close her eyes to see it: gray with purple flowers the size of her palm. A divan and two chairs. A divan instead of the two beds with worn-out mattresses: her dowry that the parents had slept on but sacrificed so they wouldn't be embarrassed "when people visited." A divan, yes. She had actually dreamed of a divan. A foldout divan, not so much for comfort but to have something new, that was truly hers, that smelled like wood and the store, and not like parental sweat that seemed to have seeped all the way through to the springs.

She and Petro had hauled the divan up to the seventh floor, since the elevator wasn't working. It had been shut off for "non-payment." The tenants all shared responsibility for making—or not making—the payments. Eventually they all got used to living without it entirely. They dragged the divan, Maria dug her nose and chin into it, and was even willing to sink her teeth into it to get it there and set it in place. She wanted to admire it, revel in the fact that you could feel the buttons on your back. Buttons—not springs. If you can dream it, you can achieve it.

She was shooting at it, imagining every flower, every stain: coffee stains, period blood, watercolor paints, Halyuska's juice spills. She was shooting at her own rants: "Why do you have to abuse the furniture? You should be ashamed of yourselves! Food stays in the kitchen!"

Into shards. One after another, Maria blasted the "discs" that represented Red Moscow perfume that was only good for poisoning cockroaches; the ones that represented the saucepans that had to be polished to a shine (since that's what good housewives do) or stockings with the holes painted with nail polish so they wouldn't get runs. She took aim at the nail polish, too. Not at hers, but at the one the girls had all lined up for, the mother-of-pearl that was the only color available. She shot fixedly at her past life, at what she had considered a life. And she never ran out of targets and they never completely disappeared.

It had happened to her suddenly. In one day, in an instant. Like an epiphany. But not like finding God, more like a sudden loss of smell and taste, anosmia. She woke up and, instead of the newly fashionable nostalgia, with its rose-colored glasses tinting the shop signs from the movie *Dva tovarishcha* (Two Comrades), and the adoring song for the Red Army soldier in his uniform, the triumphant return of the Soviet Mimosa salad, and ecstasy over boiled condensed milk...

Instead of the nostalgia that was flooding everything, worming its way in, bubbling up from all directions, Maria felt rubber: soft, liquefied, colorless rubber swallowing her and everyone else.

The rubber insidiously bound her hands, nudging her straight to a place with no address, without thought or feeling, without any of that which Maria, unfortunately, could not yet identify by taste, but she did know now for certain that it existed. The divan, the exotic sound of the word, the longing for it, to buy it, the peering into the shop window, the steady saving up for it... The memories terrified her and hit her hard. She aimed at the convenient divan first, when she didn't know yet what she was actually trying to hit.

"Divorce him, he's a bad match for you. He's not a real man. How long are you going to support the parasite? Divorce him, he's pathetic. Where are you, and where is he? You can't even take him out in public. It's embarrassing."

Or:

"Be patient. Remember, 'Love is patient, love is kind.' Keep yourself in check, don't be prideful, act like a wife and mother. Even if he's useless and a fool, someone will take him! Just wait and see. Someone will snap him up, get him all cleaned up, and you'll be left eating your heart out alone."

Nothing could be simpler than to ask, "Who are these people and why should they know best?" But not for someone who had collected enamel pins as a child.

Maria had collected the pins. For her birthday, she'd receive special albums with white foam pages to hold her pin collections of "Hero Cities," "Soviet Automobiles," "Historic Places of Our Motherland," pins from her favorite cartoon series *Nu, pogodi!* (Just You Wait!), the coats of arms for random cities, Cheburashka, Pushkin, Soviet Masters of Sports. There were also pins that would shapeshift from one picture to another. Look straight on—and there's Puss in Boots with a hat, tilt it a bit—and the hat disappears. Or a hockey player: first standing, then jumping. Not too high.

Not too high, not too proud. Everyone knew Maria collected pins. So she was easy to shop for. She'd be happy with a new collector's album, "Shock Worker of the 9th Five-Year-Plan" or "Travels around the Golden Ring."

"Okay, children, everybody take a seat. Let's look at Maria's collection," her mother would say cheerfully when Maria invited her classmates over. They were already fifteen years old by then. Some of them already had Vesna tape recorders. Everyone was listening to the Ottawan song: "Hands up, baby, hands up..." But Maria had pins. There weren't a lot of visitors.

She never once asked herself or anyone else why she was collecting them. Eventually, she came to secretly hate them and silently cry when she received pins instead of dolls, markers, hair clips, or printed T-shirts like the stylish girls wore. Everyone thought she didn't need anything but the bits of metal and plastic that peeked out of the edges of the albums like dough oozing over the edges of a pan.

Where are they now, anyway? Where are all those albums with their smell of sadness and longing? Where is that monument to hopelessness and compliance? Where is all that complicated, stupid, pointless mess?

Maria shot at the pins, too. Her personal war was fierce and didn't let up for a minute. It was easier for her.

It was easier for her than for Petro. She had money, skills, and an Audi instead of a trolley. But everyone, everyone, everyone considered her a "bad girl," a "bad woman," a "bad, mean, greedy person." Her subordinates and relatives, neighbors and acquaintances, men and other women. And no corporate relationship training could fix that. Maria was rich among the poor, ungrateful among the grateful, stingy among the generous, a "beeznesvooman" ("what a ridiculous word they came up with for you, voo-man, ha-ha-ha) among "beeznesmen," a breadwinner among dependents and housewives, exhausted among the idle, short among the tall, dyed among the natural, a wife among the divorced...

"Did you buy a gun to kill your enemies?" Bohdan asked her.

"Petro's enemies," she smiled. "Or him, if I have to. So they can't torture him."

"Well, you can delay that tender mercy for now. I'm telling you with 100% confidence."

Ten years passed before Maria and Bohdan talked about "mercy" and guns again. Halyuska-Haska had written her first book. And it got published. Not at her own expense, not twenty copies, not printed on a printer then bound in a plastic cover with black rings, "take it and don't cry, dear author." No, a real book with a real publisher. The bad woman was transformed into a good mother. A good, happy mother. With plans to buy the book and give copies to everyone. Everyone. Let them all know who the Lischkes are.

"They've published her book, Bohdan, she's been published. Can you believe it?!"

"And she probably has swearing in there, right?"

"And you don't curse?"

"Oh, I do. It's not the worst thing we taught our children."

"Come on," said Maria amicably.

"Come on," said Bohdan. "I see you're still shooting."

"Oh, absolutely. I'm the best in my age group—the champion. Not just for our club—Ukraine's national champion."

"You're simply the best. Trust me."

"What are we talking about now?"

"About the expired statute of limitations. Ten years for a felony. Will you forgive me?"

"No. I can't even forgive the divan, and how long ago was that? For me, the past isn't the past, it's an enemy."

"And for me, the past is the only thing I have. No offense, but I'm holding onto it, you know."

"It's not worth it," said Maria, shaking her head.

They were sitting in a cafe on Pushkin Boulevard. Without Haska and without the books, which hadn't arrived from Kyiv yet. And for the first time there was some kind of tension that Maria could always easily sense. Between her and Bohdan, between the coffee she was drinking and the tea he had ordered. An anxious, vile tension that Maria didn't deserve.

"Do you want to say something to me? To tell me something? Some deep, dark secret?"

"Maybe, but not today. I'm getting a headache. I'm sorry." He stood up.

"Isn't that a female excuse?"

"You would know better than me."

"Oh, come on!" Something got stuck in Maria. A strange note with a high, arrogant pitch out of her, sounding like an old gramophone. She could feel that it came out sounding fake, that she needed to grab him by his hands, his pants—what do you grab hold of in such situations?—to make him sit down, order some wine, laugh like they'd always laughed, be easy and real with each other, be honest and calmly ask, "What happened?" Instead of celebrating this genuine triumph that wasn't really hers, she looked pathetic: "Bohdan!"

He left. She stayed. A stop-frame melodrama in which neither the director nor the actors knew what they wanted to say. And the celebration of the victory of the good mother over the bad woman didn't work out.

Maria knew how to sell, organize, train, and apply makeup. But it turned out she didn't know how to share her joy so that it infected other people. She was overjoyed on her way to the village, when she gave them the book and described all the negotiations, how the editor had commended the book, and the publisher had praised it, and the review that had already come out—just one so far, but good, almost without any critique... Maria's mother-in-law turned Haska's book in her hand and said, "Our Petro wrote bad poems when he was little, too. Thank you, of course, but we don't have anywhere to put it. We've always worked so hard, never had much time for books."

But she did find a place to put it—in with the crystal goblets, deep in the heart of what they called the credenza.

Maria's mother oohed and aahed more enthusiastically and loudly. She was clearly proud, and she promised to read it because "We're different, we're educated people, we have Druon's books and Chekhov's *Complete Works*—the blue set." When Maria came back a week later to bring some medicines to her parents, Haska's book was propped in the open window frame so the wind wouldn't blow the window closed. That summer was roasting hot, but they didn't want an air conditioner. They worried they might catch colds.

Maria called Bohdan. "They stuck the book in the window. I took it back and they didn't even notice. What do I do with them?"

"Shoot them. They're your past, right?"

LYOSHA
WAR
ON LEAVE

Lyosha ate. From the twentieth to twenty-fifth anniversary of his birthday. They fed him, and he ate.

His mouth, esophagus, and stomach became the gathering places for his relatives who didn't know what to do with their guilty feelings. Mom, dad, grandmas, stepfather, his father's dates—each relied on their culinary talent to fill his stomach with their apologies, attempts to talk, their own panic attacks, anxieties, and plans for the future. He ate, chewed, swallowed, and drank, hiding silently behind the childhood rule that reigned everywhere—from kindergarten to home and afterschool: "Don't talk with your mouth full."

"Come over for breakfast," said his mother. "Let's have a beer," proposed his father. "We've got kebabs with shrimp on the grill. It'd be a shame to waste this weather," suggested Shvets, whom he referred to as a stepfather only in his private thoughts.

Cake, ice cream, salad with smoked duck and strawberries, maybe at... At the Fifth Avenue, the trendy new restaurant near the Philharmonic. "Come with us," his dad's girls would say, different ones every time. There was no point in remembering their names, so Lyosha distinguished them by the dessert: mille-feuille, pistachio cream, salted caramel. But there turned out to be a smaller variety of desserts on offer than girlfriends. And they all blended into a nauseating, sugary mass, bulging with tits, lips, and the overpowering scent of patchouli—all fried up in oil.

"Eat, honey. My poor little orphan," his grandmother would say, concealing her predatory smile of "I told you so" under the thin gray mustache that Lyosha clearly remembered her plucking, one hair at a time with the metal drawing compass from his school supplies. "Eat up," sighed his mother. "Have some more," suggested his father.

"They didn't manage to turn me into a drug addict or an alcoholic. I didn't become a hooligan, didn't steal cars, or get in bar fights—I don't even like bars. I didn't slit my wrists. I hardly even skipped class. I wasn't a teenager anymore, but I was still the golden child. They didn't know what to do with me... So they decided to feed me to death," he told Haska later. A few years later, when he'd lost most of the weight.

"So why did they do it?"

"To unite in the face of imminent threat, I think. To offer a 'united front,' as they love to do. Three divisions advancing on my fat cells. An allied command..."

"But you're the one who gobbled it all down."

"I did. I even have stretch marks on my belly—like pregnant women get. It's creepy. Aunt mille-feuille is undressing you and—oops!—blue rivers down my gut all the way to the Gulf Stream."

Of course, he'd devoured it all. When you're stuffing your face, you don't have to hide. No one tries to get fat guys into bed, you're like the ugly friend, but a guy. Have some fun together, then call a taxi. The bigger you get, the faster their eyes slide past you. Hence the conclusion: if you want to hide, blow yourself up to the size of a mountain and become part of the landscape. If you don't want to get naked, get big.

"I strongly disagree," laughed Haska. "But I'll write that down."

"Do you want to make a hero of me? For the segment 'how to throw pounds off your body, instead of Momma from the train'?"

"I just want everyone to know about you."

"Well, let's start with the juicy part, the secret part. Me and Ernest, and the birthing horse."

"What was her name?"

"Ivolha."

"Someone else got lucky with a nickname?"

"No. She's an actual horse. From the Jaguar Club on Myr Boulevard: they had hippotherapy, a boarding stable, dressage, you could even take a horse home if you had an estate. See?"

"So you took Ivolha?"

"Don't be stupid. Someone didn't look after her properly. Her boyfriend, a horse, was called Khapei. They somehow hooked up on their own. In nature. When you've got someone with a doctorate in education working as the stableboy, maybe you can expect training in good manners. But pregnancy and everything that gets you there, they generally skip that."

"Based on that logic, all of our parents must have doctorates in education."

"Fortunately, we're not all Ivolhas. The guard from the club called Ernest in the middle of the night. He was yelling: 'Something's dripping from her. First it drips, then pours, but it's not pee. Come quick, I'm scared!'"

"Don't they make *mahan* sausage out of horses?"

"Well, they don't make it out of security guards. He was worried about his own death, not the mare's. They can cost from a thousand up to a million bucks."

"You're confusing me on purpose," said Haska, getting frustrated. "You are deliberately generating new questions. Did the security guard also have a doctorate? Is he the one who hooked up with her in nature? Who's dripping what? Who's going to kill the guard? And what is hippotherapy?"

"I don't want you to make me the hero of your story. I want you to make Ernest the hero."

"I can't. I don't want to."

"So we got to Ivolha. She'd almost managed everything on her own. She was running around the stall, rubbing against the sides and moaning a little. Just a little. Ernest told her to hang in there. I wrapped her tail up in a cloth. I'd managed to google it on the way. I wrapped up her tail so it wouldn't be in the way and wouldn't get in the foal's eyes. Ivolha lay down on her side. And it started to come out—the front legs, the head between them—honestly, it looked like it was emerging from the depths of the sea into the world. After all, it wasn't pee. It was her water breaking… With horses, just a little comes out at first, and then there's a whole flood. About twenty liters in all. Maybe a little less. Both of them were lying in the damp. I waited for the placenta to come out. Ivolha bit off the umbilical cord… I don't even know what they named it. I just wanted to go to sleep. I mean, I'm a dentist."

"Not all dentists are so squeamish," said Haska.

"True. Then the mare's owner helped fund the clinic. I learned to set dislocated joints, do ultrasounds, hook up IVs. Whatever was needed. One time a dog nearly bit my hand off when we calculated the anesthesia wrong. We thought he was asleep, but he was plotting his revenge…"

"I'm not going to write about Ernest."

"Then you won't write about me, either. And you'll never know how I successfully lost all that weight. Bye-bye, sweet Halya. Our sweet, spoiled Halya."

He headed for the exit and then up the hill. Lyosha didn't know Kyiv, but he had plenty of time, he was on leave, he had friends and GPS on his phone. Haska's stubbornness was no great tragedy. Every morning he woke up stiffer than the night before. The grasses, greenery, and music that he used to have inside were gradually turning into some kind of shoddy, porous asphalt. It might still be possible to remove the top layer, open up the road, convert it back to dirt and plant some flowers on the sides. Not to walk on. Just to lie somewhere nearby and watch the breeze. A breeze and a couple of cows. That would be fine.

"Don't leave!" called Halya. "Slow down! I can't keep up! So..."

"One vet clinic. Then two, then three. And three pet stores with food, toys, diapers, dishes, scratching posts... And everything else. It was like a treasure chest. I would've played with the mice and the little balls myself. I would've eaten the canned food. It's a successful business, by the way. People need to love someone unconditionally. It doesn't work out with our parents, we don't know how with our kids, we're afraid of our next-door neighbors, we hate our coworkers and are ashamed of our city. Parrots are just the thing. Cats are good, so are fish. Dogs have to be walked, but some people manage it. Lizards are terrific—they eat flies, which are sold separately. Fortunately, you don't have to breed the flies, so you don't feel bad using them as food. Get it?"

"Do you get it?" he continued. "No? Okay, now let's talk about love and escape. About a city under Russian siege. About animals and animals. About house pets who are now homeless, may be injured and don't know how to catch mice or hunt their own food. I'm not talking about flies or lizards. I think they can manage on their own. I'm talking about Ernest. You're lucky, Haska, and I'm lucky. We can choose who we want to save and who to abandon. Ernest couldn't. He bundled help for the strays as the price for helping the house pets. 'I'm treating them for export to the territory of Ukraine.' 'Take one pet out of the occupied zone to Mariupol and get discounted pet food. Take three with you and get two pounds for free.' It's not true that people didn't leave their pets behind: you wouldn't believe how many strays there are. But you have to admit that their chances improved significantly. Their chances of survival improved significantly if they could reach a war-free zone and become homeless there, instead of being killed by our armed 'brothers' from Bryansk. That's why I want Ernest to be your hero. Will you write about him?"

"And what's the situation now?"

"I don't know. Probably the same. Just a lower volume: fewer are being abandoned, fewer killed, but more that aren't spayed. And now they'll be reproducing because the spring and autumn have been warm..."

"So now he's making money delivering the occupiers' foals, is that it?"

"The gynecologists make money delivering the occupiers' foals. And I don't really care to judge them. Creatures with tails don't know they love Hitler. Everything works differently for them."

"So, 'the horses are innocent?'" asked Haska angrily.

"Are we really going to start quoting Kotsiubynsky now? That's not the point," Lyosha answered in frustration. "That's not how it works. They have ears, little paws, tails, and eyes—they look at us and believe we're people. Dogs have dark eyes. And little arched brows. I haven't talked with Ernest in a year. I haven't written or called him once since I left in 2014. And he hasn't called me. Maybe he found out somehow that I was the one who didn't save the goat. Maybe he's mad at me now. I don't know what's going on with him now, Halya. But for that summer, just that one summer, I want him to be your hero. Is that an option?"

"Did he study finance?"

"Why?"

"Just wondering. For the full picture. It was just business from the very beginning..."

"Oh, right, he was just cashing in on someone else's misfortune. Why don't you go ahead and write that he was putting animals to sleep in his clinics. The incurable ones. Euthanasia is prohibited, so it's ecoterrorism... You're hopeless."

"And you?"

"Me, too. Thank God, we've come to the main topic: my diet." Lyosha smiled. "It's very simple: they stopped feeding me, I stopped gorging. Their love, hate, and guilt have now been upgraded to a new platform."

"Her name is Dina. She's staying with me right now. She's great."

"I believe you. I don't want to see her, and I'm not going to. Sorry."

BOHDAN
A LETTER
DECEMBER 2015

Referring to yourself in the second person using the informal form of the pronoun and grasping for letters on the page are signs of adolescent immaturity. Don't argue. They suggest unfinished childhood verses, poorly structured compositions, and a blatant hysteria that actual adults hide behind other pronouns. Or they don't hide it, making it the actual engine and chassis of the plot.

It's a sign of immaturity when you're looking for just one person in the world. Okay, two. Yourself and someone like you.

Millions of people stood on the plaza of 2014. Let's intensify that: millions of unseen people. You read up on Rwanda, the Khmer Rouge, the Indians, and the Armenians in Turkey. You read everything you can about concentration camps and learn that they weren't only places to die, but also to live. You'll read about Syria, but still won't really understand who is killing who or who's telling the truth. You'll read about all the catastrophes and mass killings, but it won't add anything.

Millions of unseen people. Also blind, deaf, and utterly naive. They had no idea that, in every maternity ward, no matter where they arrived in this world, the handwriting was on the wall indicating that they had been measured and found lacking, that their birth certificates came with reservations for the *Titanic*, which will slowly sink. It will sink for years, becoming the *Flying Dutchman*, unseen and, therefore, nonexistent.

The ones who stood on that plaza, even if they were sitting at home, running errands, or watching TV, had to choose. Can you choose in an instant?

I envy you.

At first, the old life, the past reveals itself to you in stories. In legends. Then you learn to spy it out: grandma's comb in her gray hair; the boring, musty old professor's tie with its weird length and knot; the neighbor's boots, unchanging year after year; the table crumbs scooped from the table and popped into a waiting mouth when no one's looking. You spy on the past until it starts talking to you. But what if it's mute?

What if it doesn't speak? If it hangs on the wall as a portrait, smiling in rays of sunlight? If it's mute, you just believe in those rays because you remember them yourself. And what if it's mute and dead?

You don't have anything to say to the dead. Just try it. Try to imagine that those rays could have turned into fights, alienation, boredom, hatred. Try it and you'll find yourself alone. Without the smile, without the sense of having had a winning ticket that just didn't work out.

I'm talking about Alla. About my wife. About the woman who maybe I should have learned to hate, I should have forgotten.

Some people had Lenin hanging on the wall instead of Alla. Or he was standing in a square somewhere, with his cap, hand, jacket, vest. Just standing and standing there. Like an antenna, picking up signals from the past.

You're not attached to him. You always did swim against the current, and I never asked you how that happened. We don't ask children for advice. We just lay out the facts: either you obey me, or I stop loving you. Except not really. I can't stop loving. But I always knew for sure that everything I touched would become the dead past.

Are you surprised that now, standing with the millions of other "voters," I actually picked him? It's not about the twenty-two-kopeck ice cream. In fact, I never liked the twenty-two-kopeck kind. I liked the twenty-eight-kopeck one. It was called Kashtan, and I would buy it at the intersection of Teatralnyi Avenue and Artem Street, from the kiosk right next to the Shevchenko movie theater. Or some tomato juice, just a little farther down at the produce stand. Alla and I would go buy two glasses of juice. There was a saltshaker on the counter. Salt and a spoon in another little glass filled with pink liquid for cleaning the spoon, supposedly.

It's about fear. Lenin in his cap and Alla on the wall are the reality I know. You knew a different one, didn't you? You had Chernivtsi and Lviv, your Ukrainian writer Khvyliovyi—I still don't even know who that is. But you had him. You read him with Ernest. Ernest used to cry at night, saying, "I killed my mother." And I wanted to kill your Khvyliovyi. But they beat me to it.

You had a world where the University of Vienna seemed not so far away. But, for me, for most of us, Moscow was the capital of "our homeland." Later, there were vacations to Turkey, shrimp, gin and tonics, and the music of Rammstein. Yes, Rammstein. But it all felt accidental, like it might come crashing down any minute because we hadn't earned it: the freedom, the taste, the travel, the sense of speed. You have to raise the children on it, feed it to them from the beginning, so that later, when it gets taken away, they have something to remember.

When you live on memories, the past always wins. Math was my refuge. A guaranteed shelter—even from a nuclear blast. If I'd had enough talent, I wouldn't have fled. I wouldn't even have noticed that the summer of 2014 had arrived, and a choice had to be made.

Geniuses are lucky that they can live outside of time right away. Some even live on after death and through the ages. But, believe me, while they're alive, they're outside of time. Killing a genius is like killing a child. I was like that myself for three or four years. I was awesome. And then it all went to the dogs.

I woke up one morning and I was just like everyone else. My language was lost, but I got more money instead. So there'd be enough for shrimp.

The minute we're born, we get a ticket to the great beyond. Tanya's Shvets is right about that. Then there's movement. Process. Gradually, each in his own time. Almost everyone is at least a little prepared when they go, realizing that their time has come.

In the summer of 2014, millions of people received their tickets at the same time and with a limited validity period. We were all just living our lives, just living, and then time was up—not just for me, or for you, but for everyone. But you could still choose how and where. In a basement, in your own apartment, in a bathroom somewhere, in a field, in a village, at a checkpoint, at the front, on a roof, in a pond. And you could choose your cause: for a flag, for Chernivtsi, for Stalin... For Turkey—no, that wasn't one of the options. You could die for whatever had value to you. For an apartment you didn't want to lose. For a house with sails on the veranda. A daughter who'd stepped out for a walk. For a Mercedes.

If you think about it, then all the books, and yours is no exception, are about how we'll die. With robots or without; in a spacesuit traveling to Mars; on a throne surrounded by relatives burning with hate; in a hospital surrounded by familiar faces—if you're a doctor, or among indifferent strangers if you're a nobody there. That's what all the books are about. It might be delayed until the very last page or carefully inscribed in the very center of the plot, but death is the message; it makes the story fragile and tender, ephemeral and comprehensible to all.

I'm in Moscow.

That doesn't mean I'm already dead—although, of course, you think otherwise.

There is a version of the Judas story that's a like a hard-core version of *Oedipus the King*. He was abandoned as a baby because of a curse. He was rescued, raised by a passerby, and grew up knowing nothing about himself. He returned and happened upon his own family without recognizing them. He killed his father and married his mother. He also killed his brother along the way—that's a remake of the early Biblical text. It's not canonical, but it explains a lot. You have to agree that, if somebody throws a baby in the river just because of a prophecy or a bad dream, then it's hard to expect anything good from him as an adult. Trust in the world doesn't stay afloat for long on a river and it will sink long before anyone rescues the infant. Ultimately, the infant never grows up or matures. He just floats on for his whole life, hoping to grab onto something. When I was a kid, they used to say: "It floats like shit down the Yenisei." I always thought the Yenisei was a special river of shit. Maybe it is.

I didn't kill my father. And I now have every likelihood of seeing the Yenisei.

I'm in Moscow. I haven't married my mother—God forbid.

She invited me to come live with her "for a while"—which was a complete surprise to me. She complained and is still complaining that cosmetic procedures are too expensive, "for some reason my face has to suffer because of your war down there." Mama used to visit us to get cheap facelifts and "beauty injections." Did you know that? She's seventy-eight, by the way.

But she called me to come "live for a bit," "wait things out." Does that mean she wanted, and still wants, to save my life? A late-blooming parental, maternal love? I don't know, but it's an iron-clad excuse. I could justify myself with that. But I won't.

No cover for me. I just chose not to die in Donetsk. And Ernest didn't choose me. Unfortunately, email won't let me smear tears and snot on the page or write in wavy lines as if my hand is shaking.

I haven't lost hope of manipulating Ernest. Every day, I want to force my mom to write him that I'm dying, that he needs to come immediately to see me breathe my last. I hope you won't betray my secret.

I'm afraid. I'm afraid he still wouldn't come. And one Judas (me) per family is enough. I worry about him. Traitors have feelings, too.

And, to tell the truth (we're family here, right Halyuska?): my fear of bombs turned out to be stronger than my paternal instinct. Which leads to a conclusion: I'm much more like my mother than I ever thought. Please enter this into the record as a confession.

I'm writing you because you remember me as brave. And I really was once. This isn't a reproach, it's an attempt at calculus. It's unlikely to be successful. But there's still time. There's time. I work quickly and I work from home. I have a lot of days off. Any day can be declared a Sunday. I even envy myself. I'm a freelancer now. It makes no difference to me where I write programs and who I don't pay my taxes to. I don't have a company here. Don't worry: I'm not financing the Russian army. I work for some guys in the Netherlands.

This could be interesting to you—as a writer. I'm writing you because I want to leave something behind. I've already failed to enter the ranks of history. Reproducing myself in Ernest was never the plan; I'm hardly likely to be incarnated through his children. I'll be doing well if I return as a guppy rather than a rock on the side of the road. But I want to leave something behind: be reworked, disguised under a different name, with a slightly different or not so different biography, almost unrecognizable. But to survive somehow.

You know, we always complain when we don't look like ourselves in a photo, when we age and change so much that we're the only ones who can recognize ourselves and say—that's us! You and me thirty years ago. But we want something different from a text: we expect stipple, shadow, and imprecision as a tender mercy. And, in that mercy, we still hope for a sense of presence.

It's not so much that we want to recognize ourselves: we just want to exist.

Did you notice how I got rid of that adolescent "you," and have boldly manifested myself through "I," and appropriate other people through "we?" That "we" that I never really had.

But I'm in Moscow. Here, as always, it's the tsar, the serfs, the subjects, and ladies of the demi-monde. Here "we" is expected. I easily adopt this language to blend in, I even copy the accent, but it comes out badly. The fricative Ukrainian "h," which was never my issue, slips out now from time to time. It slips out and draws me homeward.

I'm nearly fifty—don't forget to write that. And translate me from Russian. Even if it comes out wrong, even if you struggle with the structure of the language. And you'll struggle until the old Ukrainian idioms—"just like Pylyp from the hemp"—turn up in every phone call. But translate it: even if the Russian makes you sick. That will be my disguise as well.

I'm nearly fifty, but, for the first time in my life, here, in Moscow, I get called a *"khokhol."* I'm a "stubborn *khokhol*," obstinate.

And that collective pronoun that unites me with you rises up whenever I hear: "The Ukrainians are so ungrateful."

I'm furious. I didn't expect it myself, but I'm furious. I'm boiling over with unspilled blood.

So, from your perspective, does that mean I'm not hopeless?

PETRO LISCHKE
THE NUMBER 17 TROLLEY
2014–2015

Cecil the Lion had to die. He lived in the Hwange National Park in Zimbabwe under the oversight of some British scientists. Not the ones in whose name all sorts of nonsense is spread around the world, but some real British ones from real, genuine Oxford. He was thirteen. Even though Cecil never celebrated his birthday or invited guests over, the British scientists knew his exact age. He was old. Lions live to be ten to fourteen years old, so thirteen was old, indeed. But his mane was black. Surprisingly black.

The American dentist Walter James Palmer shot Cecil with a crossbow. But Cecil didn't die right away. Palmer hunted Cecil for another forty minutes before finishing him off. Then the dentist took Cecil's black-maned head home as a trophy.

Cecil was a good-natured, well-fed lion. He was the head of his pride of lions and a national star. He wasn't expecting anything like this from humans. It's just not the sort of thing one generally expects from humans. It's expected from animals. For instance, it was expected that Cecil's successor, the lion Jericho, would kill all of Cecil's cubs in order to establish his dominance over the pride and assert his power. But two years later, it wasn't Jericho who killed Cecil's descendant, Xanda; it was Robert Cook. And he did it legally, "within the stipulated hunting regulations."

Cecil the Lion had to die in order for things to improve. So his death meant something. At least that's what the newspapers wrote. His death led to the adoption of new conservation laws in the United States and France, plus millions of dollars collected by Oxford for wildlife protection. Xanda's death, however, meant nothing.

In 2015, scientists found water on Mars. American astronaut Scott Kelly reported directly from the International Space Station on how to avoid losing your socks in space. *Star Wars* finally became available to stream and broke all previous records, making a tremendous amount of money.

A princess was born in Britain. They named her Charlotte Elizabeth Diana.

The UN celebrated its 70th birthday. Seventy years, of which the last ten, or even twenty, it had existed in a state of "deep concern" that the world was going to hell in a handbasket.

What else? What else do you need in order to solemnly write that "2015 will go down in history as a year of remarkable and horrible events"? What else do you need to write that it wasn't all meaningless? That everything happened for a reason?

Charlie Hebdo and European solidarity? Russian airstrikes and Syrian refugees wherever the bombs weren't falling? Legalization of same-sex marriage in the United States? An Oscar for the movie *Birdman*?

In 2015, the Number 10 trolley route no longer went all the way to the October Coal Mine. It's quiet road life now ended at Partisan Boulevard. And not even every day or at every time. Sometimes Partisan Boulevard wasn't safe either. And even the people who walked through the morning darkness didn't dare ride to the last stop.

The Kyiv District of Donetsk was definitely in the war. But the Lenin District was like a Soviet mausoleum. It was always quiet there. The apartments were more expensive, and people weren't looking for basements, weren't trying to equip them for extended stays, although having your own garden and homestead with a bit of land for growing things was still considered an advantage. The buildings here were intact and the windows weren't even striped with tape against shelling. There was a metallurgy plant with plans for iron and steel production, the church in Lar'ïnka, schools, the "eternal flame" on the grave of the "unknown soldier," and even a cultural center that still featured songs and dances of "brotherly peoples."

The bullets weren't flying here. Of course, the construction "were flying" embodies the chthonic, impersonal nature of the war. The chaos of a war in which it was frightening to identify the guilty, since the guilty posed as saviors, and the innocent were maligned as beasts. To live in Donetsk in 2015, the year Pope Francis decided to canonize Mother Teresa, you had to use the right words. At least with strangers. Although... Everyone and everything became strangers. "The shell came flying in" means a war without an author. It's a specious claim of innocence and a consent to victimization, a curse sent on a curved trajectory, hitting "whoever."

"It came flying in," "it hit" are words of helplessness and incapacity, an inability to recognize as the enemy the person who places a mortar next to the house, on the roof of an apartment building, or in the yard in order to draw out the return fire, or simpler yet: to shoot at civilians, then film the consequences to show the whole wide world not your own villainy, of course, but the cruelty of the Ukrainians with their assigned role as "Banderites."

"Just leave. Enough already," Maria said to Petro. "I'm waiting for you."

"I don't know how to do anything, can't do anything and don't want anything other than the life I have here."

"You won't have that life."

They talked on the phone every day, sometimes twice, even three times a day. They hadn't talked this much even when they were young. And it even seemed to Petro...

It seemed like... He'd done the right thing. Fate had de-cided. To let them go. He should have let the girls go a long time ago. In peace—without worrying about whether he'd fall back into actual gambling or just continue aimlessly cheating against himself. He'd made the right decision. For maybe the first time in his life, he'd made a decision like a grown man, recognizing that he hadn't coped and couldn't have coped with a success that had first seemed unattain-able and turned out to be unnecessary to him. He hadn't always known but had known for a while now that Maria brought the sacrifices and he was the altar, and a little bit—a tiny bit—Halyuska. But it was one thing for Halyuska. For him, it was pathetic.

Both of his girls deserved to live free from the constant worry of whether he'd fall off the wagon again, or whether he'd embarrass them with his poor manners, his bad pro-nunciation, his grease-stained hands, and his ignorance of the language that Haska loved so much.

No divorce, no breakup, no betrayal, no broken promis-es... They didn't actually make promises to each other, but Petro did—all the time... mentally. Promises to himself, to Maria, to Haska. Some of them he would make, break, and make again. But the main one—"til death do us part"—that one he didn't break. He would never break that one.

Although war actually is death. It was in no rush, but it could free them from him, from his clumsiness, unworthi-ness, mediocrity, and clownishness. It offered a way out—a beautiful, honest, human way out. Adult. Manly. He repeat-ed those last words to himself often. Often and out loud. The right decision. Not a life sentence, just a present without his presence.

Maria went to Kyiv in June, when it still seemed as though the madness would end, that there would be enough Haldol for everyone who'd suddenly become obsessed with suffocating themselves in the lap of Mother Russia, leaping from a rooftop onto Lubyanskaya Square, praying to the Chekist, and dying with a bullet to the back of the head. There weren't enough anti-psychotics. And the bombings, torture, and looting had almost no effect on the course of the disease.

Since then Maria had called every day, and Petro called her, too. They talked and talked. They laughed a lot. He felt like a partisan fighter behind enemy lines. Sometimes he really was, writing "Russia" on the plastic backs of the trolley seats with Nazi lightning bolts for the double S's. He photographed his handiwork and sent it to the girls as a sign that the dark side wasn't a matter of geography, nor the light side either. He wanted Halyuska to be proud of him, and Maria to be free of him. For the first time in his life, Petro could become a hero. And he felt he had.

Maria asked him to come to Kyiv. She threatened to come get him, shoot him, and drag his carcass out, even if he resisted. "Because a carcass doesn't argue. Especially with a gag in its mouth." Petro knew for sure that Haska wouldn't allow it. Neither the gag in his mouth, nor Maria's return. Not because she's angry with him, but because she's smart and loves Maria. She loves him, too. She asks him to come, too, but it's not about her. None of this is about her.

The Russians roamed the city, introduced a curfew, exchanged "government" positions, and then fucked off to Moscow in a panic, leaving the local goons in charge. People lived, without looking up. People lived, flaring up, in spasms of hysteria and paranoia. People died. But Lischke was happy. He and Maria talked every day. More than they ever had. And almost every time, when he hung up, he would stroke the phone and say to it, "I love you." I love you.

He was already graying, short, with black eyes, black eyebrows, and a bulbous nose. He wasn't handsome, nothing like Maria and, thank goodness, nothing like his Halyuska had turned out.

It's obvious why he didn't actually say it into the receiver, to Maria. He wasn't about to derail his whole plan by summoning her back. With a stupid promise that he might not be able to keep. And now it wasn't his fault.

Why didn't he say it before? Well, there's a question. But why would he have said it? Just to hear the sound of his own voice? Wasn't it obvious already? Didn't they live together, sleep, eat, and argue together? Petro hadn't even known that this—this was the sweet part. Sweet, sad, soft as the belly of a chicken, but also solid. Because it was solid. Yes.

Petro didn't want to drive a shortened route only as far as Partisan Boulevard. He felt castrated, along with the castrated route: the severed, discarded, dangerous foreskin of this war that somewhere over there, in the UN or elsewhere, they intended to freeze and forget.

"There's a vacancy on the Number 17 route. Everyone's gone. Ran off," said one of the other drivers. "Ask for that one. It's quiet over there. It doesn't come flying over there."

The question wasn't whether shells were flying or hitting over there, though that mattered, too. Lischke wanted to understand whether this was his route: his dawns, stops, bushes, his people, and his smell in the driver's compartment. He started checking it out in December, listening closely to the names: Freedom Square, Fire Station, Miner's Hospital... He closely observed the traffic lights, most of which weren't working. And the people who were the ones Petro was used to. He started riding in December and continued into January. Not because he couldn't make up his mind, but because now there was plenty of time—for decisions, regrets, and realizations; for memories; for the path of the samurai who lives as if he is already dead.

The day the Lenin District did get hit—just so Russian television crews could film civilian deaths and then go on and on about the "crimes of the Ukrainian junta"—Petro was riding with his eyes closed so he could learn the 17 route with his body rather than just his eyes. When he got thrown out into the snow, he thought how Maria would be furious about the dirty pants that would be impossible to get clean. It was painful and sharp, but only once. Yet he didn't feel dead right away. He didn't feel anything.

When Ukrainian prisoners were brought in to be spit on, beaten, and forced to load the dead bodies, Petro felt fortunate. It's exactly what he would have wanted: to be in the hands of "his" people.

He'd once said to Maria, "You know, it would be funny if I died from our return fire." And added, "I wouldn't mind too much."

Petro Lischke didn't die in the way he would have found funny. The shelling was staged, and it was enemy fire.

"It wasn't one of ours, definitely not ours, my friend," said a gray-haired man with a dark, grieving face, through bloodied lips.

"Yeah, I know, don't worry," Petro answered. But the man couldn't hear him.

Shubin said to Babá, "Well, this one... If he wants, maybe he could cough at drivers if there's a wreck or whatever disasters they have. Methane? Explosions? No? Well, when they're about to be electrocuted, or the poles are about to slip off the wires. Or when a passenger's about to have a seizure? Or go into labor? Whatever he wants..."

"What accidents are you talking about on those trolleys? It's a joke, those accidents," Babá answered with a slight catch in her voice. "I can teach him to set fire to casinos and slot machines. If he wants to."

"And his last name is good—it works. Shubin, Babá, and Lischke for the drivers of public transport. Can there be three of us? The two of us aren't enough anymore for such a large, ill-starred territory, right?"

"Unfortunately, our numbers are growing," sighed Babá.

"But not everyone will want to be a Shubin. With my personality... Well, it's not so easy. I coughed my lungs up for them. And for what? Instead of closing the mines, they keep going in to die of accidents."

"Now the Russians have come to them, so they're dying in the war instead."

Cecil the Lion had to die.

And 2015 will be remembered as the year of Cecil's death—which had meaning.

TANYA NEFYODOVA
ALIEN
2014

"I won't bury him! I won't!" screamed Tanya. She screamed out of fear and rage at something she couldn't even name. "Tell him, Nefyodov, I'm begging you! I won't bury him, and I'll curse the both of you! To hell with everyone!"

"You're acting like your mother right now," said Nefyodov. "Stop. You'll feel ashamed later. Just stop."

They were on the phone. She couldn't see how red his face had turned. He didn't see that she'd gone white. Both of them had almost forgotten how they used to laugh after heated fights, comparing the colors of their cheeks, which Tata called "differences in autonomic responses."

Tanya had never really thought about whether a person could wake up as a Spaniard after having gone to bed the night before as no one. Wake up English, French, or Croatian. She wouldn't want to be Croatian. Nothing other than Russian. It happened to her in the spring of 2014. Right around March. It's really too bad she didn't mark the day on her calendar. She should have because she'd like to celebrate it as a second birthday. As the first day that she'd understood who she was and, finally, who was to blame for everything.

"Revolution, revolution," she repeated, smiling. Festival of the poor. Days of hope. Victories—ahead. Vitya was with her. In April, they flew to Milan and bought cheap tickets at La Scala right before the show. They saw Verdi's *Macbeth*.

"It's about fate. And power," said Tanya.

"But did Scotland gain anything from losing Macbeth, whatever he may have been?"

"What should Scotland have gained?" asked Tanya.

"Independence."

They brought their first, but very deep, mutual misunderstanding back from Milan. That spring, when Tanya woke up as a *Russian*, Vitya suddenly became a "republican"—of the "Donetsk People's Republic." She wanted Russia's warm embrace, to climb into the lap of the motherland; she wanted stability and the greatness of that half-forgotten but eternal world that included Siberia, the Decembrists, Lenin in exile, Herzen in London, the architect Barma blinded by Ivan the Terrible. It was all hers, familiar from childhood, clear, and comprehensible. Vitya wanted something different. A new world with its capital in Donetsk, sudden ascents, battles with Indians, its own Wild West and its own Far East, its own geography with borders, military uniforms, a flag, and the words of its constitution properly composed in a cafe somewhere on the corner of Pushkin Boulevard and Teatralnyi Avenue.

They fought like they were drunk. They were giddy with the richness of the moment, the sense that they could make history rather than just reading about it: bring your building supplies, draw and erase the horizons of the future; select entire neighborhoods, instead of just furniture; fill them with Red Squares, La Défenses, new Cheryomushkis. With anything. Create a new Lake Geneva there. Or even a Mediterranean. Why not?

They felt as though they'd spent their entire lives asleep. Lacking any sense of meaning or purpose, or the happiness that was now on offer. It was promised and even peered through the haze of the television news, which was now actually interesting to watch. A few times Tanya threatened Vitya with divorce. They both turned white when she shouted: "Never! I'll never agree to your Scotland! It's all or nothing. Long live the queen!" Nefyodov would have been sure to ask what the queen had to do with it and when did the General Secretary of Muscovy have his balls hacked off.

Nefyodov would have grimaced at her logic, howled and banged his head against the wall until it hurt, or at least pretended it did, while listening to her "nonsense." But Vitya wasn't like that. Sometimes it seemed like he could only hear himself, while Tanya went right past not only his ears, but past the new life he envisioned under the flag with the black stripe. According to Tanya, the new flag—with its black, blue, and red—was the height of bad taste and an affront to her newfound designer style. She and Vitya fought about the flag, too.

Before, Tanya would have called their behavior ridiculous, fanatical, and manic. But the adrenaline rush, the sense of omnipotence, the heart-stopping rapture for what was happening let her ignore the voice that occasionally whispered something like, "Stop, just don't." And then it disappeared, as though it had never existed.

The sex wasn't bad. Not bad at all. Like for the very last time, the final battle. Like boxers in the ring, like fishers who'd reeled in a shark with no more than a worm, like cooks tossing jalapeños into chicken broth. From warm to hot. And sometimes straight to hot, without any preliminaries.

Vitya declared that he wouldn't trim his beard until the independent "republic" received official recognition on the floor of the UN. "Then it's going to keep growing until you have to stuff it into your pants, and eventually into your socks," Tanya assured him. She didn't make any such threats: growing a braid would be too small a sacrifice. She was capable of more. Three times she ripped the Ukrainian flag off her neighbor's car. Twice she threw eggs at "Banderites" on bicycles. Once she went looking for a downed Russian drone on the Kalmius embankment, hoping that it required medical assistance. She didn't find it.

"Can I not write about this?" asked Haska. "My eyeballs are already bleeding, and my fingerprints have worn off.

Another thirty lines and I'll turn into Casper, bitten by the bride of Chucky! Please?"

Haska had flown to Kyiv for her birthday. For their shared birthday, though they could hardly celebrate it together now. A clean slate: clear all debts for death or war, she told herself. She lied. No one dies without debts. Moreover, death multiplies them, makes them visible and bulging. To eliminate debts, you'd have to wipe the disk. Wipe it and then smash it into pieces. With a hammer.

They did talk about that. They were already talking about it in April, in Donetsk. Physically destroy your computers, be prepared for searches and prison, escape while you still can. They talked about it but, in April, it still seemed ridiculous.

To war as if to death. With no debts. It was Haska's battle cry, her Cossack shout of "Yasa!".

She went to see Aunt Tanya to return the thousand dollars she'd stolen that New Year's Eve half a lifetime ago. She actually took the money to Nefyodov first, since it was his, really. Not Tanya's. But he wouldn't take it: "Forget it!"

Yasa! That is—with no debts.

"I stole this from you and now I'm returning it. I'm sorry." They were sitting in the kitchen. Aunt Tanya glowed with heresy, which she spat out in words that were beautiful, but terrifying to Haska. "I'm sorry," Haska repeated. "Given the circumstances, I didn't see any other way out."

"Do you always speak Ukrainian now?" asked Aunt Tanya with a mixture of sorrow and suspicion. Haska nodded.

"Did they force you to over there? Or are you a Banderite now?" Vitya was curious. Uncle Vitya.

"Can I go now?" said Haska rising, but Aunt Tanya grabbed her by the arm and sat her back down.

And the abyss opened. By the end, when she was finally running out of steam, even the beard and jalapeños had entered into it. But, at the beginning, Tanya screamed like an Alien had crawled out of her. Fed a steady diet of Prozac, sedated by streams of Haldol—now suddenly standing in a ripped straitjacket, her mouth a volcano erupting in the flames of all the unspoken words. The ones she should have said long ago to her mother, to Nefyodov, to Angelina, and to Fink, too, but Haska was the one they came flying at (in the pre-war sense of the word).

"You all stole everything from me! Everything! My fatherland, stability, faith in the future. You, all of you, you robbed me and tossed me in shit with your worthless coupon rubles, with your 'Stick with it, little Cossack, and someday you'll be an ataman.' I didn't want to be an ataman! I hate your math, your physics, your chemistry—I hate it!! Your gold medals, too. You stole my childhood! All of my memories belong on the trash heap, right? I can't have my past—my past is a big hole now. I can't go anywhere there. Bullets are whistling, aiming at my head. But I want it to be comfortable there. I want to take pride in how I lived my life. But you took it all away from me. Stole it. You stole it, Halya! And now I don't need your money. You won't humiliate me. Hands off! Hands off my history. I know, and only I know how it was and how to... Get out!"

Three times Haska tried to walk away. Three times Aunt Tanya beat her to the door, blocking it with her body, continuing her recitation:

"You're not going anywhere until I let you! You stole from me, so listen here now, you Banderite! You want to kill me? And how will you live with that? How will all of you live with yourselves after you kill us, your own parents? You're scum, not people. Ungrateful, disgusting... Pieces of shit..."

When an Alien emerges from a person, the buttons pop off first—the buttons that kept the human skin fastened on, pressed under the abdominal muscles, under the ribs somewhere, maybe even near the heart. The buttons pop off with flesh attached. Small, even tiny, they fly off in all directions, fall under the table, roll into corners. They disappear from sight. Then they disappear entirely. You should have used a zipper instead of buttons to contain your Alien. It's easier to fix if anything goes wrong, thought Haska. She also thought about Tanya's temperament. About the strength of Aunt Tanya, who had seemed so boring, buttoned-up tight, stern, sometimes boastful, but still just a boring, gray, nearly invisible older woman. They were all old to Haska. They only got younger when she herself got older.

Aunt Tanya was impressive. The Bickford fuse inserted up the butt of her Alien was long like sparklers. He, it, they, she scattered sparks but hardly ever burned you, saving the explosion for later.

"Can I please not write about it?" Haska asks again. "I don't know how to describe how I wanted to kill her, but also to hold her and comfort her. And I still don't know which I wanted more at that moment."

Aunt Tanya coughed, poured and drank some water, then paused to catch her breath. And Haska poured words into that pause like oil onto a bonfire. She asked,

"And where's Les living now?"

"Who's that?" wheezed Tanya.

"Oleksii. Your son," answered Galya blithely.

"His name is Aleksei, you stupid fuckface... duckface!" answered Aunt Tanya. In Ukrainian. The words didn't even have to be translated. It turns out that, in the new *russkiy mir*—"Russian world"—of Donetsk, just like in the old world, you couldn't buy Russian *svekla*, beets. You couldn't even buy "svyokla"—if you wanted to try it with a Ukrainian accent. You couldn't buy them or even to ask the saleswoman for them. If you wanted to buy a beet, you would have to use the Ukrainian word: *buryak*. Apparently, "duckface" was best said in Ukrainian, too.

"I won't bury him." It wasn't spring when Tanya said it, and she wasn't talking to Haska. It was already that summer when drones had been replaced by tanks; "carnations," "peonies," "acacias," and "tulips," were no longer the names of flowers but varieties of self-propelled mortars that kept rolling in from Russia, bringing death. And bringing her choice, which could still be made.

It was Nefyodov. Tanya shouted it at Nefyodov. In fear and rage, despair and disillusionment. In the voice of the disaster she'd called forth and viewed as the price of her new happiness. Tanya had never considered that this might be the price. Her Lyosha would never betray his mother. He was always on her side. He'd always hugged her and, after his years of adolescent "don't touch me" rebellion, he always kissed her on the forehead. She would blink happily and wonder whether her hair was clean enough and whether her roots were freshly colored enough for Lyosha not to be embarrassed by her gray hair. She screamed "I won't bury him" because parents shouldn't have to bury their children. It's against the order of things, against the laws of nature. Not honest, not right, not happening to her. Though the Alien which she could no longer shove back in shrieked in disgust and shame that this was how he'd turned out. She was torn between loving and cursing him.

"Your damned Polacks won't help him. Tell him that. You tell him."

"Tata," said Nefyodov. "You're not Taras Bulba. I'm telling you for sure."

"I'm not Tata."

"I already gathered that. I hear you. But stop flipping out. Our child is at the front."

"Do you know what I regret, Nefyodov?" asked Tanya in the vicious, icy tone she knew he hated because it scared him. "I regret that you didn't let me name our son Ernest.

In honor of the German anti-fascist Ernst Thälmann. If you even remember that name. With that name, my son definitely wouldn't have betrayed us. He would have been on our side."

"You've lost your mind, Tanya, your whole fucking mind."

Yes, he used to shout. Loudly, harshly, with his deep voice occasionally breaking into a falsetto. He used to turn red like a "million roses." He might flip a chair or break a plate. But never once did he lay a finger on her. And never once did he swear. Never. He always had some other mean and insulting words. That, and the roar, just the roar itself, had been plenty.

There's a first time for everything.

And Vitya said that there were issues with Communism, whether it was ours or the German variety. So they didn't need Thälmann or Lenin.

Not only Lenin, as it turned out. Designers also fell into the category of "not needed." Tanya went back to practicing medicine. She worked in the district clinic. And she didn't want to read graffiti in entryways anymore.

THELMA
2015–2020

Thelma, where are you? Say something. Just give us a sign. Write, call, manifest yourself somehow. Be a voice in someone's head even, send a signal. We'll hear you. We'll understand it the right way. We're all crazy enough now to believe whatever you believe. Maybe you could appear in a dream or something? Drop a Kinder egg toy, leave some tacky pink lipstick in the bathroom, turn on a light in the middle of the night. Appear in a watermelon; as a snowflake flying in my mouth and all the way to my lungs; toss a video at our feet. You can do it.

Just make it clear: you still exist. Here, not there. Speak.

Thelma. Where should we look for you? I could kill you for all this stress, but please just be alive. That formula hasn't changed since 2015, but the list of possibilities varies.

Killed at a checkpoint and buried in a ditch.

Hit in a bombing and suffering amnesia.

Detained "in a basement" and denied contact with your family.

Working for the intelligence services.

Went to Syria seeking revenge against Assad for killing Maryam.

Fled to Siberia, to your grandparents, answering the call of blood, which suddenly started speaking Russian.

Made it to Europe, changed your name, severed ties with your past, cursed everyone, and forgot.

Raped by our "brotherly Buryats" and now too ashamed to come back.

Killed and unidentified.

Killed and misidentified, then buried under a different name.

Someone else compared to who you were yesterday.
Compared to a world in which war is impossible, and so it
isn't happening. Someone else in relation to time, which
now goes in circles, is no longer linear and irreversible,
which now stutters and repeats, not sure whether it's passing at all. But you can do it, Thelma.

You brought Ernest a carload... Well, not a whole carload
but a trunkful of dry animal feed. He thinks you stole it. Maybe you looted some bombed-out warehouse. There's no shame
in that. It's a good deed. Don't worry, little bird. Be proud.

You tossed a mortar off the roof. Well, not the whole
mortar. Part of it. As much as you could. It certainly couldn't
shoot anymore. Which means it didn't fire a shell at the
peaceful Lenin neighborhood. At least not in July.

You painted your nails—and those of the grannies who
spent all of August 2014 in the basement of their own building. Maybe you should have fed them first. But your silly
manicure definitely brought them back to life. Because the
dead don't shriek, "Petrivna, have you lost your mind? What
are you thinking—red? At our age! You need something
simple and modest!"

You robbed your own mother and took a load of cookies
out of the shop heading in an unknown direction. No one
believes you ate them all yourself. But even if you did—enjoy! Enjoy.

The logic of your hatred made no sense. It was twisted
and misdirected. That's how it seemed then. I'm sorry. But
to hate Putin for supporting that "sadist Assad" who was
torturing Syrians and not see his other "exploits"... That
seemed beside the point in 2014... Off-topic... It didn't fit
the narrative. Now everything's been rewritten. Completely destroyed by the howitzer of our current experience. It's

like shooting at yesterday from today. Shoot first, before the stupid thing gets said, before the irrevocable is done. The right hatred with the wrong roots? The wrong motive? But who's to say?

Killed for your organs to be sold on the black market.

Hit by a missile. A Tochka-U. Fell under artillery fire somewhere near Debaltseve. And there was nothing left of your body. Ashes to ashes. Dust to dust.

Did you fall in love with the enemy? Move to Pskov? Or Ryazan? Are you ashamed?

An overdose? Did you do drugs? Drink rubbing alcohol? Or drain cleaner?

A nunnery?

A refugee camp somewhere in Europe... Oh sorry, I already said Europe.

In a globalized world where people are no longer tied to a certain place, war restores the meaning of home. It relentlessly draws us back to the one place we can't go. But you can come back. Could you give us a sign with some stupid prank? Make us stop in the middle of the street and suddenly burst out laughing, or fly into a rage, or want to throw ourselves under a car.

We might not have the strength to throw ourselves under a car. Plenty of stupidity, but we're not resourceful, we're tired. We're more "frozen" at this point. Frozen in a thousand-yard stare. But if you're suddenly aroused by the sensation of a miracle, some irreality, if you're absolutely certain that it will definitely happen, then you will happen: in a few minutes, or months, or centuries, and then it won't be any problem to come alive.

Where are you? Nowhere. There.

Alas, Thelma, alas. That's how it is. That's how it is and how it falls and falls into an abyss of silence and evil, an evil that conceals its own existence in a cloud of deceit.

You're like a manifesto of absence. Our shared absence. Although ours takes on a hysterical, sometimes convulsive form. Whereas you are actually gone. To disappear in the age of social media, total surveillance, GPS, bank cards, wiretapping, "bugs," space stations that can see a matchbox tossed under a bench in Comrade Shcherbakov Park... It's an accomplishment. Kudos to you, Thelma, kudos and respect.

Every year that you're gone, there is less and less hope of your return. Because even someone as obsessive as you, someone who has, at times, lacked any sense of proportion (okay, always lacked, if we're going to be honest), even you would have gotten tired of "showing" us with this silence. And someone as kind-hearted as you, Thelma, would have taken pity on us a long time ago.

So let's agree: you've lost your memory. And now you'll never tell what went on with you and Lyosha-Oles, or with you and Ernest, and what they are to you. And I can't tell you. Since you've lost your memory, you don't care who all these people are and why we're stuck together for life.

Okay then, little fish, this will be about memory. It may be a bit melodramatic, but Hollywood, Netflix, and Showtime aren't embarrassed—why should we be?

Let's dial down the drama for a moment: we'll turn Leonardo into a ninja turtle. And Casper into a ghost. I just recently found out that one of the wise men bearing gifts was named Caspar. I mean, it's not actually canonical. Their names aren't listed in the Bible, but that's what people said and how they were remembered. And just in case, to avoid going into the past without a name, he became a friendly cartoon ghost on TV. Turtles are much more likely to arrive in the future than ghosts. There's no debating that. And there's also good news. Thelma has a much better chance of arriving in the future than Thälmann.

In the absence of a dead body for either one.

Childhood friends don't really have a "physical description." If they're real friends and we're not jealous or wanting their lives for ourselves. They're not blondes or brunettes, not skinny or fat, not beautiful or ugly. Our friends are a part of the general landscape—like molecules of oxygen, tap water, chalk, jump ropes, hair ties, pillow forts, skinned knees, hair-pulling fights, Barbie and Sindy dolls, and dreams of Ken ("Let's see if he has a penis!"). Our friends have no physical description until we first see ourselves in the mirror.

Thelma's face is kind of long with a sharp chin, and she thinks it's ugly. Maybe it is. But her beautiful lips... You notice them right away. Her full lips would make you think she was more African than Boiko. Those lips won't need any "beauty injections" in old age. You won't see anything beyond those lips, much less a pointy chin. Where would she get African blood in her lips? But what do we even know about our blood?

...Her nose has a hump. Acquired, not congenital. She was riding her tricycle and smashed into the desk as she was rounding the corner between the hallway and the living room. It might have been broken. There was definitely a bruise: first on the bridge of her nose and then two ponds filled in under her eyes. It looked like she was wearing glasses. Ernest teased her, "Let me wear them!" There was no trip to the doctor, of course. But after the bruise had faded, the bump was still there. And Ernest immediately stopped teasing.

If you see Thelma somewhere in a sunny square, in spring or summer, whether it's actual summer or what Americans call Indian summer, she'll have freckles on her face. On her forehead, her cheeks, and below her eyes. If she's not wearing makeup or powder (she'd rather pull your leg than powder her face), then the freckles will glow—lazily, reluctantly, lightly—like amber. You won't need to squint to see them. Look at her carefully. Thelma simply is.

She could be bald, or brunette, or a redhead; she might have long braids with green strands, or maybe blue. Maybe platinum. The hair won't help you; you can never tell with her hair. But her eyes are gray, always ready to laugh, so she already has some crow's feet, barely noticeable lacy traces at the corners. But those eyes can also kill—with one sharp shot from under the brows. And a fist, of course. Because a fist is more reliable. I won't be surprised if she's armed. Some sort of service weapon purchased on the spur of the moment in the spring of 2014 at a local police department. In the spring of '14, the Donetsk and Luhansk police sold off pretty much everything: armor, billy clubs, pistols (those were expensive), helmets, uniforms, the city, their fatherland. Not all of them did. But it was easier to find the ones who were selling stuff than not. So she's probably armed. Don't get too close, keep your distance. Take a good look. Thelma simply is.

This definitely isn't how she planned to manifest herself: stuck somewhere between probably dead in a ditch and silenced by amnesia. Thelma wanted to be a manicurist, a model, a pastry chef, the head of an illegal bank, a biker (that didn't last long), a veterinary nurse (that one was about love, it seems). "Nothing dependable," her mother Angelina sighed. "Three generations of women without higher education. Dina's our only hope."

Thelma didn't like Dina, carrots, or thinking too hard. But her borscht, if she sets about making it for you, is music. Music, aged wine from the foothills of the Alps and the blind colonel's tango from *Scent of a Woman*.

Jamais vu: never seen. A sensation that your normal life is unfamiliar, like it's not your life and you can't understand it.

"Missing" is not a form of immortality. It's a torment that is never over, that never transitions into sadness and grief. "Missing" is fruitless, bloody hope. Peering into unfamiliar faces, listening to footsteps on the stairs, seeing an unfamiliar number on the phone and shouting: "Somebody answer it! Somebody else answer it! I can't do it." That's what Angelina yells and will keep yelling until Thelma's been seen. Dead or alive. Preferably alive.

But, until then, today and tomorrow, *jamais vu*. Tormenting these people, diffused and scattered like spores in the heart of Europe, unseen and mute, even when they're talking a lot, but that's not the point... They seem to see the people around them but no longer know the rules, don't recognize people or signals, don't pick up on hints; the world has become dangerous in ways they never foresaw and they have very few wishes left. One of which is a photo. A photo with everyone. A selfie with Thelma. With Dad. With all the parents. With Ernest and Lyosha. With Grandpa Fink. Get him in the frame, too.

A selfie with everyone.

"He's asking what you used to do and what you want to do next." *Pani* Khrystyna translates conscientiously.

"In what sense?" asks Les.

"In every sense. Don't be shy, child. Just speak honestly and tell it like it is. He's German, he'll write it all down, don't you worry. He'll write it all down and answer every question."

"So, Doctor, will I be able to play the violin?" asks Les with a smile.

"He says it will require some thought," says *pani* Khrystyna. "But..."

Her "but" always implies a plan. Lyosha already knows this, but he still falls for it every time. Falls into Khrystyna's hat, from which she pulls not just rabbits, but all sorts of other wonders, somewhat similar to rabbits. You can't always adopt them, but it would be a shame to say "no." Next to pani Khrystyna, Lyosha is all fur and ears.

Sometimes he's still Lyosha. But more and more often he uses the more Ukrainian-sounding Les. He signs letters as Les, introduces himself as Les, responds when someone shouts it in the street. He's still Lyosha when he's sleeping, lost, or embarrassed, when he wants to hide from everyone, when he lifts himself up from bed to deliver the brilliant observation, his "exit line," as his mom used to say: "life goes on."

"My sweet son works at the opera. Here in Munich. It's too bad you're not a girl, since I can't stand his wife, so I'm always looking for a replacement. I even have girls come live at my place practically for free. Students, waitresses. Our people—from Ukraine. I keep thinking that he'll meet someone normal and ditch his... his kitten. Or if he were gay," pani Khrystyna sighs dreamily. "If he were gay... and you were gay... I could introduce the two of you and life would be great. You'd make a good couple. You'll see!"

Pani Khrystyna is getting sidetracked and the doctor values his time and wants to be effective. In the face of Pani Khrystyna's magical and chatty realism, where nothing is trivial and everything is significant, the best approach is to keep things formal. Move the conversation to paper.

"You can send me an email," the doctor says in English, looking Les in the eye. "Don't be embarrassed. Write exactly what you want. Write it however you want. Be honest. Your honesty and openness will help us choose the best option, okay?"

"What's he saying to you?" asks pani Khrystyna. "Anyway... just say '*Danke*' and let's go. We'll go to the opera. My son is a conductor, just so you know. Not the chief conductor, he's here on contract. Violin is fine, though I like piano better. We had one in the village growing up, at the school. I learned to play Chopsticks without anything written down. Listen, here's a funny thing: why does it say 'for fortepiano' on the sheet music sometimes, when it's actually just called a piano? I never got that. But my son did. And he even learned to read music. He studied it. Just wait, for him to set up a violin for you—well, at least to figure out how it could work—easy-peasy! You'll see."

There is no tiny crack, no moment, absolutely no opportunity to interfere with pani Khrystyna's plan. She's happy and excited and can't stop. She talks about the Grosshadern Clinic that she likes because it's close, and another clinic on the other side, near the Isar River, whose name she'll find later on Google Maps; about the Ottobock company

and bionics that she didn't know about before, but now—
"they've made so much progress, child, these Germans have
made so much progress in medicine, it's just incredible."
Pani Khrystyna drives and talks. Les doesn't have anywhere
he needs to be and is embarrassed to interrupt and confess
that he was just repeating the old joke at the doctor's office. Before having his appendix removed, the patient asks:
"Doctor, will I be able to play the violin after the operation?"
"Yes, of course!" "Amazing! I couldn't before!"

Pani Khrystyna's son isn't at the opera. The opera house
is cool, quiet, and dark, with an air of solemnity in the
morning. Les doesn't get a chance to relish the silence that
is uncharacteristic for both the opera and pani Khrystyna.

"What an idiot I am. What a total idiot. Who holds re-
hearsals in the morning? They don't even get to bed until
2 a.m. We'll go to their place. It's a gorgeous apartment, they
have these cypresses in red boxes on the roof. I wrap them
in plastic for the winter, so they don't freeze. But my son,
Pavlyk—well, here they call him Paul, that's the German
version of Pavlo—he didn't want nasturtiums."

"I've never played the violin," announces Les in a firm
voice on the steps of the opera house, to which Duke Maxi-
milian I Joseph has his back turned. In a chair.

"So what? If a person wants something, they can figure
it out. What difference does it make whether you've played
before or not? We'll just walk there. It's not far."

Five minutes later, pani Khrystyna and Les reach the
apartment on the fourth floor of a building that has been
occupied since long before a Welshman named John Hughes
arrived in the steppes of Ukraine and built the first metal-
works plant in Donbas.

Pavlyk is older than Les. Forty? Fifty? He's slim, with
a short, simple haircut that wouldn't look out of place on
the front line, and a nice smile that immediately makes

him look like pani Khrystyna. He offers his hand to Les. And then gets embarrassed, just like everyone does.

"Damn, sorry. I'm always a bit stupid in the morning. Will you join us for breakfast?"

"Good housewives are already serving lunch at this time of day," pani Khrystyna observes. "Perhaps yours is still sleeping?"

"No." She floats into the large room that Les isn't even sure what to call. The living room? Dining room? Hall? She floats into the room, then kisses Paul on the cheek and pani Khrystyna on the crown of her head. She places her left hand on Lyosha's shoulder and squeezes lightly, her hand lingering a bit longer than necessary. A bit longer than a gesture of simple politeness would suggest. "I'm Nastya."

Her left hand on his right shoulder. The shoulder that no longer ends in an arm.

So, to hell with the violin. With dentistry. With hugs and handshakes. To hell with the future.

The choice is between "mechanical" and "bionic." A mechanical prosthesis can rotate almost like a screwdriver: 180 degrees. You can use it to hold a glass or a bat, grip a steering wheel and do magic tricks. A bionic one is soft, responsive, and more like a human body part. It has the capacity for finer movements, and you can even control the fingers… It's sensitive to rain, dust, and heat. Like a living thing.

The choice is between describing how his personnel carrier hit a mine and just saying it was a car accident. A car accident doesn't unnerve people. It spares them.

The choice is between a jacket with long sleeves or a T-shirt. Between the delayed shock that the sleeve is empty and the instantaneous, here and now, "Look, everyone! No arm!"

Lyosha has breakfast with Paul, Nastya, and pani Khrystyna. In a jacket. The left hand is enough for him to pick up toast, smear it with butter, and cut an omelet into pieces (fried eggs would be harder). It's all easy. Paul laughs at the old joke about the violin. Pani Khrystyna is a bit offended, but then she laughs too, insisting that he should think about music anyway. "It's not like you have to crawl on your stomach like Maresyev." Lyosha has no idea who Maresyev is.

There's a patio on the roof. Lyosha asks if he can go take a look at the cypresses and have a smoke. Pavlo doesn't smoke, but Nastya goes outside with Lyosha. His left hand is enough for him to take out the pack and lighter; to tap out a cigarette and grab it with his teeth. Nastya doesn't look at his empty sleeve. She looks at him. Greedily and tenderly. Her gaze travels slowly, like a camera, as if she were enlarging his neck, Adam's apple, shoulders, chest. Nastya takes the biggest close-up as she directs her optics at his pants just below the belt. The pants respond, straining and bulging, giving a sense they might burst open. Without raising her eyes, she whispers,

"You're so handsome. So handsome."

She sniffs at the air and starts to resemble a dog. The comparison is a compliment for Les. She really does look like a dog—with beautiful, moist, dark eyes.

"You're handsome and smell the way I love."

"A pervert," thinks Lyosha. He hides behind what he's studied, not in medical school but currently. Acrotomophilia. Sexual attraction to amputees. Deviant. Not treated. More common in men. There are movies about it. Mainly horror movies: *Boxing Helena*, *The Butterfly Room*. There are more but Lyosha hasn't managed to see them.

"Are you a pervert?" He decides to be bold and rises to his full height from the trench, ready to throw some sort of offensive grenade if necessary.

"Are you stupid? Sick?" Nastya asks gently.

"You finally noticed. Thank God," says Lyosha, forcefully exhaling a stream of smoke.

"I'm not the only one, you know," says Nastya, sitting down on the patio tiles. She draws her knees up to her chin and looks up. "There's tons of us perverts. Every day, hundreds of us stand in Pio Clementino waiting for the Belvedere torso to give us our certification. And if one isn't enough, then we hop right on a plane to Paris. We bypass the Lafayette Gallery, even though it's hard. We have to get to the Louvre: the Venus de Milo gives it to everyone who wants. And you wouldn't believe how many people there are: thousands. And they're all perverts, such perverts..."

She doesn't get up, but sits looking past him, smiling... She's younger than either Pavlo or Les. She's about twenty-seven, thin, delicate, fragile. Lyosha doesn't know what Pio Clementino is, or why it's hard to bypass the Lafayette Gallery. The Venus de Milo is perfectly clear, though.

Lyosha wants to kiss her. Not the de Milo. Nastya. Lyosha wants her.

"So? Didn't I tell you? Such a prostitute!" An enraged pani Khrystyna brakes sharply at the traffic light and, delaying the main topic of her presentation for a few minutes, gets into a heated fight with the driver of the car that's stopped in front of her. The driver can't hear her, but that's not important. "Well, Russian plates, what do you expect? Bought his license from the FSB in Moscow and now he's sabotaging the traffic here. So? Did you see what I told you? She practically set your pants on fire. You were great, though. You stood your ground nobly. I don't know what I'd do if someone undressed me and caressed me like that with those hussy eyes. And it's all fake. Don't fall for it. Dyed hair, fake extensions. I mean, if you want to change your hair, just wear a wig. Right? It's more economical. And you always have it in the closet. And her tits—I'm 100% certain she had them done before she met Pavlyk, to catch a husband with them. My sweet boy. I won't say anything about the lips. Did you get a look at her lips?"

Lyosha shakes his head. He really didn't see. Not the tits or the lips. He saw something else, for sure, but he can't talk to pani Khrystyna about that.

"That's right," she sighs. "Exactly right. What is there to see when the obscenity is just pouring off of her? What a bitch. Well, fine. I'll give you some valerian drops now. And I'll brew you some motherwort for the night. We can also look for some bromine. We'll take care of it, child. For you and for Pavlyk. We'll find him a good little girl. I promise you that."

That night, it occurs to Lyosha that Les is short for Oleksandr, not Oleksii. He texts Haska: "That's an 'F' for you, girlfriend."

"Well, you can't return it. Just keep it," she answers. And includes a smiley face: the colon and a parenthesis which now get instantly converted to an emoji.

"But what if I wanted to be Oleksii?"

"As long as it's not Alyosha."

But, at night, he is still Lyosha. His thoughts are slow and dull. It's the first time since the war, but not the first time in his life. Thirty-three years old. A dangerous age. "There you have it," as pani Khrystyna would say.

His hand... Maybe he should have buried his hand. With some sort of tombstone? Bring it flowers, talk to it, make promises? What would he promise? To clip his nails, maybe—and other peoples', too. To work out with the remaining arm so that everyone envies his biceps. Maybe the violin after all. Learn to play violin... "We love to make promises to the dead," Lyosha thinks. "I should have buried it. What did they do with it anyway? Where do the arms, legs, burned off chunks of skin, and pieces of bone go? Where do they go from the Dnipro Hospital? Into a pit for no longer useful body parts? It's like something straight out of a horror movie. The winner."

He can't fill out the German doctor's questionnaire—it feels like fortune-telling: what he used to do, what he's doing now, what he'd like to do in the future, what makes him feel calm and happy...

The mechanical prosthesis seems like the best option. It's cheaper. He could take two. To alternate. He could wear a ring on one. He had once dreamed of a gold ring with a skull and a deep red inscription around it, but he'd never figured out the inscription.

"You're handsome and you smell the way I love." He could live with that.

Those words aren't more powerful than a personnel carrier that suddenly, in the middle of the day, when it's relatively quiet and you start getting used to it, even though you know not to trust it... In the middle of the day, it hits a mine. And, instead of the quiet, there's dirt trickling into your ears, your back and chest burn and, from somewhere in the background, like music in a bar, you hear: "Marshal, Marshal, you goddamned sissy, are you alive?"

Not more powerful than that.

But still.

ANGELINA
DAUGHTERS
2011–2020

Long, grown-up fingers. Just like a grown-up hand—you could film it for a wedding movie. Tiny nails perfect for a French manicure. They have to be trimmed so she doesn't scratch her face, but it'd be so nice to keep them the way they are... and paint them.

The top of her head smells like home, milk, and peace. You could live forever there. If Angelina could fit, if she could turn into a grain of rice, she'd hide away on top of the baby's head and never go anywhere ever again.

Or in her eyelashes. Or cheeks. Or under her lower lip, that starts trembling first, proclaiming an imminent attack of immense grief that will overflow with tears if someone doesn't feed her, pick her up, and pour kisses on this beautiful little girl who was born to make everyone happy but is lying here wet, unfed for half an hour, and unpraised for five minutes.

The instant Angelina and Dina set eyes on each other, it was clear who was the boss and who would melt beyond recognition and stop fooling around in her efforts to improve her fate.

The sense of it—the size, weight, length—was calculated at six pounds, ten ounces and twenty inches. And growing by the month. It should have been another twenty-one ounces, another twenty-eight, plus twenty-one ounces again—and then total hysterics because it was ten ounces instead of the expected fifteen.

It's all like the sea that Angelina still hadn't seen but could easily imagine. Waves, sand, sun, the shade of the

palm trees, the intoxicating scent of flowers, never quiet—
but quiet, too...

Her first teeth, lifting her head, sitting propped up with
pillows, an awkward crawl with the left leg dragging behind
like a tail and never catching up to the right. Broccoli, the
broccoli puree which was a favorite and didn't get spit out,
unlike carrot juice or the baby food kefir.

The sling that Dina and Angelina wore to work together: one walking, the other riding. A cradle for the office,
a playpen, a rocking cradle for home, a stroller, a kangaroo
carrier, too, but Angelina preferred the sling. Dina on her
belly was like a continuation of pregnancy, but now on the
outside instead of the inside.

"So they call it a sling now?" said the woman who Angelina had hired for kitchen work off the labor exchange with
the promise of good money and an easy schedule. "In the
old days, they used to say that a child with no father was
carried in on the hem."

Angelina laughed hard at that one. She'd heard all kinds
of things about herself: about retirement and gray hairs
(that she should be thinking about them), about the devel-
opmental risks for the "offspring of older mothers," about
irresponsibility, and also—that people would shout "Grandma and granddaughter!" at her and the baby. It was never
quite clear who'd be doing all the shouting.

But "in on the hem"—that was actually kind of cute.
Mainly because it was unexpected. But Angelina fired her
anyway. She doesn't need that crap.

So she fired the baker. She turned Nefyodov down again.
And she didn't take maternity leave because the cookies ar-
en't going to bake themselves and the tax documents have
to be filed. And so? A cradle in the office, diapers on the
bum—it's a great big world. And it all belongs to Dina. Make
sure she knows it. Make sure she knows.

Broccoli, avocado, asparagus... Dina's food, just the food, brought on a nagging sense of guilt. It attacked sharply, jabbing her in the ribs and then lurking behind the pots on the shelves. The sense of guilt was called "Thelma." Thelma didn't get avocados as a child, Thelma collected those "poverty toys" from Kinder Surprise eggs, Thelma struggled with those tights that usually ended up with the heels on the front...

There had never been time for Thelma, but now it was entirely unclear what had been so important. How had the time trickled out and poured away? Where had it gone? There wasn't enough time, but there was more than enough screaming—harsh and ugly. "Don't stand, don't climb, don't touch, don't move, don't whine..." It was easy to yell at Thelma when it started raining and the umbrella had been left at home; it was fine to yank her along at the store, so she didn't ask for anything; it was natural to give her a smack on the butt, just smack her on the butt, just to... When her baba was alive, she used to grumble at Angelina: "Stop hounding the child!" And Angelina, fool that she was, would answer, "She's my kid, I'll do what I want."

Now, whenever the fatal broccoli caught her eye, either under the knife or already in the pot, the words "I'm sorry, Thelma" would bubble up in Angelina, but she never let them slip out. Absolutely not.

Instead... And, this is the worst, horrible, shameful "instead"—instead, Angelina would wait for the chance to be alone with Dina. To bring the baby into her bed and watch how Dina slowly fell asleep with her fingers in her mouth; how her forehead would sweat sometimes; how her lips would twitch in her sleep from a smile or tears, and she'd say to her, to Dina: "Sweetheart, my one and only, my sweet baby."

She thought then and always had thought that full, true love isn't shared with everyone. A love in which my "one and only" is secured with hugs, kisses, shared breath, and the fear of possible loss, and grows into a cosmic exclusivity, total isolation, without room for anyone else... Only love that excludes and blocks out the entire world is true love.

While Thelma disappeared into her apparently grown-up and perhaps already womanly affairs, Angelina embarked on a festival of rebellion. The older Dina got, the more the festival was marked by chaos "on the streets of home." A toy railroad, races on two red Ferraris, feeding the dolls real, freshly cooked kasha; hours on the iPad; making cloth napkins out of old skirts (and sometimes even new skirts—is that a problem?); cartoons until midnight; drawing on the wallpaper—at first with markers, then watercolors... A life in which anything was possible. And Dina wasn't the one starting over from the beginning, it was Angelina.

Angelina and, sometimes, Nefyodov, too, was choosing their future, drawing it broadly, going not just beyond the boundaries of what was formerly "impossible" but beyond all visible horizons. She was betting, no they were betting on robots and molecular genetics, on diving and whale research, on a flamenco school that Dina could open some day in Madrid. On Oxford—and why not? On Oxford, with Latin and Ancient Greek, or the Massachusetts Institute of Technology and the construction of air bridges. Ballet, cosmonauts, and figure skating, along with piano, were out due to their association with oppression and mothballs. Chinese was an open question—difficult, but possibly promising. Sports and aviation were also questionable, along with law: too many lawyers, not enough laws.

There was still some time. Some time during which Angelina froze, listening and observing Dina's wishes and talents. In January of 2014, Dina turned three. She was already going to preschool and had happily reported: "There are more children there, but not as many cookies." Angelina easily corrected the deficit.

For the New Year's party, Dina refused to dress up as a snowflake, a fox, a squirrel, or Barbie doll.

"I want to be a zombie. A sad zombie. So we feel sorry for it."

"But that's so ugly, it's not festive at all. It doesn't really suit little girls, right, Dina?"

"It doesn't suit anyone. But we have to do something…" she responded sadly and insistently.

After "being a zombie" became all the rage in Donetsk, Nefyodov took Dina to the coast, to Berdyansk. Angelina wouldn't go: she was worried about Thelma, who was running all over the place, and it was completely unclear whether in that "all over the place" she would be hurt by a missile, Motorola's filthy dick, the Isolation torture camp, or the ruins of a house in Pisky. She needed to look out for Thelma.

Angelina did a poor job of it.

And that's all.

The only bit of life she still had was through her phone and laptop. The existence of a connection is like the existence of blood. Not the blood that was being shed everywhere, the other kind. The blood that creates a bit of normality. Call Dina, write Dina, listen to Dina, and worry about her. Love her.

Everything else became waiting.

A year, two, three, four, five years. First it was days. Then weeks. Then months.

Bounty chocolate bars. Potatoes and milk for mashed potatoes. Soup with sautéed onions added for flavor at the end—once every three days. On the evening of the third day, Angelina would boil it, taste it, pour it into a liter jar and take it down to the alley. It wasn't fresh, but it was still edible. The people who came for the soup

were called bums. They hadn't gone anywhere just because there was a war. Angelina would bring out pieces
of bread in plastic wrap with the soup, and also a napkin
and plastic spoon.

And then she made more. At first once every three days.
Then twice a week. Then ten times in a month. Then 523
per year.

At the end of the year, Angelina didn't multiply the soups,
she just reset the counter. Once every three days.

She wasn't sure what Thelma liked to eat. She wasn't even
sure what she herself liked to eat. But they both seemed to
like soup, mashed potatoes, and Bounty bars. Meatballs,
sausage, pasta. Pizza.

They started making the pizza at the bakery. Which was
still open. Not because she needed the money. Although she
did. The bakery was open because Thelma might come back
here. Either to the apartment or here. Thelma loved the bakery: the rolls, the smell of vanilla, the rise of the dough—
first rise, second rise, flour dust, sugar that was measured
not in spoonfuls but by the sack. She liked it all better than
the apartment cluttered with Dina's toys. Where there was
no space for Thelma.

On Thelma's birthday in April, Angelina baked cakes. She
baked all kinds of cakes, all day long. In the morning, she
took Napoleons and Sacher Torte to the hospitals. And not
only cakes and not only on her birthday. She delivered
anything she baked to the doctors. A girl with amnesia, in
a coma, unconscious, without ID, could turn up in any ward.
Or in the morgue. Angelina took sweets to the morgue, too.

But not to the prisons. No one knew exactly how many
there were now, but everyone knew for sure that it was
easier to get in than to get out. Angelina couldn't afford to
disappear behind bars somewhere. She had Dina in the evening. And every day, every minute—Thelma.

Angelina listened to footsteps. She peered into the darkness of the courtyard. She sniffed the air in the entryway; she smelled sweaters, T-shirts, pillowcases. Sweaters in the winter. T-shirts in the spring. Thelma had always been the first to "shed layers." All the girls would still be wearing tights, and she would have already switched to socks; everyone would still be wearing winter coats, and she would be the one in just a shirt—with long-sleeves, at least. Everyone took their winter hats off in the spring. She took hers off at the age of fourteen and never put it on again. The pillowcase still smelled like her hair for a year or two. And then the smell was gone: it had aired out. And Angelina wailed for the first and last time.

Little Thelma's hands had always been warm. She would stroke Angelina's face before going to sleep, patting it in amazement, as if it were an unexpected gift, a stroke of luck. As she took her hands away, Thelma would give a ragged exhalation, like after crying, and Angelina would give her a quick kiss on the cheek: "Now go to sleep." She was hurrying to get somewhere.

Soup with sautéed onions added at the end. Footsteps outside the door. There's plenty of time now. Angelina's living it backwards. In the past, there is so much of Thelma that she never saw earlier. All the yesterdays and the days before yesterdays, and the ten years before that are permeated with her. Enough to live on for a long time.

Kind people tell Angelina: "Go to Dina. Or bring her here. One daughter is better than none. You're going to lose this one, too."

"Fuck off, kind people," Angelina answers silently—and often out loud. "Fuck off. You're just jealous. I have two daughters. And I'll wait for both of them as long as I have to."

MARIA

ON LEAVE
AND A LITTLE BEFORE
2015–2016

"You whore, I'll claw your eyes out, you hear me? I'll rip your hair out..."

"Is that a promise?" asks Maria.

"What?" The woman across from her falls silent and blinks her black lashes, with their clumpy mascara. The clumps are the result of a low-quality brush. It could also be the properties of the mascara itself. Or maybe she's just ham-handed. The most common issue, by the way. Any makeup can be ruined if you have hams for hands.

The woman sitting across from her is probably named Natalka. But that "couldn't be verified," as they say now. It also couldn't be verified that she has a brother named Mykola, who is currently in training, but could be sent any minute to Shyrokyne, or Bakhmut, or Novotoshkivka, or Avdiïvka. Or... No one knows exactly where since it's a "military secret." The probable Natalka asked to meet. She'd said on the phone, "I want to send some Easter babkas to my brother. And a few gifts from the family, from the children. Some drawings..." You could hear that Natalka was crying and sniffling. A bit overdone, but Maria now knew for a fact that people cry all different ways. Sometimes people even cry when they laugh.

"Alright, let's meet. Does the coffee shop on Obolon work for you?"

Clumpy eyelashes, cleavage, high heels, a tiny bag on a long, shiny chain. Maybe she left the cakes, gifts, and drawings in the car. She sat down and ordered coffee and a glass of white wine. She put an iPhone on the table, and her hand on the iPhone—a hand with nails that seemed longer than the fingers. She tossed her black hair. Licked her lips.

Stupid with bad taste. But Maria had learned to respect the "leopard leggings" crowd. They usually brought much more help to the front than the sophisticated girlfriends who indefatigably complained of war fatigue while sunbathing on beaches in Turkey.

"My leave is short and I don't have much time. What's your brother's last name? And give me his phone number."

Instead of the phone number, Maria was treated to a brief solo about how she was a whore, and she wasn't going to hear it. But, though Natalka was knocked off stride, she wasn't stopping.

"How old are you, woman? Fifty? Sixty? You need to have your organs harvested before the flesh falls off them. You hear me? If you see my husband once more, I'll burn your ugly mug off with acid!"

"Just not in our establishment, if you don't mind," said the waiter as he approached the table. "Shall I call the police?"

"I'll tell you when," said Maria smiling. "For now, I propose we hear our speaker out."

"You slut!" gasped the almost certainly Natalka. "You old nag. You army whore!"

Not convincing. All the words are right, but the screeching, the intonation, the semantic emphases... No. Not convincing.

"Who is this performance for? Someone on the phone? Who's the third party?" Maria stretched out her hand. Natalka swatted it.

"Is it a fight yet? Should I call the police?" asked the waiter, and then, leaning a bit toward Natalka, added, "I really wouldn't recommend it. She could kick, too, and take a look at those combat boots…"

"Alright then, you tell me," says Natalka, grabbing him by the pants. "What about sleeping with other people's husbands? How's that? What do you think about that?"

"Sleeping is a waste of time. It's better not to sleep. I agree. Now, can I get you anything?"

Alarm. Ihor called it "alarm." When you wandered into something and unexpectedly got stuck. The word was hilarious and everyone adopted it. When the dugout got covered in snow that then melted and poured from the roof—alarm. When a general, some Soviet idiot from headquarters, arrived to do a spot check—alarm. When a mine fragment hit the armor plate—how the fuck did you come flying in all the way here—alarm. Birds, flood, heat. The onions in the trench garden hit by missiles, Buryats on skis—that was back in 2014—in the mud, because it was still autumn, the freaks. Maria didn't see it with her own eyes. But the guys swore it was true. "Such an alarm, we nearly pissed ourselves laughing." Ihor hadn't seen the Buryats with his own eyes either.

They arrived at the front after the worst of it. After Ilovaisk, after Debaltseve, after the Donetsk airport. They arrived in the grassy spring, abloom with tiny poppies, wild tulips, shy buttercups, and the scent of artemisia that promised fields of feather grass (though not for everyone everywhere) and, if the summer came fast and hot, one more wonder: tumbleweed. "If you see it, you won't even believe it. You'll get scared," said Maria.

"You'll get scared"—those are words of love. There was no talk of love itself, of course. Maybe because there was nothing that looked like love. Nothing that would be worth feeling, that was recorded in the statutes, that should be recognized and proclaimed as love.

There was fear. Maria woke up every morning and went
to sleep every night afraid. She was ashamed to admit it.
After all, she chose this herself. She was exactly where she
wanted to be, had fought for this, argued that people needed to learn to shoot not just on the training range, and that
she could do this. In a combat zone. With deep knowledge
of the local terrain. With a unique knowledge, acquired
through years of picnics, children's camps, and trips to the
surrounding villages. Be so kind! Kindness happened. But
being didn't really work out.

On days when the birds were singing and the sun was
so bright it was blinding, Maria taught them how to make
a "nest" and how to lie in it without moving. How to become
a bush, a snowdrift, or part of a shed, and how to hold a target. How to breathe in unison with that other person, over
there, who's ready to kill you. How to spot his movement:
"And he'll definitely move! One instant and, if you catch it,
you're alive. And he's dead." She taught them to calculate
the wind, to adjust for dawn and dusk, for rain and cold,
which, of course, are not your allies, but you can come to
an agreement.

Maria explained what it meant to be both "sharp" and
"slow," what it meant to shoot without emotion, without
malice, or anxiety, or vengeance. To just shoot as if it were
merely a plastic disc a kilometer away, or two kilometers
away. A disc without a conscience or brain, but with a Russian passport.

She also taught them not to pee. Or to pee in your pants
or adult diapers. In her previous life, she hadn't known that:
that knowledge wasn't needed in sport shooting. She'd been
taught, also. And, at first, it was cold and humiliating. Even
on a hot, sunny summer day, it's still cold.

"It doesn't come out right away and it doesn't always
have to," Maria reassured them. While she was teaching,

she had the strength she needed. But the fear never let up. It was always lurking, a quiet jangle—one, single, alarming note—but it didn't beat against her ribcage or pluck at her temples. It waited. It waited for Mama to come home from work and feed it a porridge of panic, pressure, pounding heart, sudden blindness, and sometimes even shaking hands. A mediocre dessert.

On quiet days, she wanted to take off and run. Across the steppe, toward the slag heaps. Home. She was seven kilometers from Mar'ïnka. To run screaming. Or just to scream. She wanted a toilet, hot water, and a body scrub. And these wishes just made her want to run, hide, and scream all over again.

On the not so quiet days, when everything rumbled and flew, when they had to wait for approval to return fire in the face of what felt like nonstop artillery barrages, Maria wanted to die quickly. First. Immediately. Instantaneously. So there wouldn't be time for her to shit herself and die in filth, rather than with the dignity she promises everyone who makes it through ten hours in the "nest."

Ihor was like that, too. Maria saw right away how afraid he was and how ashamed he was to be afraid. Maybe everyone was afraid. But she sensed how that same tedious note was relentlessly chirping in his head, telling him to run, but he would freeze so that no one would see the fear, or throw himself into battle first, even when there was no battle and wouldn't be. Instead, there was the unexpected quiet that you couldn't trust. He didn't say, "I'm scared." He said, "Lean against my back. Like I'm a chair." Maria leaned. Back-to-back. It was the end of spring. The end of a day that had not been quiet, but also not bloody. There were stars in an infinite sky. Somewhere in the pond, out of sight, frogs were croaking.

Lost children. Not forgotten, still needed by someone. He was thirty-seven. A driver. "A driver. It's karma," thought

Maria. She was forty-nine. She had the emerald star and the diamond bumblebee. She'd gotten the "star consultant" car out of the Donbas last summer and quickly sold it.

He was from Ternopil Oblast.

"We have waterfalls there and a lake that never freezes. And a village called 'Rai'—paradise."

"You've seen everything we have here," she said. "But if it's a hot summer…" Maria promises him tumbleweed. He doesn't believe her and laughs. "You'll see—you'll be scared," she threatens.

They fall silent and the summoned-promised fear suddenly retreats. Maria and Ihor laugh. They're cowards. It's a secret, but now a shared one. And the whole night lies ahead, after which everything will go back to how it was. And there won't be anything more.

"The Sarmatian Sea used to be where the lake is now."

"And the Wild Field used to be right here."

"You make it sound like it's civilized now," he laughs.

"I'm not going to be offended by someone whose sea ran off," teases Maria.

"Alarm," he says and puts his hands up. Apparently.

Back-to-back. The sky is their go-between. The words come out slowly and quietly. Time passes slowly and quietly. Sometimes it stops entirely. Unintentionally stops and unintentionally creates eternity. So…

He's a driver, his wife is in Spain, the children are with his parents. They text every day. Text and send selfies. They're growing quickly.

She's Maria. A respectable woman. She has a daughter, but no husband. Her husband was killed. "You know, for some reason, I always evaluated life in terms of war. I always knew. I wasn't wrong."

"Damn," Igor's back smiled sadly.

"Damn," answers Maria.

"Your wild poppies look like paprika for seasoning chicken."

"I could definitely eat something fried and unhealthy right about now."

"Another time..." he says. Not talking about food.

"Another time..." she seems to agree, blushing for no reason.

But there won't be any other time. Can't be. Only here and now next to the croaking frogs. Where for the very first time since the war started she's not afraid.

Maria leaves at the end of the week. Back to the training ground and then on to another sector of the front. Everyone exchanges phone numbers. No one is sure whether they'll use the numbers. God forbid if they use them in the near future. God forbid...

And a group photo.

"If I get drunk and pee in the bed like a baby, I'll tell my wife it's your fault, you taught it to me," laughs one of Maria's students.

"Come to a sharpshooting competition after the war," she says. "I'll give you a handicap. But I'll still win."

"No doubt about it."

She takes pictures with Ihor, too. As she's leaving, he posts one of them. "What a hag," Maria thinks when she sees herself, enlarging the image. "Wrinkles, spots, some kind of weird eruptions on my forehead, bags under my eyes... What a nightmare." She looks for pictures of his children and parents. And, of course, his wife. Tanned, pretty, plump, blonde. Young.

"Who are you anyway?" Maria asks the probable Natalka threateningly. "Who are you? A terrorist?" Maria can be threatening, especially when she's locked in on the target, right between the eyes of the person she's getting ready to hit. "Did they tell you, you little shit-for-brains, who I am?

Did they tell you I can hit your ear from two kilometers away? And then you'll have to live with only one. Who are you?"

"I'm a friend," Natalka quickly admits. "I came with an assignment. Here... do you want to see my ID?"

"What kind of assignment?"

"Well, Natalya, my friend asked me to get a look at you and scare you. She's Natalka and I'm also named Natalka. See? She's in Spain right now, so she couldn't come herself. But she wanted me to check. It's her husband... They have a family... She loves him. She's jealous. What does my ear have to do with anything?"

"Stand up," says Maria. "Stand up and go to the bathroom."

"Are we going to fight? Without any witnesses?" sighs Natalka with a tone of resignation.

"No. You're going to wash your face with soap. And then I'm going to do your makeup. Without these clumps. You'll be beautiful."

The thing is that
I don't have a home
Whether out of good manners
Or the threat of the belt
I'll remember the tribe I'm from
I'll remember the city I'm from

"I Don't Have a Home," Odyn v kanoe

"The thing is that / I don't have a home," sings Nefyodov. "'I just don't have a seat / to write out my speech.' I can't get the song out of my head; it just keeps playing on and on. On and on. Like I'm in prison. Morning, noon, and night on Radio Repeat. Maybe until the day I die, do you think? And I don't have any words of my own. I only think of myself in someone else's words. Either lines of poetry or this song. Or something hits home from my childhood: 'lie there quiet.' 'Lie there quiet' may be worse than 'I don't have a home.' What is it they say now? There's so many goodies, so many goodies that I don't even know what to choose. But the words actually choose me. Do you know what a mercury thermometer is?"

"Of course I do," says Haska. "I'm a woolly mammoth, too."

"One time I was telling Dina all sorts of general safety rules: 'Don't stick your fingers in the electric outlet.' 'Don't accept anything from strangers.' And I added, 'Matches aren't toys.' And she asks me, 'What are matches?'"

"Even Dina knows about mercury thermometers. Fink says they're more reliable—like a hammer."

"I must have broken a hundred of them. When I was little, on purpose, just to cause chaos and get the floor cleaned at the sanatorium. Since then it's like I'm jinxed. Doctor Alla Stepanovna's delayed revenge. Don't ask who that is. It's not important. Splattered beads... Oh boy, oh boy. And Tata yells out: 'Nobody move! Lyosha – don't swallow the mercury, your kidneys will fail!' Lyosha shouts: 'I'm not eating it! It doesn't taste good.' Tata pulls out a couple of tampons, dips them in oil and uses them to clean the drops up off the floor. And Lyosha jokes: 'Wow, I've never seen a thermometer with such a heavy period.' Then Tata says, 'Where'd you get that from?' He laughs, 'My mom's a doctor.' But no, it turns out it was all about me. I'm the one rolling into the cracks of the floor, pausing at the edge of the veranda, sparkling on the rug, rolling out into the kitchen. And I can't be put back in. None of us can be pushed back in. I think, if we were spores, or some kind of mushrooms or bacteria, we'd scatter around the world, multiplying somewhere without sexual partners... That would be something. But we're mercury. Pretty and silvery but actually poisonous, toxic droplets. For disposal only. Let Dina live with you for a little longer, okay? I can't come and get her right now. The thing is that I don't have a home. I'll buy an apartment as soon as I get things together, we'll have everything. But for now—no. The thing is... I get this call from 'Unknown Number.' A voice from hell, Moscow accent. It says, 'You can have your house back. We're leaving. The climate here doesn't suit us anymore.' I say, 'Fuck the hell off.' And they say, 'Geez, you khokhols are so rude.' Isn't that great? 'You can have your house back.' They move in there, steal everything, shit on everything, file a record somewhere that my property is 'expropriated,' and now 'the climate doesn't suit them.' And you want to know the funny thing? The funny thing is they named a price. There's a lock on the gates, the fence is repaired, full landscape design, windows replaced, a boiler and three hundred thousand rubles a year for 'property protection.' That comes to two million up to the present. Seven hundred thousand hryvnias. Twenty-five thousand dollars. And everything else adds up to about a hundred. I. Am. Supposed. To pay. Them. For. My. House. This fucker said he'll come to Donetsk and we can finalize it there. According to their fake laws.

"'Now I don't owe anything to anyone, ever.' That's how the song goes anyway. There was this Sprinter refrigerated truck. This was before my time. The guy I drove with later told me about it. He started with this truck in 2014, all covered with pictures. Not the guy—the truck. He showed me a photo. It was covered with pictures of ice cream. Some kind of Mickey Mouses or somebody holding up chocolate, vanilla... Nice. Romchyk said, 'Suddenly, these kids came running up to us. Where'd they come from in this little village? Maybe their moms got distracted and they escaped the basements. Anyway, they came running up all happy. 'Ice cream! The volunteers brought ice cream! Have you got any Plombir?' But we didn't bring anything, we were just picking up. And not ice cream. It was early September. That endless hot summer. They'd already had one body explode in the heat. Refrigeration (not Pushkin!) is our everything. We collected the body and loaded it into the Mickey Mouse... Instead of ice cream.' Ours was just a plain truck, though— no cartoons. The one I drove with Romchyk.

"Here's what I think, Haska. It's a good thing that my Fuji Studios weren't popular anymore. If they were still going... Well, just imagine... It's all actual photos in photo albums, right next to the baby pictures, right next to the wedding photos. All this... We're so idiotic, we would absolutely print out photos of bombed-out streets, dead bodies, severed hands... We'd print them to remember. As keepsakes. So there's Lyosha's blown-off hand on one page and Lyosha in diapers on another. Somewhere near the beginning, right after Fink's picture, there's little Lyosha, a little bit further there's him at graduation, then, fucking A, the hand. Hello! I mean, we still take pictures. But on the computer or phone, they just disappear when you get a new device, lost to the mists of time. It just sits somewhere in the archive. Of course, a photo album doesn't chase you down or force you to look. But a photo album is like a museum. From the dinosaur in diapers at the start to the very end. Did you bring your photo albums with you from Donetsk? I didn't. I'm telling you, they're pure mercury.

"I've had funny stuff happen, too—not just the awful stuff. We gave some fighters a ride to the checkpoint one time. So they wouldn't have to walk. It was about three miles, maybe four, or five. It wasn't so far that they'd freeze in our truck, though even when you turn off the refrigeration, it stays cold for a while. There were three of them. They asked us, 'Hey, can you give us a ride? We're not superstitious.' And Romchyk talks like he's threatening them, 'You can only get a ride in our van one time!' They cracked up, 'Perfect! Now you're talking!' So we get to the checkpoint. And the guys there already knew our truck. Yeah... Everyone recognizes those trucks. 'And people like that, and people like that...' See how the song's stuck in my head?

"Sometimes I think it's a good thing. It used to be that in the damaged regions of our brains, we'd always be quoting Pushkin, or Mayakovsky: 'I clean myself under Lenin, to sail on into the Revolution.' And now, sometimes, you stumble over it in your head, because it's still sitting in there, lurking, and you just want to hide from your own self. 'Clean myself under Lenin...' Cleaning, fricking hell, I'm cleaning...

It's like an abortion on the leader's orders. A self-abortion, you know?"

Haska shakes her head, "No."

"Well, good. So the guys at the checkpoint don't even look. They just look down at their feet. It's always like that with me and Romchyk. People just want us to be gone. They're glad we're there, but not for them. On the other hand, anywhere we go there's always respect for the people we're carrying. We never have to wait in traffic. In the little towns, we can even run the red lights. We don't destroy—we're the end of the line of destruction. Me, Romchyk, and death in the refrigeration truck. 'How many?' one of the dudes asks. And Romchyk laughs, 'Three. They're about to get out.' 'Um, do you think maybe you should rest here for a while?' asks one of the checkpoint guards cautiously. His patch says Kyivan Rus´, rank, name... 'Where can you go when you're this tired? Huh? I can't offer you any booze, but you definitely need some sleep.' 'What, you think you're gonna stick me in the fucking crazy house?' Romchyk shouts, jumps out, throws open the back doors and orders, 'Get out, guys!'

"I can't even tell you what their faces looked like. Not because there aren't words to describe it, but because it was like a full rainbow. Those Kyivan Rus´ guys turned red, yellow, green, and blue all at once. They didn't quite reach lilac. One of them definitely wanted to run. Another one, the one who suggested we rest, calmly pulled out his radio. To call in some Haldol. And the third, the youngest, already got it probably. He's smiling. Everyone smiles at the living. Then the guys climb out. And he says to them, 'Greetings, brother-zombies!' You don't think it's funny? Such a good story... I thought it would be funny.

"I'm not making those trips anymore. They're hardly finding any of the missing now. The other side doesn't even look for them. And, fortunately, our guys aren't dying unidentified anymore. Did I say 'fortunately'? I said that because I know what I'm talking about. They have it all set up now: who, where, and how to collect them. They've worked it out.

"I've been working through the morgues since sometime in 2017. I have lots of contacts.

"Let Dina live with you a little longer. We opened a business in Zaporizhzhia. We were bringing people out of the occupied areas. There's a client base. At first, we were just middlemen, like traders, making money on the difference in prices, on old connections. They took over the factory that year. Candy wrappers: a longing for the sweet life—turns out we're all longing for a bit of sweetness... I had calls from the morgues forwarded to the office. I asked them not to call me on my cell phone, but to call the managers at the office. I'm educating the 'vata.' If you call every office once a week and say, 'This is the morgue of the military hospital calling. You can come and collect the material for evaluation,' the war stops being invisible. A morgue is like a mortar. It's impossible to ignore.

"We're getting fewer calls now. And sometimes the bones might date back to World War II. They're only finding them now that they're looking for our guys.

"I'm a lousy dad to Dina now. Angelina and I are phone parents. It's awful. The last time I saw Angelina, when I was still going back and forth, I was thinking about selling the house and trying to extract the business... I proposed to her for the second time. We should get married for Dina's sake. And she spat right in my face. A lot of spit. And I just thought, 'Excellent.' I went to the bathroom and collected some of the spit into a plastic baggie left on the counter from a pack of cotton swabs. I also rubbed some of it on one of the little cotton swabs, just like in the movies. And I took a comb with her hair on it. Tata always cleaned out her brush, but I don't. And Angelina doesn't. We're collecting the hairs to knit socks out of someday. DNA, Halyuska, I collected DNA. And it turned out fine that way, just calm and quiet, like maybe I'm a perverted scumbag, but it doesn't hurt her.

"And then the specialists said that blood would have been better. I laughed so hard—trying to imagine how I would get blood out of Angelina and what she'd do to me after that. I laughed so hard. The first analysis came back as a solid negative. Zero DNA match. It definitely wasn't our body. Ninety-nine point nine percent that it's not ours. And I kept laughing.

"I still have a baggie of Angelina's spit. It's dried up, but still toxic to enemies. You can be sure of that. I have the comb, too. It's pretty big—it won't fit in my pocket, so I keep it at home.

"Although, I actually don't have a home. I have a place for storing DNA samples.

"I talk a lot, don't I? I used to just yell, but now I'm constantly saying something. Because I don't have the words. I've stopped recognizing them. It's like they're all strangers. I don't know which ones I can rely on and which ones will definitely betray me. I just pour out words because I'm afraid of silence."

"Like my dad," says Haska. "He never liked silence either."

"I'm sorry," says Nefyodov. "Another idiot competition where I take second place. I'm sorry. I always just whip everything into butter, and never think about who gets hit with the spatter. I'm almost sixty, and I act like I'm five years old. Again and again, I'm just a loser and a bungler. Surrounded by abandoned children, incurable people, and me, completely sick in the head. When the war is over... After our victory... I'll write a book: *How to Fuck up Your Life in*

A Few Short Decades. It won't compete with your book, but it'll sell well."

"You know, Halyuska, the fact that I'm a loser—no, don't interrupt or contradict me, this is my tried and true theory, and I want it to work... The secret of my little pact with the universe lies in the fact that I'm a loser and never find what I'm looking for. I've intentionally set out to look for Thelma among the dead, to make sure that I'll never, ever find her. Among them."

ERNEST
SWINGS
OCCUPATION

Everyone starts getting nervous at nine-thirty. In the summer, at a quarter to ten. But in the winter, it's consistent. Nine-thirty. If it's snowing and the roads haven't been cleared, and it falls and falls, like an accident victim, who knows why or where to... If it's really slippery, if it's dark, if the electricity's been shut off somewhere, then there definitely won't be a trolley. And probably not a bus, either. And then taxis charge triple for the risk, the bad roads and "you should have planned better" and "you need to get together closer to home." It's a good thing the city isn't so big anymore and is partially destroyed. In any case, not every neighborhood is suited to restaurants and safe home gatherings. It's good that it's not so big anymore. In theory, he can make it on foot in an hour and a half. Not from everywhere, of course. You can get from Budyonnyi District, where the big garage used to be and is now a shelter, to the Kosmos Arena. If you run at least halfway. You definitely couldn't make it to the train station. Although, who needs to go to the train station now? What's the point of a station if no trains ever leave?

The orcs stole and outlawed everything. They didn't just steal the trains. For some reason they fucking pilfered the nights, too—from 2300 to 0500 hours. Well, and everything else, too. So nothing matters anymore. Except maybe time.

Casual sex, for instance, becomes some endless preschool show-and-tell. Before curfew starts, you have to meet someone and then also have sex, so that you don't wake up in the morning in an awkward situation... To avoid waking up in the morning next to a stranger who wants a husband, a relationship, coffee in bed, and long, intimate conversations. Have sex and make it to the bus. Say goodbye and catch a taxi. Run away from alien territory before it all starts up.

Ernest isn't sure he could maintain an erection listening to the confessions of a girl who turns into a St. George ribbon right before his eyes. He still likes cartoons, not horror movies. Cartoons, sex, and animals.

He doesn't answer the question, "Why haven't you left?" He doesn't answer it anymore. Because no one's asking anymore. Because he doesn't want to. Because there is no answer. Because the answers are always different. Because fuck the hell off, that's why.

On the other hand, to meet a girl at five in the evening and be completely done at ten, isn't that the dream of any single guy? There's no obligation to remember names. Everything is temporary and brittle, with no obligations and for just a little while. Except the old lapdog whose teeth are falling out. Except the barky, ill-tempered, hundred-year-old (in dog years) Pinscher with an intestinal obstruction. Even his own mother couldn't have told you who fathered that scruffy mutt who was born at the dawn of the new millenium that had promised progress, humaneness, and flourishing beyond our wildest dreams. But the mutt wasn't merely the product of some mass dog wedding. He was also Granddad Marat's only friend. The anchor holding Granddad Marat to life. Maybe anchoring him to the bottom. But whose business is that?

Ernest can't treat animals. But he can look for and find, bring and take away the people who can. Even at night. Sorry, girls, but Ernest has permission to move about the city during curfew in the event of urgently required veterinary care. Well, you're not cows, right? So that permission doesn't extend to you. What you and Ernest have is a show-and-tell.

But Motya the Pinscher and Ernest have a life.

The orc bitches are also some of the answers he doesn't give. And their male dogs, too.

Those tender-hearted murderers carried in by the north wind also loved dogs, acquired iguanas, fell in love with pet rabbits left behind by their owners in occupied homes. The animals got sick, gave birth, refused to eat, and vomited at night, making awful noises. The "generalissimos" from the town dumps, car washes, and neighboring country wept out of love for their pets. They seemed to love their Rottweiler bitches more than the girls they'd hooked up with here or brought "from there" as wives and camp followers. If it weren't for the Rottweiler bitches giving birth in pain, then the Pinscher Motya, along with his grandma Katya and the animal shelter in Budyonnovsk, would have died long since.

The transaction was simple, though hard to explain in the free world. An orc Rottweiler (hamster, parrot, lizard, ferret, cat, or canary) became a solution for the neighboring mutt, the homeless and legless cat, or the blind stallion who had once lived in an excellent private stable.

The "trolley problem" isn't a matter of choosing who to save but choosing who to kill: one or five. And even if you do nothing, you're still responsible. If you do nothing, someone will die anyway. More likely the five on the rails than the one asleep in the hammock.

"And it's also a good thing I'm not Abraham," Ernest will say. "I'm just flat out lucky that I'm not Abraham, that I don't have and don't plan to have a son named Isaac whom I'll have to slaughter to prove the strength of my faith. I'm lucky. A lucky man. All I have is the Maltese problem... You should see her. She's not a Maltese. She's vintage."

"Well, we're all vintage here—right out of a book on World War II," Babá chimes in.

"And, anyway, that Maltese is the head of the family. If you really think it through."

"If you really think it through," isn't a great method. It might work forever, or it might never even start working.

The view from the window hasn't changed except for its seasonal attire. For spring, grass, swings, broken asphalt, and the flowers that grow now without any assistance. For winter, snow with black patches, puddles, and swings like a broken hanger. Across the way, there's a nine-story building with balconies dressed as if the outside world doesn't exist. There are some balconies dressed in plastic chic according to the latest "fashion." Others look ancient with wooden frames and broken windows. The lower floors have "boat" balconies that stick their noses well beyond the limits of the decks and common sense. Some have flowers, and underwear hanging up to dry. Others are always empty and always lonely. Ernest always greets them. But balconies aren't Babá, they just hang there silently. Feigning muteness.

But how can he abandon them?

His father brought the skillet back from the Emirates. It had been white at one time. Later, it had hardened, exchanging its attire for something darker and more generic, like everything else. An omelet in the morning. Nothing for the evening. In the evenings, Ernest has show-and-tell. Either show-and-tell or house calls. Animals are like people. They feel worse at night. Or maybe in the silence it's easier to hear them whimper, belch, and vomit. To hear and see how they start to die.

Donetsk isn't an animal. Or maybe it's this way: ever since the orcs have fucking pilfered the Donetsk nights, no one can hear it moaning in pain.

There's no answer to the question, "Why haven't you left?" But maybe there's an answer for "Why are you here?"

The answer of a coward whose life is postponed until tomorrow. It's weird: it used to be almost fun to put things off until tomorrow. Not even almost. Just fun. Not to get married, not fall in love, not look for a career, not long for adventures, not engage with the incomprehensible world and not be afraid of getting nowhere.

Now "tomorrow" is the only real time. The "great tomorrow," in which Ernest plans to march by Aunt Tanya's house, assaulting her ears with that sweet Kharkiv chant of *"Putin Khuylo!"*—Putin's a dickhead! And the "lesser tomorrow," in which Ernest will fight for Uncle Petro's coffin. Not so much for the coffin as against Aunt Tanya's plan to bury him covered in the tricolor flag of the crucified chicken.

"Oh, that was a good one—proposing the German flag," Babá smiles approvingly. "A little bit more and Tanya would have been the one lying under the crucified chicken."

"Yup, that's us, German fascist-communists," roars Ernest.

His plans for the "great tomorrow" include a new hairstyle, renovating the apartment, and restoring the pet cemetery, with a memorial to all the mutts who didn't let their old, very old, and not very healthy masters go into the light. For the "lesser tomorrow," an omelet, a call to his father, a letter from Fink, a Zoom call with Dina, a run around the pond in Shcherbakov Park. Instead of "inhale-exhale," Ernest whispers to himself: "Rename, rename." Here, the greater and lesser tomorrow meet for an instant, but don't pair up, don't merge in ecstasy, don't become a present-day where it's possible to live.

It's not possible.

But Ernest lives. Like a coward and like the giant *Zhdun*, the famous waiting statue.

"So, does this Dutch *Homunculus loxodontus*—"The One Who Waits"—look like a giant pile of shit to you, too?" asks Ernest.

Baba says nothing. She does think so, too. But she doesn't admit it because Ernest is nothing like a pile of shit. Babá can't hold her tongue for long. She's not a saint, she doesn't have to sit back and patiently wait while the stupid devils devour themselves. She explodes in anger:

"Do you really think in Paris or some quiet, peaceful little Longwy commune there are no miserable fools wanting to throw themselves from a bridge or under a car, or slit their wrists? Really? Do you think that someone with my personality and background hasn't been to Paris? Or that anyone could have forced me out of there? That I wouldn't have business to take care of there? Not to mention Canada! Who did you just call a pile of shit?"

"Then why are you still here?" asks Ernest.

"Don't you think you need to apologize first?" snaps Babá. She's silent again, and again she can't stand her own silence. "I'm here out of spite. That's right—out of spite. So all the good ones don't kill themselves, so you won't cry, so there's someone to drink with... Even if you leave, I'll still stay here. I still have to teach Shubin Ukrainian. So much to do, so much to do. Who's got time for Paris?"

"Maybe I'll go," says Ernest. "If I'm alive, and after the 'great tomorrow.'"

"By the way, after a series of pointless victories, the Duke of Alba did leave the Netherlands. Left them in peace..."

"I'm not the Duke of Alba."

"And I'm not talking about you, moron."

Well, maybe he is a moron. A coward, *zhdun*, and moron. Besides taking things to the animal shelter, Ernest also brings food and hygiene items to the psychiatric hospital. He feels good with people who can't be rational. He's at home with them. With the speechless and the mad.

In the "great tomorrow," the landscape outside the window never changes. Dressed for the seasons, it will reflect thousands of other city landscapes—deserted islands, filthy, artificial concrete islands, that no one with any common sense would ever miss. To run away and forget. To choose bright streets and clean squares with domed cathedrals instead, to walk along Parisian boulevards, to drink water from Roman fountains.

"Oh, it's our old swings," Haska will say, as she looks out the window of the "great tomorrow." She'll already be forty then. Hopefully not fifty.

"It's you who's old," Ernest will say, thinking he'd saved them.

The swings, that is.

I wish I could embrace you like an ivy,
So close and tight, and shield you from the world,
I'm not afraid to take your life away,
You'll be like that old ruin, dressed in leaves—
She gets her life from ivy, as he hugs her,
And shelters her naked walls from storms,
While steadily the ruin holds her friend,
Protecting him from falling to the ground.

"I Wish I Could…" (1900),
Lesia Ukrainka (Larysa Kosach)

Dina isn't interested in boys and weddings anymore. "That's over and done with," she says. "It's time to leave childhood behind and take on something serious."

Something serious includes taking care of the zombie apocalypse. Well, "taking care" how? A zombie isn't a puppy, you can't drag it home. Dina doesn't dress up as a zombie for New Year's parties anymore. It's all more serious now, no joking: she's studying the issue. She watches shows, searches on Google, compares their types, behavior, and means of spreading the infection. She hopes to find a vaccine that will restore not only zombies' human appearance but also body parts that were bitten off at the moment of virus transmission. She is in no way on the side of the zombies or their holy apocalypse these days. "A vaccine is more effective than a bullet to the head. You could make lots and lots of vaccines and spray them from a plane. Pour it over them like a shower. Kle?"

"Kle" means *klas*, great. There's also "kool," "awesome," and "nu." If one of the so-called adults tries to choose words for Dina, she rejects them because they "get worn out and smell like armpits." No one knows for sure where words have armpits. It's a secret.

"If you look, you can always see a miracle," instructs Dina on the Zoom call. She teaches everyone who shows up. "You just don't notice. And when you close your eyes, it's like ivy. And I want to embrace you all, like ivy."

None of the participants recognizes Lesia Ukrainka in this "ivy," so Dina gets mad. She complains to Haska about her Russified relatives. And Haska admits that she is also... Russified without realizing it.

"The verse is about love. About how this woman wants to hug her beloved who she sees as a ruin."

"Thanks," says Haska. "For the ruin. That was nice."

"You said yourself that we have to call things by their right names," says Dina, upset. "Especially since I meant it in a good way. I want to hug all of you. You're my old ruins..."

Dina invites people to video conferences on Saturdays and Sundays. Angelina joins reluctantly, but she can't resist Dina. "Mama and Ernest from Donetsk, Papa from Zaporizhzhia... If he's not at the morgue. Is the morgue open on Saturdays? Let's assume that there's Internet there. Grandma Maria from Shyrokyi Lan, or sometimes from "location can't be disclosed." Grandpa Fink from Munich. With Khrystyna. That's fine. We're in Kyiv. We'll put Grandpa Petro and my sister Thelma in the picture here. But not next to each other—on different sides. We won't bother Les, okay? He'll come to us one day."

Dina is quiet for a moment and then sternly concludes her weekly speech: "I don't want to talk with the Ruscist part of our family yet. Quarantine."

"By the way..."

Dina always has various "by the ways." Sometimes it's a cake that you can eat virtually—everyone their own. So you have to buy one.

Sometimes it's about words: "If my father's next wife is called a stepmother, then who is his former wife? A beforemother? So is Aunt Tanya my beforemother—or just nobody?" Or: "Why are we called 'dis-placed' persons? Why are we not called 're-placed' or 're-turning'? Is dis-placed forever?"

Sometimes it's about politics: "So, if Putin is like Voldemort, then who are his Horcruxes? Who still has parts of him inside them? Can our Harry Potter be a girl from Donetsk?"

The participants report to Dina on various topics: appetite and weather, body temperature and sunrise times, the price of sausage and purchasing logistics, neighbors, a song that's stuck in their heads, Pinschers, poppies on the steppe and nasturtiums in the courtyard, TV shows, dreams; about what life was like before her. They report the good and the bad. Sly Dina waits until everyone is relaxed before she starts extracting promises from them. The sea, Disneyland, permission to not go to school tomorrow or to never go at all, and to dye one tiny little strand blue... Doll parts. Or some sort of bioconstructor she can use to make them.

Two years ago, all of Dina's dolls lost an arm. Elegant, dressed-up dolls, dolls with ribbons, some dolls with teased hair and others with braids, dolls with eyeshadow and lipstick in high heels, some in stockings. They are all beautiful and well-groomed. And they are all missing an arm.

"And—it's not scary," announced Dina. "He needs to come and see that it's not scary at all. Only, just at first, it's a little strange, so you want to close your eyes or look away sometimes. But once you get used to it, it's not scary."

Later, Dina began looking for supplies to make spare parts. She made hands from Legos, from clay, from wire. She sewed one and immediately threw it away, because she couldn't find flesh-colored fabric, and the blue one with flowers looked tacky and was insulting to the chic Barbie. The hand she made out of Legos that turned Barbie into the Terminator was not insulting, according to Dina's standards. Sometimes Dina bragged about her inventions and would seat the dolls next to the computer. She sighed, "Technology doesn't stand still. I need to move along with it. I need something bionic. Can one of you give me that?"

Nefyodov couldn't bear this part of the conversation. He would turn off his camera and sound for a few minutes. When he got back, it was already too late: the restless Khrystyna was blocking Fink and making Angelina agree to the blue streak for her hair.

Last week, Dina had asked, "Who is Vatman? Is that a special nickname for the vata we're kicking out?"

"Stop lying, Haska," says Dina, peering into the monitor. "I didn't say 'kicking out,' I said 'fucking up.'" And then everyone turned red and started shouting, "Halya, what are you teaching her? What are you thinking?! She's too young! She's just a little girl! She'll start cursing at school, too!" And only Fink's Khrystyna said, "What's the problem?" "And now you're ashamed of me, and you'll lie about me in your book. If that's how things are here, I'll go live in Munich. They understand me there!"

"Oh, honey," says Khrystyna, peering out menacingly from behind Fink, "Whatman isn't a nickname or a last name. It's the type of paper that they used for wall newspapers under the Soviets."

"Wall newspapers? You mean murals and graffiti? They had those in the former life, too?" Dina was surprised. "See, there was something good even in that millennium you were all born in. But why'd they call it Vatman if it's so useful?"

Dina's tricking them. ("And Haska is a tattletale!") Dina's fooling them. She already read all about that Whatman-Vatman. And even talked it over with her teacher and classmates. She's tricking them. She wants to "maintain attention" on a topic that no one else seems to want to focus on anymore. No one wants to hear about it, focus on it, remember it. Except for the ones on Zoom. Dina's fighting. Sometimes she gets called to the principal's office for it. So, sometimes she changes schools but never the war that she definitely intends to win.

She doesn't really remember Donetsk anymore. And Haska makes a concerted effort not to let it become some sort of lost paradise in her imagination. ("Haska's a traitor.") She runs it down, she rubs Dina's nose in the battered "Khrushchevka" apartment blocks; in the broken asphalt riddled with potholes; in the pathetic Lenin in his cap; in the statue of the revolutionary Artem whose dangling finger, from a certain angle, looks like a dick. Haska "travels" the Number 10 route with Dina and, at what was the final stop in her previous life, the October Coal Mine, they both break down crying. Haska starts first and can't stop, swallowing the words she still can't utter, swallowing her love, longing, helplessness, loneliness, and love again. So, so much love. "Daddy, my Daddy."

Dina hugs Haska, strokes her head and hums a little lullaby. Then she gets tired of being adult and wise and begins to wail in unison with Haska, crying, "My brother doesn't love me, he never comes to see me... I'm not a sister to him, just a piece of shit... Everyone's gone and abandoned me. And, dear Haska, you're the only one left..."

Somewhere there, far away and out of reach, under a spell and raped by strangers, the city is still the promised land. It's not right. But it can't be fixed.

She needs the Whatman paper to make her family tree. Because Dina's tree won't fit on a standard-sized sheet. How could it?

"If they wanted me to make a coat-of-arms, the motto would be 'It's complicated,'" laughs Dina. "But, for now, that's just my hashtag online."

The tree has a lot of issues. Too many holes, killed and abandoned offshoots, too many disruptions at the roots. Only Angelina's roots reach as far as the "great-greats." And that's only for the female line. The rest of them are short and uncertain. Maybe they're ours, but maybe not. Definitely not strangers. Dina covers the branches and roots in question marks, but she claims them all. She makes everyone brothers and sisters, grandmothers and grandfathers, and pencils in the ones she sent to quarantine. "We won't cross them out for now," she declares and puts not just Bohdan and Aunt Tanya in the gray zone, but also the bearded Vitya and Ernest's Moscow grandma.

Grandpa Fink has a special place. And Khrystyna is like an addition to him, they make a pair. Dina's only seen her on the video calls. "The Internet is like blood ties now," says Angelina. And Dina likes everything about this statement, since it makes Khrystyna one of her own.

Fink and Khrystyna are on the trunk of the tree. Their names stretch in capital letters from the bottom to the very top. "That's going to be hard to explain," warns Haska.

"To who?" asks Dina.

True. Who needs to hear that the flat, colored figures can move, that those caught by Haska's master eye may not be exactly like she sees them, that they—photographed so long ago on the steps of the maternity hospital—are alive? Alive even when they're dead. Who needs to hear that they've lost words, time, and space, and are still trying to breathe?

Unseen, wrapped in hundreds of layers of polyethylene, almost crossed out, doomed to be losers or weirdos, they exist, emerging as unseen trees. Trees. Not tumbleweed.

"You know, Ernest," says Haska. "On Dina's drawing of 'My Family and Other Animals,' there's a weird splotch in the upper left corner. It's like someone spilled a bit of yellow paint and then tried to wipe it off but couldn't. Or maybe I'm imagining it? The longer I look, the clearer it is..."

"Congratulations. Finally. That's Babá. She really loves having her picture taken. And now, look, she's switched to painting..."

"She never came to me," says Haska, in a hurt tone.

"You always had too many bats in your belfry. Babá is a soloist. She doesn't do choirs," laughs Ernest.

The yellow paint on Dina's tree isn't only in the upper left corner. Haska sees the same thing around the words "Grandpa Petro."

But not around Thelma. And Haska and Thelma's own faces look slightly blue, like anyone in the city who rarely gets out for fresh air.

Recent Titles in the Series
Harvard Library of Ukrainian Literature

Forest Song:
A Fairy Play in Three Acts

Lesia Ukrainka (Larysa Kosach)

Translated by Virlana Tkacz and Wanda Phipps
Introduced by George G. Grabowicz

This play represents the crowning achievement of Lesia Ukrainka's (Larysa Kosach's) mature period and is a uniquely powerful poetic text. Here, the author presents a symbolist meditation on the interaction of mankind and nature set in a world of primal forces and pure feelings as seen through childhood memories and the re-creation of local Volhynian folklore.

2024	appr. 240 pp.	
ISBN 9780674291874 (cloth)		$29.95
9780674291881 (paperback)		$19.95
9780674291898 (epub)		
9780674291904 (PDF)		

Harvard Library of Ukrainian Literature, vol. 13

Read
the book
online

Love Life: A Novel

Oksana Lutsyshyna

Translated by Nina Murray
Introduced by Marko Pavlyshyn

The second novel of the award-winning Ukrainian writer and poet Oksana Lutsyshyna writes the story of Yora, an immigrant to the United States from Ukraine. A delicate soul that's finely attuned to the nuances of human relations, Yora becomes enmeshed in a relationship with Sebastian, a seductive acquaintance who seems to be suggesting that they share a deep bond. After a period of despair and complex grief that follows the end of the relationship, Yora is able to emerge stronger, in part thanks to the support from a friendly neighbor who has adapted well to life on the margins of society.

2024	276 pp.	
ISBN 9780674297159 (cloth)		$39.95
9780674297166 (paperback)		$19.95
9780674297173 (epub)		
9780674297180 (PDF)		

Harvard Library of Ukrainian Literature, vol. 12

Read
the book
online

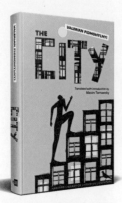

The City: A Novel
Valerian Pidmohylnyi

Translated with an introduction by Maxim Tarnawsky

This novel was a landmark event in the history of Ukrainian literature. Written by a master craftsman in full control of the texture, rhythm, and tone of the text, the novel tells the story of Stepan, a young man from the provinces who moves to the capital of Ukraine, Kyiv, and achieves success as a writer through a succession of romantic encounters with women.

2024	496 pp.	
ISBN 9780674291119 (cloth)		$39.95
9780674291126 (paperback)		$19.95
9780674291133 (epub)		
9780674291140 (PDF)		

Harvard Library of Ukrainian Literature, vol. 10

Read the book online

A Harvest Truce: A Play
Serhiy Zhadan

Translated by Nina Murray

Brothers Anton and Tolik reunite at their family home to bury their recently deceased mother. An otherwise natural ritual unfolds under extraordinary circumstances: their house is on the front line of a war ignited by Russian-backed separatists in eastern Ukraine. Isolated without power or running water, the brothers' best hope for success and survival lies in the declared cease fire—the harvest truce.

Spring 2024	196 pp.	
ISBN 9780674291997 (hardcover)		$29.95
9780674292017 (paperback)		$19.95
9780674292024 (epub)		
9780674292031 (PDF)		

Harvard Library of Ukrainian Literature, vol. 9

Read the book online

Cassandra:
A Dramatic Poem,

Lesia Ukrainka (Larysa Kosach)

Translated by Nina Murray, introduction by Marko Pavlyshyn

The classic myth of Cassandra turns into much more in Lesia Ukrainka's rendering: Cassandra's prophecies are uttered in highly poetic language— fitting to the genre of the dramatic poem that Ukrainka crafts for this work—and are not believed for that very reason, rather than because of Apollo's curse. Cassandra's being a poet and a woman are therefore the two focal points of the drama.

2024	263 pp, bilingual ed. (Ukrainian, English)
ISBN 9780674291775 (hardcover)	$29.95
9780674291782 (paperback)	$19.95
9780674291799 (epub)	
9780674291805 (PDF)	

Harvard Library of Ukrainian Literature, vol. 8

Read
the book
online

Ukraine, War, Love:
A Donetsk Diary

Olena Stiazhkina

Translated by Anne O. Fisher

In this war-time diary, Olena Stiazhkina depicts day-to-day developments in and around her beloved hometown during Russia's 2014 invasion and occupation of the Ukrainian city of Donetsk.

Summer 2023

ISBN 9780674291690 (hardcover)	$39.95
9780674291706 (paperback)	$19.95
9780674291713 (epub)	
9780674291768 (PDF)	

Harvard Library of Ukrainian Literature, vol. 7

Read
the book
online

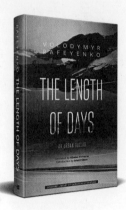

The Length of Days: An Urban Ballad

Volodymyr Rafeyenko

Translated by Sibelan Forrester
Afterword and interview with the author by Marci Shore

This novel is set mostly in the composite Donbas city of Z—an uncanny foretelling of what this letter has come to symbolize since February 24, 2022, when Russia launched a full-scale invasion of Ukraine. Several embedded narratives attributed to an alcoholic chemist-turned-massage therapist give insight into the funny, ironic, or tragic lives of people who remained in the occupied Donbas after Russia's initial aggression in 2014.

2023	349 pp.	
ISBN 780674291201 (cloth)		$39.95
9780674291218 (paper)		$19.95
9780674291225 (epub)		
9780674291232 (PDF)		

Harvard Library of Ukrainian Literature, vol. 6

Read
the book
online

The Torture Camp on Paradise Street

Stanislav Aseyev

Translated by Zenia Tompkins and Nina Murray

Ukrainian journalist and writer Stanislav Aseyev details his experience as a prisoner from 2015 to 2017 in a modern-day concentration camp overseen by the Federal Security Bureau of the Russian Federation (FSB) in the Russian-controlled city of Donetsk. This memoir recounts an endless ordeal of psychological and physical abuse, including torture and rape, inflicted upon the author and his fellow inmates over the course of nearly three years of illegal incarceration spent largely in the prison called Izoliatsiia (Isolation).

2023	300 pp., 1 map, 18 ill.	
ISBN 9780674291072 (cloth)		$39.95
9780674291089 (paper)		$19.95
9780674291102 (epub)		
9780674291096 (PDF)		

Harvard Library of Ukrainian Literature, vol. 5

Read
the book
online

Babyn Yar:
Ukrainian Poets Respond

Edited with introduction by Ostap Kin

Translated by John Hennessy and Ostap Kin

In 2021, the world commemorated the 80th anniversary of the massacres of Jews at Babyn Yar. The present collection brings together for the first time the responses to the tragic events of September 1941 by Ukrainian Jewish and non-Jewish poets of the Soviet and post-Soviet periods, presented here in the original and in English translation by Ostap Kin and John Hennessy.

2022 | 282 pp.

ISBN 9780674275591 (hardcover)	$39.95
9780674271692 (paperback)	$16.00
9780674271722 (epub)	
9780674271739 (PDF)	

Harvard Library of Ukrainian Literature, vol. 4

Read
the book
online

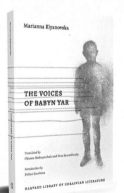

The Voices of Babyn Yar

Marianna Kiyanovska

Translated by Oksana Maksymchuk and Max Rosochinsky
Introduced by Polina Barskova

With this collection of stirring poems, the award-winning Ukrainian poet honors the victims of the Holocaust by writing their stories of horror, death, and survival in their own imagined voices.

2022 | 192 pp.

ISBN 9780674268760 (hardcover)	$39.95
9780674268869 (paperback)	$16.00
9780674268876 (epub)	
9780674268883 (PDF)	

Harvard Library of Ukrainian Literature, vol. 3

Read
the book
online

Mondegreen: Songs about Death and Love

Volodymyr Rafeyenko

Translated and introduced by Mark Andryczyk

Volodymyr Rafeyenko's novel Mondegreen: Songs about Death and Love explores the ways that memory and language construct our identity, and how we hold on to it no matter what. The novel tells the story of Haba Habinsky, a refugee from Ukraine's Donbas region, who has escaped to the capital city of Kyiv at the onset of the Ukrainian-Russian war.

2022	204 pp.	
ISBN 9780674275577 (hardcover)		$39.95
9780674271708 (paperback)		$19.95
9780674271746 (epub)		
9780674271760 (PDF)		

Harvard Library of Ukrainian Literature, vol. 2

Read the book online

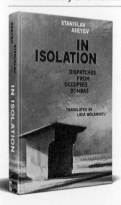

In Isolation: Dispatches from Occupied Donbas

Stanislav Aseyev

Translated by Lidia Wolanskyj

In this exceptional collection of dispatches from occupied Donbas, writer and journalist Stanislav Aseyev details the internal and external changes observed in the cities of Makiïvka and Donetsk in eastern Ukraine.

2022	320 pp., 42 photos, 2 maps	
ISBN 9780674268784 (hardcover)		$39.95
9780674268791 (paperback)		$19.95
9780674268814 (epub)		
9780674268807 (PDF)		

Harvard Library of Ukrainian Literature, vol. 1

Read the book online

Recent Titles in the Harvard Series in Ukrainian Studies

The Frontline: Essays on Ukraine's Past and Present

Serhii Plokhy

The Frontline presents a selection of essays drawn together for the first time to form a companion volume to Serhii Plokhy's *The Gates of Europe* and *Chernobyl*. Here he expands upon his analysis in earlier works of key events in Ukrainian history, including Ukraine's complex relations with Russia and the West, the burden of tragedies such as the Holodomor and World War II, the impact of the Chernobyl nuclear disaster, and Ukraine's contribution to the collapse of the Soviet Union.

2021 (HC) / 2023 (PB) | 416 pp. / 420 pp.

10 color photos, 9 color maps

ISBN 9780674268821 (hardcover)	$64.00
9780674268838 (paperback)	$19.95
9780674268845 (epub)	
9780674268852 (PDF)	

Read all chapters online

Harvard Series in Ukrainian Studies, vol. 81

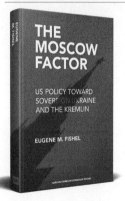

The Moscow Factor: US Policy toward Sovereign Ukraine and the Kremlin

Eugene M. Fishel

Russia's war on Ukraine did not start on February 24, 2022 with the full-scale invasion. Over eight years ago, in 2014, Russia illegally annexed Crimea from Ukraine, fanned a separatist conflict in the Donbas region, and attacked Ukraine with units of its regular army and special forces. In each instance of Russian aggression, the U.S. response has often been criticized as inadequate, insufficient, or hesitant.

2022 | 324 pp., 2 photos

ISBN 9780674279179 (hardcover)	$59.95
9780674279186 (paperback)	$29.95
9780674279421 (epub)	
9780674279193 (PDF)	

Read all chapters online

Harvard Series in Ukrainian Studies, vol. 82

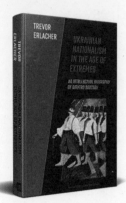

Ukrainian Nationalism in the Age of Extremes: An Intellectual Biography of Dmytro Dontsov

Trevor Erlacher

Ukrainian nationalism made worldwide news after the Euromaidan revolution and the outbreak of the Russo-Ukrainian war in 2014. Invoked by regional actors and international commentators, the "integral" Ukrainian nationalism of the 1930s has moved to the center of debates about Eastern Europe, but the history of this divisive ideology remains poorly understood.

2021 | 658 pp., 34 photos, 5 illustr.

ISBN 9780674250932 (hardcover)	$84.00
9780674250949 (epub)	
9780674250956 (Kindle)	
9780674250963 (PDF)	

Read all chapters online

Harvard Series in Ukrainian Studies, vol. 80

Survival as Victory: Ukrainian Women in the Gulag

Oksana Kis

Translated by Lidia Wolanskyj

Hundreds of thousands of Ukrainian women were sentenced to the GULAG in the 1940s and 1950s. Only about half of them survived. With this book, Oksana Kis has produced the first anthropological study of daily life in the Soviet forced labor camps as experienced by Ukrainian women prisoners.
Based on the written memoirs, autobiographies, and oral histories of over 150 survivors, this book fills a lacuna in the scholarship regarding Ukrainian experience.

2020 | 652 pp., 78 color photos, 10 b/w photos

ISBN 9780674258280 (hardcover)	$94.00
9780674258327 (epub)	
9780674258334 (Kindle)	
9780674258341 (PDF)	

Read all chapters online

Harvard Series in Ukrainian Studies, vol. 79